MAGGIE CHRISTENSEN

Christmas in
Bellbird
Bay

Christmas in Bellbird Bay

Maggie Christensen

Cover and interior design: J D Smith Design
Editing: John Hudspith Editing Services

Dedication

To Jim, my own soulmate

Also by Maggie Christensen

Oregon Coast Series
The Sand Dollar
The Dreamcatcher
Madeline House

Sunshine Coast books
A Brahminy Sunrise
Champagne for Breakfast

Sydney Collection
Band of Gold
Broken Threads
Isobel's Promise
A Model Wife

Scottish Collection
The Good Sister
Isobel's Promise
A Single Woman

Granite Springs
The Life She Deserves
The Life She Chooses
The Life She Wants
The Life She Finds
The Life She Imagines
A Granite Springs Christmas
The Life She Creates
The Life She Regrets
The Life She Dreams

A Mother's Story

Bellbird Bay
Summer in Bellbird Bay
Coming Home to Bellbird Bay
Starting Over in Bellbird Bay

One

Libby Walker brushed the sand from her feet and slipped them into her canvas sneakers before crossing the coastal pathway and running up the steps to her home.

The renovated weatherboard cottage overlooking the ocean in Bellbird Bay was the one she and Bernie bought together for their retirement. But it was not to be. Bernie had died two years earlier, after a lengthy and painful pancreatic cancer drained his energy and will to live. It had been his last wish that she move here, to the place where they often escaped from the city, and which they both loved.

So, although only in her mid-fifties, Libby moved there alone, except for Milo, the dog she'd rescued when he was only a pup, a tiny ball of fluff. He had grown into a much larger dog than she'd anticipated, but she loved him. She had no regrets. The tranquillity of the ocean town soothed her, and Milo's companionship helped her through the grief of losing her soulmate.

Libby found a part time job in the local library, enabling her to utilise her skills and qualifications while giving her time to take stock of her new life. Now, after two years, she'd made many good friends and no longer regarded herself as a newcomer.

This was her favourite time of year, late spring, early November, before the intense heat of summer began to bite, and the beach and town were filled with holidaymakers. She smiled to herself as she pushed open the back gate. In the past two years, she'd managed to come to grips with her grief, even though it did sometimes overwhelm her. The town was filled with memories of happier times, times when she and Bernie had wandered hand-in-hand along the beach, explored the narrow streets crammed with interesting shops, visited the weekend markets and relaxed away from the hustle and bustle of everyday life.

As she opened the door, Libby heard the strident ring of her mobile which she'd left on the kitchen bench. She picked it up with a sigh. She'd been planning to make herself a cup of tea, toast a slice of the seeded sour dough loaf she'd bought the day before, perhaps spread with some of the fig and ginger jam she loved, and settle down to enjoy the view and the new Marcia Willett novel she'd brought home from the library the night before.

'Mum! It's Matt! He's gone! He's left me!'

Libby sat down with a thump at the sound of her daughter's voice muffled by tears.

Emma started to speak again, but Libby couldn't make out what she was saying.

'Slow down, sweetheart. I can't understand you.'

Emma continued to speak through her tears and by the time the call finished, Libby had promised to drive to the city as soon as she could get organised. She looked out at the waves breaking on the shore, the view she loved so much. It normally had a calming effect on her, but not today. It was only now, when she could hear the alarm in Emma's voice, she wished she lived closer, regretted moving from Brisbane to this tropical paradise.

Libby stared at the phone, trying to work out what to do first. Matt had walked out on Emma, told her he had found someone else, packed his bags and left. It was hard to comprehend that the lively, charming young man her daughter had married had left his wife and daughter. At the thought of Clancy, the tears Libby had been stifling started to trickle down her cheeks. The poor little mite was only four. How was she going to cope without the father she loved, and how was Emma going to manage on her own? Despite his outward charm, Libby had never warmed to the real estate salesman who won her daughter's heart, but she knew what it was like to lose a soulmate. At least she and Bernie had enjoyed several decades together, and his illness had prepared her for the loss. Emma and Matt had only been married for seven years. According to Emma, Matt's pronouncement had come out of the blue. Emma would need all the help Libby could give her.

Giving herself a shake, Libby dropped a lemon and ginger teabag into a mug and made the toast she'd been anticipating. There was no sense in trying to do anything on an empty stomach. She fed Milo while the water for the tea was boiling and started to make a list. Making lists was her thing, something both Bernie and Emma had often teased her about. But she found it useful, especially as she got older and tended to forget things if she hadn't written them down.

First, Libby needed to find someone to take care of Milo. He normally went everywhere with her, but he'd be in the way at Emma's, even if his presence might help comfort Clancy. Eddie might be the answer. The woman who was her next-door neighbour had become a good friend over the past two years, someone Libby knew she could depend on. She didn't have a pet of her own and when Paula, her long-time partner, died a year earlier, Milo had proved a comfort to her.

Next there was the library. She knew her boss would understand. Rachel had grown children of her own and knew how close Libby was to her daughter. But it would leave a gap in the library schedule which would cause problems for other staff. Libby sighed, wishing she could just lock up and head off down the highway. But there were things to be taken care of first.

Quickly downing her tea and taking a last bite of toast, Libby headed next door leaving Milo sitting by the kitchen bench. The dog could tell something was wrong. He'd always been good at sensing her moods, a blessing during Bernie's sickness when he knew exactly when to comfort her and when she needed to be alone. This morning, after putting one paw on her lap and whining softly, he'd settled down at her feet, head on his paws, waiting for her instructions.

'I'm sorry, Milo,' she said before she left. 'But I'm sure Eddie will take good care of you while I'm gone.' Milo whined again as if, while acknowledging her words, he wasn't going to be happy about being left behind.

'Libby!' One look at Libby's face must have told her neighbour all was not well. 'What's up?' Eddie tried to draw Libby inside. 'Come sit down.'

'No. I can't stop.' Libby could feel her heart pounding. 'It's Matt, Emma's husband. He's left her, Eddie. I never did completely trust him, but Emma loved him, and they seemed to be happy together. He's Clancy's dad.' Having said her piece, Libby did take a seat, dropping onto the yellow painted bench on Eddie's veranda.

'Oh, no! Poor Emma.' Eddie joined her and put a hand on Libby's shoulder. 'You'll be going to Brisbane to be with her. She'll need your support. Would you like me to look after Milo while you're gone, or will you take him with you?'

'Would you? I need to get on the road, and I can't take him, not this time.' Libby couldn't imagine the sort of uproar Emma's house would be in. She'd heard Clancy crying in the background when she was talking with Emma. At only four, the little girl wouldn't be able to understand why her daddy had left her.

'Of course. We'll be company for each other. I've been thinking maybe I should get a dog of my own. It's been lonely since Paula went.' She gazed into the distance.

Libby knew exactly what she meant. It was how she felt every morning when she awoke to the empty space in the bed. Even after two years, she still expected to see Bernie lying beside her, to feel his lips on hers, his arms around her, providing a loving ear to share her thoughts with. Now Emma would experience these same emotions. It wasn't fair. But life wasn't fair. She'd discovered that long ago, when they'd lost their infant son to a cot death, followed by three miscarriages. She and Bernie had almost given up hope of another child when Emma was born. Then she'd worried herself sick until she was sure her daughter was going to survive.

'Thanks a million. I'll drop him round before I leave. I can let you have his bed and food and water bowls, too. And I have a bag of dogfood.' She fell silent, knowing she was babbling.

'We'll be fine. He can come with me on my morning run and keep me company when I'm working.'

'Thanks, and could you maybe...?'

'I'll water your garden, too,' Eddie said, before Libby could finish. 'And if there's anything else, just let me know.'

'Thanks. I'm not sure how long I'll be.' Emma had sounded so distraught on the phone, Libby couldn't imagine how her normally super-efficient daughter was going to cope.

'Don't worry.' Eddie gave her a hug. 'Now, on you go and do what you need to before you leave. I'll be here.'

Two

Tears filled Adam Holland's eyes as his friend's frail hand grasped his. 'You'll do it for me, mate, won't you? You won't let me down.'

Adam nodded his head, too overcome to speak. He knew Greg had come to the end. After fighting the cancer for three years, he'd declined rapidly over the past few weeks. This would probably be the last time Adam saw him alive, the last words he'd have with his old friend.

'Say it,' Greg insisted, his voice barely audible.

'I promise. I'll take your ashes back to Bellbird Bay. I'll do what you want, Greg. I might even spend the summer there.' Adam tried to inject a lighter note. 'You've bored me with tales of the place for so long, it's about time I saw it for myself.'

A slight smile crossed Greg's face, before his eyes closed, his breathing becoming ragged.

Adam gently extricated his hand. He patted Greg's shoulder. 'Goodbye, Greg, you've been a good mate to me. The best.' With unshed tears in his eyes, he made his way out of the hospital room and stood, his back against the closed door, to take a deep breath.

'Are you all right?' A passing nurse gave him a strange look. Surely she was used to seeing grieving friends and relatives?

Adam nodded and walked off, his eyes blurring so much he had trouble finding the lift button for the ground floor.

Knowing he was in no state to drive, Adam headed for the hospital cafeteria hoping no one would notice the tears which he was trying unsuccessfully to stem. Damn! He didn't often give way to emotion, but Greg was still a young man. He didn't deserve to die like this. They'd spent two years together in war zones, managing to evade bullets, bombs and other catastrophes, before returning to the country's capital to focus on Australia's political leaders.

*

It was strange to think it was only a week since he'd attended Greg's funeral. Greg and he had gone through a lot together, but his friend's final fight with cancer had tested them more than anything else. Adam had shed more than a few tears during the service, and now here he was, in Bellbird Bay, the small town on Queensland's Sunshine Coast where Greg had grown up.

Adam fitted the key into the door of the small weatherboard house he'd rented for the next few months. He pushed open the door, and immediately felt a sense of release. He dropped his bags and went straight to open the window, breathing in the scent of the ocean.

As a writer, Adam could work anywhere. But it had suited him to live in Australia's capital. His political thrillers were mostly based there, and he loved soaking up the ambiance of the city. Now, conscious of his promise to Greg, he had locked up his unit in the city and rented this seaside cottage for the summer. He'd come to fulfil his promise to his friend, to scatter his ashes in the ocean at Bellbird Bay on Christmas Eve.

He pushed the window wide open and gazed out at the wide stretch of white sand. There were only a few early morning walkers around, one a woman with a large dog, who climbed up the pathway from the beach as he watched. It was still early in the season. He had no doubt things would become busier closer to Christmas.

After bringing in the rest of his luggage from the car, Adam moved a table under the open window and set up his laptop. Perhaps the new location – and the view – would inspire a new direction in his writing. If he was honest with himself, he was feeling a tad stale with his current series. Maybe it was time for a change. But how would his readers react if their favourite author suddenly deserted them to write murder mysteries set on the Queensland Coast? Would they follow him, or would he need to develop a whole new readership?

He knew what his agent would say, but Julian English had a stake in Adam continuing in his current vein. His latest book would be released in January. It would be fun to take the risk.

*

It was still early by the time Adam had unpacked his few possessions. He travelled light, a legacy of his years in war zones and the days he'd been a political journalist following politicians around the country, sometimes overseas. He was glad those days were over. It had been fine when he was in his thirties and early forties, exciting even, to feel part of what some called the Canberra bubble. But he'd soon become tired of the interminable hustle and bustle of political life, preferring to sit alone in his room. It was then, when his colleagues were out drinking and sharing gossip, that he started what he called his scribbling.

At first it had only been for his own enjoyment, a way of filling the evenings after the hurly-burly of the day. Then, on an impulse, he'd sent off one of his manuscripts to an agent. To his surprise, it had been accepted, and he was soon the recipient of a six-figure advance on a three-book contract.

That had been over ten years ago, and he'd gone from strength to strength, becoming one of the stars of his publishing house, fêted at book signings and conferences, and top of the best-seller list with each new release. But now he was becoming jaded again. Perhaps this change of scene was exactly what he needed. It would be good to have a couple of months alone to consider his options.

Adam was tired of the inevitable round of events his writing generated, and of the attraction his so-called fame had for the opposite sex. Coming from a broken home he'd avoided any permanent relationship, preferring to accept the favours that were offered. They'd become fewer of recent years, too, or perhaps he'd just become more adroit at avoiding them. He thought back to his last night in Canberra.

Yvette was the latest in a series of women who'd pursued him relentlessly. She was the only one who'd managed to break through the barrier he'd erected over the years, the barrier which kept such women at bay. Adam wasn't sure why he'd allowed Yvette into the more private part of his life. Maybe she'd been more persistent than the others who thronged around him at literary events, maybe she'd caught him at a weak moment, or maybe he'd just been tired of fending off the others. At least her presence gave him breathing space, and she was good company. He knew she wanted something more permanent than the few nights each week they managed to spend together. But did he?

After his unhappy childhood, Adam had fought shy of commitment, choosing a career that didn't lend itself to sharing his life with anyone.

Following years of vicious wrangling which caused both Adam and his sister to hide from their quarrels, his mother had left, taking his little sister with her and leaving him and his father alone. They'd muddled through, but his father had practically ignored the teenage boy who needed his love, who missed his mother and sister. His father was now dead, and he presumed his mother might be, too. There had been no word from her since she left. At first, Adam had watched for the postman every day. But as time passed with no letter, he'd gradually forced himself to try to forget, though he never had. And he had no idea where his little sister was. When he returned from the war zones, more conscious than ever of the fleeting nature of human life, he'd tried to find her on social media and other agencies available to him as a journalist, but there was no sign of Alison Holland. For all he knew she might have emigrated, married or died.

Yvette was a lovely woman, independent, intelligent, not too demanding. She owned a string of boutiques in the capital. She ticked all the boxes, but Adam wasn't convinced he wanted to share his life with anyone ever again. He'd become used to his solitary existence and didn't trust himself to form a permanent relationship.

Before leaving Canberra, he'd tried to let her down lightly, to explain he needed this respite from the city, and the mission his friend had left him. She'd taken it hard, but he had finally managed to convince her of his determination to do this by himself. Canberra emptied out at this time of year anyway. If he was to spend a couple of months away, there was no better time to do it. And it would give him time to consider whether there was a place in his life for Yvette, if she meant more to him than the occasional bed mate and dinner companion. Although he'd vowed never to marry and enjoyed his own company, there were times when the thought of a companion to share his days held some attraction. He was in his mid-fifties. Did he really want to face old age alone?

Impatient to see the place Greg had raved about when he'd had a few too many, Adam decided to investigate this town where he intended to spend the next two months. He knew he wouldn't get any writing done today – he planned to take a day or two to acclimatise himself before sitting down at his laptop. It was something he always did. He called it his thinking time, and often ideas would come to him in the strangest places. There was the time he'd been worrying about a fight scene when, walking along the banks of Lake Burley Griffin, it came to him. He couldn't get home fast enough to put words on the page. Another time, he and Yvette had been enjoying dinner when his eyes fell on a couple at a neighbouring table. They were engaged in what looked like an argument, and he'd ended up jotting down a few notes about their body language on a paper napkin.

Adam strolled down the boardwalk to the esplanade, the sun beating down on him, reminding him one of his first purchases should be a hat. The place had a holiday atmosphere with shops selling hats of every variety, tee-shirts with the Bellbird logo, and buckets and spades reminding him of his own youth and holidays spent on the south coast of New South Wales.

Eschewing the plethora of caps, also featuring the Bellbird logo, he purchased a wide-brimmed straw hat and walked towards an open-air café with the name *The Bay Café* emblazoned on the sign. He had just ordered a burger with the lot and a long black and was settling to read a copy of the local paper he'd picked up at the counter, when there was a scuffling at his feet. Looking down he saw a large long-haired dog of indeterminate breed sniffing at his feet. Since Adam was wearing sandals, it wasn't long before he felt his toes being tickled by the animal's tongue.

'Hey! Shoo!' He tried to move his feet out of the way, but the dog was persistent.

'Sorry. Milo, here boy!' A woman with short grey hair wearing jeans. a tee-shirt proclaiming her to be a lover of Bellbird Bay, and a cap with the now familiar town logo, yanked on the dog's lead. 'Sorry,' she repeated, 'he's just curious. He wants to make friends. He knows you're a stranger.'

'Is he like this with everyone he meets?' Adam asked, wondering how the animal could survive in a town which attracted holidaymakers the year round but especially in summer and school holidays.

'He's not mine,' the woman replied. 'I'm minding him for a friend, but he's a friendly soul. He may look fierce but he's really quite gentle.'

Adam didn't doubt it, his now damp toes bearing testament to the fact.

With a smile, she pulled the dog away, and Adam was able to settle down and enjoy his coffee and burger in peace. He stretched out his legs, finding himself able to relax. For once, there was no agent snapping at him, no deadline to meet, no... He stopped himself. He'd been about to think, *no Yvette to annoy him*. Was that what she did? Not annoy exactly, but she did have a habit of contacting him or turning up just when he wanted to be alone. He sighed. He'd probably miss her, but the next few months would be a good test of their relationship.

Three

The sun was already beginning to set as Libby drove her white Mazda 3 through the outer suburbs of Brisbane, the sky turning shades of pink, orange and red. It had taken her longer than she anticipated to make all her arrangements. Then the traffic on the motorway had been nose-to-tail, signalling the end of the weekend. Everyone was intent on making the most of their time on the coast before returning to the city for the start of the working week.

As she made her way through the crush of traffic on the northern access to the city, Libby was reminded why she and Bernie had chosen to retire farther north, to the sleepy coastal town of Bellbird Bay. She still came to the city to visit her daughter, but usually chose to do so on a weekday, when the traffic was lighter.

Finally, she drew up outside the federation home Emma and Matt had taken such pride in renovating. From the car, she could see the still half-painted veranda posts. Damn Matt for leaving Emma with the house half-finished. But really, there was no good time for him to leave. She stepped out and hurried to the door. It opened immediately to reveal a tearstained Emma, little Clancy clinging to her legs.

Libby enveloped them both in a warm hug.

'Mum, I'm so glad you're here,' Emma murmured into Libby's shoulder, while Clancy whimpered, 'Grandma!'

Realising she was going to have to take charge, Libby gradually extricated herself from the pair. 'Have you eaten?' she asked, to see Emma shake her head.

'I haven't been able to think straight since Matt left. I keep thinking it was a bad dream, that I'll wake up and everything will be as it was… but he's not going to come back, is he? He even took his old surfboard.'

Libby knew how her son-in-law had valued his surfboard, even if he hadn't used it since Clancy was born, so wasn't as surprised as Emma, but it did signal he had no intention of returning.

'Oh, Mum, what am I going to do without him?' Emma broke into tears, soon joined by Clancy.

Putting an arm around her daughter's shoulders, Libby led her through the house and to a seat on the sofa. Joining her, Libby was shocked to see the change in Emma since she had last seen her. The normally happy and lively young woman was a shadow of her former self, the dark circles under her puffy eyes a sign of the trauma she was going through.

'I'm so sorry, Emma.' Libby hugged her again, Clancy climbing up to join them. They sat like that for some time, Emma sobbing into her mother's shoulder, Clancy's tears leaving a wet patch on her sleeve.

Finally, Emma raised her head. 'I don't know what to do, Mum. Matt was my life. I don't think…' She began to sob again.

Libby's heart sank. She wanted to tell her daughter to buck up, that he wasn't worth it, but knew it would only bring a fresh bout of tears. She attempted to sound positive. 'Let's see what you have in to eat. Are you hungry, Clancy?'

Hiccupping, the little girl nodded.

Libby made her way to the kitchen, Emma and Clancy trailing behind her. Tea first, she decided, turning on the electric jug and taking a couple of mugs from the cupboard. Lacing one mug of tea with several spoonsful of sugar, she set it down in front of Emma, and gave Clancy her sippy cup filled with milky tea. Then she made one for herself.

Checking the fridge, she found some chicken breasts defrosting, probably intended for last night's dinner. She took these out, deciding to fry them along with onions and some tomatoes and mushrooms she found there too. Then she peeled several potatoes and put them on to boil.

'I'm sorry, Mum, I'm not hungry.' Emma toyed with the food on her plate.

Libby understood. She could remember what it was like for her when Bernie died.

But Matt hadn't died. He was off somewhere enjoying life with his new partner while Emma and Clancy were left to try to put their lives back together.

Libby knew she had to help her daughter, but how? 'You need something in your stomach,' she said, hearing her own mother's voice in her head. 'Clancy needs to eat, and she will if she sees you.' She nodded to her granddaughter who was also playing with her food.

Libby sighed. Maybe it would all look better in the morning.

*

Next morning when she awoke, Libby found Clancy curled up beside her. Watching the little girl sleep, her blonde curls so like her mother's when she was the same age, Libby felt a bolt of anger rise up. She felt her hands clench, as if she could punch Matt for being so heartless as to ruin his daughter's life.

Clancy's eyes opened. 'Grandma?'

'You must have snuck in here during the night, sweetheart. Shall we see if Mummy's up yet?'

'Daddy?'

'No. Daddy's not here.'

Libby pulled her granddaughter into a hug and lifted her out of the bed, popping her down on her feet. Clancy ran out of the bedroom. Libby could hear her footsteps go down the hall and her voice calling, 'Mummy!'

After a quick shower and dressed in a pair of jeans and her favourite pink linen shirt, Libby made her way to the kitchen from where she could hear Emma and Clancy's voices. So, Emma was up. That was a good sign. Hopefully, she managed to get a good night's sleep and was feeling better.

In the hallway, Libby paused to check in the mirror, seeing a slight woman in her mid-fifties with worry lines around her eyes and mouth. She patted her hair. When it had started to turn grey, she'd taken the advice of her hairdresser to add blonde streaks and now, her once light brown hair had become a fashionable shade of ash-blonde.

'Hi, darling. Did you sleep well?' she asked, seeing Clancy already seated at the table spooning up Weet-Bix, a rim of milk around her mouth. It all looked so normal.

'Sort of. I think I dropped off around one. I woke early. I've had time to think about things, Mum. I still can't believe what he's done to us. I'd like to wring his neck, and the neck of that slut he's with. How could he?'

'You know her?' Libby was glad to see Emma's grief had turned into anger. It would help her move forward, even though she was sure tears still weren't far from the surface.

'Know her? Of course I do. April Clarke is the newest addition to the staff in his office. I should have guessed something was up when he kept singing her praises, and he was working late so often. But don't they say the wife's the last to know?' There was a bitter note in her voice Libby hadn't heard before. 'When he came home from the office on Saturday night, he packed then left. I didn't sleep a wink and called you in the morning.'

'Oh sweetie!' Libby went over to give Emma a hug.

'It's okay, Mum.' She shrugged out of Libby's embrace. 'I have to get used to it. But I don't know how we'll manage. Matt was so adamant I shouldn't go back to work till Clancy went to school. We managed on his salary and commissions and planned to use mine for holidays and perhaps a private school for Clancy further down the track. Now...' She spread her hands.

'Well, it's early days.' Libby tried to sound sensible. 'Did Matt say anything about money?'

Emma shook her head. 'Everything's in a joint account. I suppose I can still draw on it.'

But for how long? 'I think you need to talk with him,' Libby said. 'You have Clancy to think of, and I presume there's a mortgage and bills.'

'I don't want to think about any of that, not yet.'

Libby bit her lip. She didn't want to push her daughter. But there was no sense in her hiding her head in the sand. Libby had heard too many tales of women left destitute when their husbands left. 'Do I smell coffee?' she asked, wary of upsetting Emma.

'Like some?' Emma headed towards the espresso machine which

Libby knew had been bought at Matt's insistence. At least he hadn't taken that with him. Not yet anyway. Libby looked around the kitchen, thought of the furniture carefully chosen by both Emma and Matt. What would happen to it now? Would Emma be able to remain here?

She opened the fridge and took out a loaf of bread, sliding one slice into the toaster, then standing waiting for it to pop up.

'Mum?'

'Yes?'

'I can't stay here waiting for Matt to come back. Can I come to Bellbird Bay with you?'

Libby's mouth dropped open. She hadn't expected this.

'Just for a few weeks, until I get my head around everything. Clancy loves it there. I need some space.' Emma turned to face Libby, her eyes pleading.

'Of course you can.'

'I'll need to come back to find a job. Clancy will be starting school in January. We'd talked about me going back to work, doing casual teaching a few days a week, easing myself in gently. I guess that won't be possible now. I'll need to look for something more permanent. Oh, Mum!' Emma's apparent confidence disappeared. 'What am I going to do?'

'You're going to come to Bellbird Bay with me, stay till after Christmas. You won't be able to find anything before then, anyway. Things will look different there, I promise.'

Libby knew how the small beachside town had nurtured her. Maybe it could do the same for her daughter.

Four

Adam had been in Bellbird Bay for a week and had already developed a routine. He rose early for a walk along the beach, finishing with a swim. Being here took him back to his teenage years, to holidays with his mates, camping by the beach, spending all day on the sand, swimming and playing beach cricket, his skin slick with saltwater, sand and sun.

Then, he'd head to *The Bay Café* for breakfast, sitting at one of the sun-bleached wooden outdoor tables and enjoying one of the various egg dishes the café provided, accompanied by a large mug of coffee. It was a great way to start the day, vastly different to his normal routine in Canberra.

It was only when he'd satisfied the inner man, that he'd return to his temporary home and settle down at his laptop to write. To his surprise, the words were flowing. He was becoming attached to his new hero, a retired journalist who uncovers a drug ring in a sleepy seaside town – not unlike Bellbird Bay. He barely spared a thought for what his agent would think. He didn't care. It was as if, here in Bellbird Bay, he'd been able to slough off his previous existence and become a new person.

Today, he'd decided to visit Greg's old home. He'd been putting it off, knowing it was no longer in the family – all Greg's family were long gone, his parents killed in a crash when Greg was overseas. He had no siblings and had never married. Adam supposed that was why his friend had chosen him to dispose of his ashes. He was the closest thing to a brother Greg had.

Today, like every other morning since Adam arrived in Bellbird Bay, the sun was blazing down, the sky was clear and blue, and he was filled with a sense of wellbeing. He ordered his usual mug of long black, today choosing eggs benedict to accompany it, and settled back with a copy of the local paper.

As he drained his coffee, he checked Google Maps for the address he'd looked up the night before. Seaview Crescent sounded as if it should be close to the beach, but Adam knew from experience names could be deceiving. He had grown up in a suburb named Greenfields, and there hadn't been a green field in sight.

But, this time, the name proved to be in synch with reality. Seaview Crescent did have sea views, although many of the homes had seen better days and were being overshadowed by newly built mansions which towered over them. It was actually not far from the one he was renting and might even back onto the same boardwalk.

Adam made his way to number seven, one of the older houses which had so far managed to escape renovation. He stood outside, unsure what to do. Would Greg have wanted him to make himself known? What would he say?

Annoyed with himself for being so apprehensive, Adam pushed open the gate and knocked on the door, surprised to recognise the woman who answered.

'Hello again, how can I help you?' she asked.

Adam didn't know what to say. The words he'd carefully prepared flew out of his head. He, who lived by his words, was tongue-tied. He stood looking at the grey-haired woman who he'd last seen with the large friendly dog. What were the chances? 'I...' he stuttered.

'We met in the café a week ago,' she said with a puzzled expression.

'Sorry.' Adam took another deep breath. 'You must think me a fool. I have no real reason for being here apart from... a friend of mine grew up here in Bellbird Bay. This house is where he lived.'

'Oh!'

Adam could see understanding dawning on the woman.

'Perhaps you'd like to come in.' She stood aside to allow him to enter.

Today there was no sign of the dog, for which he was grateful. But hadn't she said it didn't belong to her?

'Would you like some tea?' Not waiting for a reply, she walked out, presumably to go to the kitchen.

While she was gone, Adam looked around the room. It was sparsely furnished in stark primary colours, a few cushions on the sofa but apart from them the furniture was pale blond wood, perfectly suited to the coastal landscape outside. On one wall hung a large photograph of two women smiling at each other, one of whom looked like a younger version of the woman in the kitchen.

By the time she returned, carrying two mugs of tea and a plate of Tim Tams, Adam had recovered his equilibrium. 'Sorry, what must you think of me,' he said. 'I'm Adam Holland.'

'Eddie Armstrong,' she said, holding out her hand. 'I know who you are, I recognised you in the café,' she said with a chuckle. 'My partner enjoyed your books and spent hours trying to persuade me to read them. What brings you to Bellbird Bay? You mentioned a friend.' She raised one eyebrow.

'Greg Holmes. He passed away a short time ago and… his last wish was that I come here.' He picked up his mug and took a sip, grimacing at the unfamiliar aroma of some herbal infusion. But it tasted okay.

'Fennel and cardamon,' she said, seeing his expression. 'It's one of my favourites – good for the digestion.

'Milo's back with his owner,' she added, seeing him glance around the room. 'So, you're on a remembrance trip for your friend?'

'Something like that.' Adam shifted uncomfortably in his chair, wondering why he was here. 'Sorry, this was a mistake.' He started to rise.

Eddie put up her hand. 'No, please don't go. He must have been a good friend. Why don't you tell me about him?'

Adam took another sip of the tea, trying not to grimace and seeing a faint smile on Eddie's lips. 'We were both journalists, covered a few war zones together. It brings you close. We were like brothers.' Adam looked down. He hadn't spoken to anyone about Greg, not since his friend died, but there was something about Eddie that encouraged confidences. 'He developed cancer a few years ago. It was an aggressive one.' Adam paused, his eyes moistening as he remembered his old friend. 'He asked me…' He knuckled away a tear. 'He asked me to scatter his ashes here in Bellbird Bay, where he was happy.' Adam looked up to see Eddie's eyes filled with compassion.

'I lost a good friend a couple of years ago,' she said, her voice filled with emotion. 'I know what it's like. It's not easy. I can understand why you'd want to spend time where your friend was happy and to fulfil his last request.'

Adam was startled. It suddenly struck him that the other woman in the photo was the friend Eddie was speaking about, that she'd been more than a friend; she'd been her partner. Did she think he and Greg…? He was about to correct her but decided not to. What did it matter? It would have amused Greg to think he was being considered Adam's partner.

'I'm sorry I didn't know your friend's family. Will you be staying for long?'

'A couple of months. I've rented a place for the summer. I was in need of a break and I can write anywhere.'

Eddie nodded sagely.

Adam wanted to put her right, to explain, but it was all too hard. What did it matter if this old woman thought he was gay? 'Have you lived here long?' he asked.

'Long enough to see the place change. When Paula and I moved to Bellbird Bay, it was more of a village. There was just the town square, a few shops and the cottages along the shoreline. Then the moneyed folk from the city moved in, built their holiday homes. They were followed by the hotels you see now.' She sighed. 'You can't halt progress, but I like to think Bellbird Bay has managed to retain some of its former atmosphere. At least we've been spared the high-rise apartments you see all along the rest of the coast.'

When Adam finally rose to leave, he knew a lot more about the history of the seaside town than he'd been able to glean from his reading or the Internet. He was filled with the desire to know even more and determined to revisit all of Greg's former haunts. Maybe this town could provide the answer to the malaise that had been creeping up on him in the city.

Five

'It's lovely here, Mum.' Emma leant her arms on the table, looking more cheerful than she had in the past week. Ever since they arrived back in Bellbird Bay, she'd been moping around unable to settle to anything.

Libby was glad she'd been able to take more time off. She needed to care for Clancy while Emma was in this state. The little girl was proving more resilient. After her initial questions about when her daddy was coming to join them, she'd accepted the explanation he was working. She loved her grandmother and loved Bellbird Bay. For Libby, every day with her granddaughter was a bonus, but she knew life couldn't continue like this for ever.

'It really is. I love it,' she replied to her daughter. 'Have you thought what you're going to do?' She held her breath, wondering if she'd spoken too soon.

'He's not coming back, is he?' Emma turned to meet Libby's eyes. 'I think I've finally come to accept that. So, I do need to make plans. But…' her eyes flitted around the room. 'Oh, Mum. It's so easy here… to forget… to pretend I'm a different person. I know when we go back to Brisbane, it'll all hit me. Everyone will know. It'll be horrible.'

This was something Libby had been thinking about ever since they returned to Bellbird Bay but had been loath to broach the subject with her daughter. It would be a huge disruption to her life, but Emma and Clancy were family, the only family she had. 'Why don't you move up here?' she asked.

Emma looked at her in dismay. 'I couldn't. Brisbane's home. It's where I grew up, where all my friends are, where...' Her voice trailed off. 'What's going to happen with the house?' she asked. 'Matt won't... He wouldn't...' Her eyes widened as she read the answer in Libby's eyes. 'Oh, Mum!'

At the note of distress in her mother's voice, Clancy ran towards her and wrapped her arms around Emma's legs. 'Mummy?'

'I'm all right, sweetheart.' Emma lifted the little girl up and hugged her tightly. 'Clancy's little friends are all in Brisbane, too, aren't they, honey?'

Libby bit her lip. She was well aware Emma's life revolved around the group of mothers she'd met when Clancy was a baby, women who lived close to her house in the leafy suburb of The Gap. How long would she be able to keep the house, even if Matt didn't demand they sell it? But now wasn't the time to bring it up.

'Let's wait and see, shall we?' she said, trying to inject a cheerful note into her voice. 'You can stay here till after Christmas, anyway. It'll be lovely to be able to have you both all to myself.'

'Christmas? That's...'

'Less than six weeks away. The shops are already selling mince pies and putting up Christmas decorations. We can have a beach Christmas. How does that sound?'

'It sounds good. Thanks, Mum. Maybe I can find some casual work till then, if you can look after Clancy. If I can keep busy, maybe it'll stop me thinking about Matt and *her*.'

Emma hadn't said any more about Matt's new partner since they left Brisbane. Libby wondered what she was like. No doubt she was younger, without the trappings of a child demanding her time. She looked across at her daughter and granddaughter and cursed Matt for his stupidity. He had a lovely wife, a delightful daughter and had chosen to throw it all away for a roll in the hay with a... colleague.

'I'll be going back to work, Em,' Libby said, as gently as she could. 'But perhaps you could book Clancy into childcare on the days I'll be at the library – even find something part-time yourself?'

'I'd forgotten you work,' Emma said, looking downcast. 'Couldn't you...? No, I guess you couldn't.'

'Em, I have my life here – a life I had to make when your dad died.

It's not easy to start again. I know that, but it can be done. I'll help you all I can, but I can't turn my whole life around because Matt has left you.'

'Thanks, Mum. I'm sorry.' But she still looked mulish. 'I don't know what I can do.'

'Let me ask around. I know a few people in town, and with the influx of holidaymakers, there are always openings coming up. I think you're right. It's best to keep busy. It's a pity it's so close to the end of the school year.' Libby frowned. 'I wonder…'

'What?'

'Give me a couple of days. No need to rush into anything. Now, how about a cup of tea then we could all go to the beach?'

'Yay!' Clancy slid out of her mother's grasp. 'Can we go swimming, Grandma?'

'I don't see why not. It's such a lovely day.' Libby glanced out the window to where the sun was shining on the ocean, making it sparkle. She hadn't taken her walk this morning, hadn't managed her usual walk since Emma and Clancy came to Bellbird Bay. She was missing that early morning time on the beach, just her and Milo and the stretch of empty sand. It kept her fit and gave her thinking time, time to prepare for the day ahead.

*

Accustomed to only having herself and Milo to worry about, Libby hadn't realised how much time it would take for Emma and Clancy to get ready for a trip to the beach. But finally they were ready and the trio, accompanied by Milo, his tail waving wildly with pleasure, made their way across the boardwalk and down the steps to the beach.

After some time, during which Emma fussed about shade and distance from the water, they spread out the rug Libby kept for such occasions. Libby had a refreshing swim while Emma and Clancy paddled at the edge of the water with Milo. She was finally able to relax.

'I think I'll go for a walk, Mum,' Emma said, when they were once again sitting on the sand. She seemed unable to sit still. 'Can you keep an eye on Clancy?' Without waiting for a reply, she picked up her hat and strode off, leaving Libby gazing after her.

Clancy busied herself making sand pies while Milo lay watching her.

Enjoying the unexpected reprieve from Emma's company – her continual negativity was becoming wearing – Libby closed her eyes for a moment and lifted her face to the sun. That one moment was enough. When she opened them again, both Milo and Clancy had disappeared. The bucket and spade had been abandoned and, raising her eyes, Libby could see the pair running along the beach.

'Clancy! Milo!' As the two hared off along the beach, Libby tried to catch up. It wasn't till she saw first Milo, then Clancy, stop in front of a man sitting on a rock outcrop that she drew breath.

'I'm sorry they disturbed you,' she said, panting as she reached them, one hand going up to shade her eyes from the sun.

Six

'Hello?'

Adam looked up from his laptop to see a small girl standing in front of him. She was wearing a pair of shorts with a pink seahorse design and a matching blue rashie. A large brown longhaired dog was standing panting behind her. He winced. Unless he was mistaken – or there were two of them – it was the same dog that had proved to be so overly friendly in the café on the day he arrived in town.

'What are you doing?' The girl had blonde curls which were peeking out from under a white sunhat. She was a cutie, the sort of child who made him regret not having any of his own. Though he was old enough to be this one's grandfather.

He was about to ask where her mother was, when an older woman came rushing up, yelling. The girl turned towards the voice, and the dog leapt off to meet the woman, jumping up excitedly.

The little girl immediately looked anxious. 'We're all right, Grandma. Milo and me wanted to have a run.'

'So I see. I'm sorry they disturbed you.' The woman appeared flustered.

From what Adam could see, she must be in her forties or early fifties. She was wearing a large sunhat from which a few blonde curls were escaping, and a well-fitting one-piece swimsuit in a shade of what Yvette would call electric blue. A sarong in another shade of blue was wrapped around her waist and hung almost to her ankles. He noticed all this in one glance. 'It's not a problem,' he said, trying to sound casual. It actually *was* a problem. He'd been lost in the world of Jay Bolton, his new protagonist. The journalist had been about to enter the house of a suspect and Adam had lost his train of thought when the girl and dog appeared.

As if sensing he wanted rid of them, the woman took the little girl's hand. 'Sorry,' she said again, and they walked off, the large dog ambling beside them.

For a moment, Adam wished he'd been more welcoming. He didn't know anyone here in Bellbird Bay unless he counted the woman living in Greg's old home. At another time, the woman might have intrigued him. He might have wondered if she was married or available – though marriage had never stopped him in the past. But those days were long gone. Now all he wanted was to be alone, and he was finding that easy to do in Bellbird Bay. No one knew him here. He was spared the type of adulation his writing had brought him, and he was enjoying the anonymity.

He returned to his work in progress and was soon once again lost in the world of intrigue he was creating.

*

It wasn't till later in the day, when Adam was enjoying a beer on the back deck as the sun was setting, that he remembered the incident on the beach. Despite the interruption, he had a productive day's writing and was feeling good about meeting the deadline he'd set himself. He had deliberately kept the news of his new direction from his agent, but knew he'd have to let him know soon. Julian would be clamouring for his next offering, eager to capitalise on the sales of his *popular* series. What would his reaction be when he learnt what Adam was writing?

It had definitely been the same dog, he decided. Surely there couldn't be two of them? And, although he'd pretended to be annoyed, there was something about the tableau of the woman, the child and the dog that had intrigued him. Maybe he could use it in his book, he mused, trying to figure out how such a domestic scene could fit into his storyline.

The ringing of his phone interrupted him, and he forced himself out of his musing to see Yvette's number on the screen. He sighed and accepted the call.

'Adam, I'm missing you so much.' The familiar husky voice of the woman who'd shared his bed only a few weeks ago failed to arouse its usual reaction. Instead, all Adam felt was a sense of release, relief he was here in Bellbird Bay, away from Canberra and its intricate web of eclectic humanity.

As he listened to Yvette share gossip which would once have interested him, he was struck by how easily he'd managed to shed his city persona in this small coastal town. It was as if he'd become a different person. Greg had been right, he thought, as Yvette's voice bubbled away, reporting the antics of various political figures and who said what to whom. Bellbird Bay was a refuge from the world.

It was over an hour later when the call finished, and in that time, Adam had barely spoken, sometimes even holding the phone away from his ear, Yvette's voice rising to a crescendo as she expressed her annoyance at one thing or other. Pleased he'd managed to calm her pleadings to join him for 'at least a weekend, darling', he contemplated how much he was enjoying having this time to himself. But he was unsure for how long he'd manage to avoid the disruption of her arriving here.

Had he been too cowardly, he wondered? Should he have finished the relationship before leaving? In retrospect, he could see how he'd taken the easy way out, assuming – or hoping – distance would lend itself to her finding someone new to squire her around. But, although Yvette was an attractive, elegant and successful woman, she was in her forties, and he supposed that, unlike him, most men would be looking for a younger partner to share their evenings and their bed. He castigated himself for his selfishness. He should have been honest with Yvette – or did he really want to keep her hanging on in case he decided he did want her in his future? It was all too hard, he decided, going back inside to pour himself a measure of scotch, before returning to the deck to stare out toward the ocean where he could see the lights of a ship anchored out on the horizon.

*

Next morning, there were no thoughts of Yvette or Canberra in Adam's mind as he made his way across the boardwalk and down to the beach for an early morning swim. As he powered through the waves, he felt a sense of wellbeing he hadn't experienced for years.

Back home, he had just showered and dressed in a pair of shorts and tee-shirt, so different to his normal city garb, when his phone rang. Fearing it was Yvette again, renewing her pleas to be allowed to visit, Adam was almost pleased to see his agent's number on the screen. He should have known he wouldn't escape Julian for long. With a sigh, he accepted the call.

Half an hour later, Adam finished the call. Julian had been the bearer of good news. He'd succeeded in selling the first of Adam's political thrillers to Channel Six. They planned to make a pilot which, if successful, would become a series, attracting a mind-blowing sum.

Julian was thrilled, expecting Adam to be the same. But, while he'd made all the right noises on the phone, for Adam, it was one more nail in his coffin, in his desire to avoid the hype of being a public figure who couldn't walk down the street without being recognised. Why, even here in Bellbird Bay, Eddie Armstrong had recognised his face. He'd give anything to be able to become anonymous. Maybe he should write his new series under a pen name. But he knew Julian would never agree, claiming he needed to satisfy his existing readers.

At least, in the excitement of his announcement, Julian had forgotten to ask Adam what he was currently working on. But it wouldn't be long before he did. And by then, Adam wanted to have made more progress. He couldn't allow himself to be distracted by dogs or their owners, no matter how attractive they were. He caught himself up. Attractive? He'd noticed more about the woman than he thought. Despite his annoyance at his train of thought being interrupted, the image of her was still strong in his mind.

By the time he was seated at his usual table at *The Bay Café*, he was again working out how he could insert the dog and its owner into his novel.

Seven

'Who was that man, Grandma?'

'What man, sweetheart?' Libby asked. They were enjoying breakfast in Libby's sun-filled kitchen. Libby was due to start work again today and was trying to persuade her daughter to think more positively and perhaps enrol Clancy in the local childcare centre. *Kiddie Korner*, run by Kate Henderson was close to the library, and it would give Emma time to look around for something to do herself. She needed to fill her time to prevent her from brooding over Matt and her uncertain future.

'The man on the beach yesterday. He looked angry with us. I didn't like him.' Clancy pouted.

'I think he was just upset at being interrupted, honey. He looked as if he might have been working.' Libby hadn't paid much attention to the man but thought she'd spotted a laptop.

'What man, Mum?' Emma asked, echoing Libby's words. 'You didn't say you'd seen anyone on the beach.'

Libby hadn't thought it important enough to mention. When Emma finally returned from her walk, they'd packed up and walked to the esplanade for ice cream. She'd completely forgotten about the incident. 'It was nothing,' she said in a conciliatory tone. 'Clancy and Milo decided to go for a stroll and disturbed a man who I think was working on his laptop. It was over in a flash. There wasn't a problem.'

Libby put a comforting hand on her daughter's arm, aware Emma was still reeling from Matt's defection and particularly sensitive to anything happening to Clancy. 'Clancy wasn't in any danger.'

'If you say so.' But Emma didn't look convinced. 'You need to stay close to Grandma or me,' she said to Clancy. 'This is a strange place. It's not like home where we know all the neighbours, where your little friends live.' She glared at her mother.

'I'd never let anything happen to Clancy, Em. You know that.' Libby gave a sigh.

'I know, Mum. It's just… with Matt gone… Clancy's all I have left. Sorry.' She looked so woebegone, Libby wanted to hug her. Then she shrugged. 'I will go to that place you were talking about,' she said, referring to their earlier conversation. 'It would be good for Clancy to be with other children, and it'll give me some space to…' She stopped as if unsure what she'd do with herself.

'Feel free to pop into the library. You can check out the local paper there. Or perhaps you'd prefer to just have a wander around town to get your bearings. We haven't been out much since we got back.' Libby worried about the way her daughter tended to cling to her and prefer to stay close to home. It wasn't healthy for her or for Clancy. 'There are some good cafés and several boutiques on the esplanade…' Libby's voice trailed off as she saw her daughter's eyes glaze over.

*

The morning passed slowly as Libby sorted out the book club boxes for the month. For her own book club, she'd chosen Erica James' latest, entitled *Mothers and Daughters* – surely appropriate for her own life at present. She was looking forward to reading it and to the discussion in the group. They were sure to enjoy it, even though not everyone in the group was a mother with a daughter. Grace would be sure to relate with two of her own, and Cleo had her Hannah, but Libby wasn't sure about the others.

It was close to lunchtime, and Libby was thinking of taking a break when she heard footsteps and a small voice say, 'Grandma'. Looking up, Libby saw Clancy standing beside her flourishing a copy of *Are You My Mother?* Libby smiled at her granddaughter, remembering the many times she'd read this book to her – and to Emma before her. Bernie had always heaved a sigh when Emma chose it as her bedtime read complaining it was so long.

'I can read it all by myself,' Clancy announced, opening the book and beginning to read. She had got as far as *'He will want to eat'* when Emma rushed up.

'Don't disturb Grandma,' she said. 'She's working.'

'She's not disturbing me, Em. I'm impressed,' she said to Clancy. 'I didn't know you could read.' She raised an eyebrow at her daughter.

'She just picked it up,' Emma said proudly. 'She knows most of her Dr Seuss books really well.'

'Can I have this one?' Clancy asked. 'I left all my books at home.' Her bottom lip trembled, and the colour drained from Emma's face.

'Of course, you can borrow it,' Libby said. 'I was about to have lunch, and I don't have to work this afternoon. Why don't we go to *The Bay Café*? There's a bookshop close by. Maybe we can find copies of your favourite books there?'

'Yes please, Grandma,' Clancy said with a smile.

'You don't need to do that, Mum,' Emma objected. 'We can…' Her eyes began to moisten, as if remembering why they'd left home.

'I know I don't, but I'd like to. Clancy needs books when she's here in Bellbird Bay and I can keep them here for her.'

'Thanks, Mum.'

'Lunch?'

'Yes. Nice idea. Thanks for that, too.'

A few minutes later they were seated at a window table in the small café on the esplanade, close to the bookshop.

'How was your morning?' Libby asked Emma when they'd ordered – panini stuffed with eggplant, tomato and fetta for Libby, a chicken salad wrap for Emma and a ham and cheese sandwich for Clancy, with coffees for the adults and milk for the little girl. Emma had been looking happier when she arrived in the library – until the unfortunate reminder about Clancy's books. 'Did you manage to pop into the childcare centre?'

'We did. Not on the table, Clancy,' Emma told her daughter who was opening her library book.

Libby bit her tongue. There was no harm in Clancy having her book on the café table while they waited for their lunch to be served. But there was no sense in aggravating Emma. She gave her granddaughter a reassuring smile. 'Maybe later, sweetheart.'

Then she realised what Emma had said. 'You did? What did you think? Did you talk to Kate? We're in the same book club.'

'Yes, so she said.' Emma appeared to be working out what to say.

'I liked Kate,' Clancy piped up.

Emma looked down at her daughter and smiled. 'She seems nice, and it all looked very well organised,' she admitted. 'In fact...' she took a deep breath, '...Kate suggested I could help out – just till Christmas.'

'She did? Why, that's wonderful, honey. Don't you think so?' she asked, seeing Emma frown.

'I'm not sure. Clancy would love it there. There are lots of activities for her – and other children her age – but... I'm not preschool trained.'

'But you have taught infants, haven't you? And this would only be a short-term thing. It would help take your mind off...' Libby didn't want to mention her son-in-law's name.

'I haven't heard from Matt if that's what you want to know.' Emma rearranged the salt and pepper on the table.

Libby's heart went out to her daughter. She'd seen the way Emma kept checking her phone, no doubt hoping to see a missed call or a message from her husband.

'I've booked Clancy in for two days next week, and told Kate I'd think about her offer,' Emma said.

'Oh, I'm glad, honey.' Libby was about to say more when a smiling waitress appeared with their meals, preventing any further comment on the subject.

'Can we go to get the books now?' Clancy asked, when they had finished eating and were about to leave the café. 'Can we get *Green Eggs and Ham*, and *The Cat in the Hat* and *Duck Feet* and *Mulberry Street* and...'

'That's enough, Clancy. Your Grandma isn't made of money,' Emma said.

'Let's see what they have,' Libby said as she paid the bill.

The three left the café and walked to the bookshop, Clancy holding hands with both her mother and Grandma and skipping along between them, reciting '*I do not like green eggs and ham, I do not like them, Sam I am.*'

Once inside the bookshop, Clancy dropped Libby and Emma's hands and made her way to the back of the shop where there was a display of children's books and a large cardboard cut-out of the cat from *The Cat in the Hat*, complete with his red and white striped scarf.

Emma made to follow her, but Libby held her back. 'She'll be fine,' she said. 'Why don't you find something for yourself?'

Emma gave her mother a strange look. 'It's ages since I had time to read,' she said.

'All the more reason to find something now.'

Looking unsure, Emma drifted off.

'You have company today.'

Libby looked up to see a smiling face surrounded by a mop of white hair. She had come to know Harry Simpson quite well during her time in Bellbird Bay, and he and Bernie had loved to discuss books before Bernie was taken from her. 'My daughter and granddaughter are staying with me for a bit,' she said. 'We need to replace Clancy's collection of Dr Seuss books… and I should get one for myself,' she added, seeing a display of new titles on a table in the middle of the shop.

'Go for it. I think we have most of the Dr Seuss titles in stock, and you may want to pick up a copy of the latest Liz Byrski.' He grinned.

Libby grinned back. Harry knew her taste so well. She headed off in the direction of the display to pick up the one he referred to. She didn't need to read the blurb, knowing she'd enjoy this novel by one of her favourite authors. Although working in the library, she still liked to add to her own collection and was glad her granddaughter had inherited her love of books and reading.

She heard Clancy's excited voice call her and was about to join her granddaughter when her hand hovered over a book by an author who Bernie had loved. Libby had never been a fan of political thrillers, but recognised Adam Holland was a master of his craft. His books flew off the library shelves. Her eyes flitted over the photo of the author, thinking he looked vaguely familiar, as if she'd seen him somewhere recently. Then Clancy was beside her, pulling her towards the pile of books she'd amassed on a small table at the rear of the store.

A short time later, all three left the store, Emma and Clancy each carrying a bag bearing the *Bay Books* logo, and Libby carrying one of her own and another filled with books for Clancy.

'Thanks, Grandma,' Clancy burbled, skipping along again and trying to jump over the cracks on the footpath.

'Thanks, Mum,' Emma said. 'I've been thinking. You're right. I'm going to accept Kate's offer. I think I'd enjoy working there.'

Libby gave a sigh of relief. Maybe she could stop worrying about Emma, at least for a little while.

Eight

Adam stared at the group leaving the bookshop. It was the same woman and child he'd seen on the beach. At least they didn't have the dog with them today, but they were accompanied by a younger woman. Glad to have avoided another encounter, though curious about the woman who today was dressed in a smart pair of pants with a white shirt, he pushed open the bookshop door. As always when he entered a bookshop, Adam stopped just inside the door for a moment to inhale the familiar aroma of books, which never failed to lift his spirits.

An elderly man with a mop of white hair and neatly trimmed beard greeted him in a lively voice. He could have walked out of one of the Charles Dickens volumes displayed behind the counter, Adam thought.

'Good afternoon. Visiting Bellbird Bay?' the man asked. 'Are you looking for anything in particular?'

'No, just browsing,' Adam muttered, catching sight of his latest release prominently displayed with other new titles. While it was always a thrill to see his books on display, he'd have preferred to remain anonymous. He knew it was only a matter of time before he was recognised. He was right.

'Harry Simpson.' The man left his spot behind the counter to join Adam at the display, holding out his hand. He peered at Adam, then back to the copy of Adam's latest book which had a younger version of Adam's face emblazoned on the cover. 'It's Adam Holland, isn't it? Welcome to Bellbird Bay. What a pleasure to meet you. We don't often see our popular authors in our small town.'

Adam shook Harry's hand, stifling a sigh. He could guess what was coming next.

'Will you be here for long? Could I persuade you to do an event for us – perhaps a meet the author evening or lunch, or even a book signing,' he finished, perhaps seeing Adam's eyes glaze over.

'Umm, this is a personal visit,' he said, giving Harry the professional smile he'd perfected over the years. 'I was hoping to avoid any publicity.' Then, seeing Harry's disappointed expression, he added, 'I could sign the books you have in stock.'

'That would be grand. I can find a space for you right here or... would you prefer to do it through the back?'

'Please.' Adam couldn't think of anything worse than sitting here in the middle of the store where he'd be a target for anyone to see. Although the place was empty right now, there was no guarantee it would stay that way. As he followed Harry through to a large storeroom-cum-office, Adam reflected that Julian would be ropable if he heard. His agent was always encouraging him to get about more, to do a tour for each book. So far, he'd managed to avoid most of his suggestions – and his books sold. Though maybe they'd sell more if he agreed to the publicity stunts he saw other authors participate in. Then he remembered Julian's latest news – the television deal. It was what most authors would give their back teeth for, but did he really want the publicity it would attract?

Sometime later, Adam finished signing a large stack of books. It appeared his novels were popular in this small coastal town. He supposed the place would attract lots of tourists, and it was coming up to holiday season. He checked out his photo on the cover of the novel again. It was an old one, taken before his hair started to go grey. It was surprising Harry had recognised him, but he supposed he hadn't changed too much over the years. Still, he was glad he'd consistently resisted Julian's urging to update his author profile picture. Maybe he could remain incognito here during his visit.

Leaving the bookshop after purchasing a book of photographs by Martin Cooper whose work he knew of from *Destination* magazine and who, he learned from Harry, was a local, he realised he was hungry, and it was well past lunchtime.

Eschewing *The Bay Café* which was his daily haunt for breakfast,

Adam decided to try out the surf club. Not a surfer himself, he admired the skill required and had a lot of respect for the surf lifesavers who risked their own lives to save others.

He signed in and climbed the stairs, pausing halfway to admire a mural depicting a surfer with his board on top of a wave. Must be a local hero, he thought, as he moved on up to the bar and restaurant area.

'Afternoon, sir. What will it be?' a young man with dark hair greeted him at the bar.

'Beer, thanks. A small one. Is lunch still available?'

'We serve food all day. I can recommend the burger with chips. It's a favourite around here.'

'Thanks. I'll have that. I'll be out on the deck,' Adam said, seeing the wide empty area outside the sliding glass doors.

He carried his beer outside, glad to have the deck to himself, and took out his phone. He'd heard it pinging with messages while he was in the bookshop but had ignored it, suspecting it was either Julian, Yvette or both, neither of whom he wanted to hear from.

He was right. Three messages from Julian and two from Yvette. He opened Julian's first.

You didn't get back to me re the TV deal. It's def going ahead. I need your signature on the contract. Call me.

Are you deliberately ignoring me? And what's happening with the new book? Hope you're getting stuck into it.

For Christ's sake call me!

Adam chuckled as he composed a reply asking Julian to email him the contract. He ignored the request for information about his current work, knowing it would only provoke at best a stream of abuse, and at worst a series of threats to cut ties with him. Neither would have any effect. Adam was enjoying writing his new protagonist. He leant back in his seat intent on drinking in the atmosphere – the ocean, the beach, the surfers he could see way out in the distance – and making mental notes for his writing.

It wasn't till he had finished his meal – the bartender hadn't been wrong about the burger and chips, they were delicious – that he took time to read the messages from Yvette. They were as expected. In the first one she sounded upbeat asking him about Bellbird Bay, mentioning some mutual friends, a couple of gallery openings she'd attended, wishing he'd been with her. In the second, she sounded more needy, pleading with him to call, asking again if she could join him, repeating her desire for them to spend Christmas and New Year together.

Adam sighed. He would reply, but not yet. He needed to decide how to let her down gently, try to communicate his need to be here alone, to fulfil his promise to Greg, to… This was where he had the problem. He wasn't sure why, but he felt a sense of release knowing she was over 1200 kilometres away in Canberra.

Nine

Libby was sitting on her deck in her robe with a cup of liquorice tea, enjoying the unexpected pleasure of being alone. As she listened to the waves pounding on the shore, the cries of the seabirds flying overhead and Milo snoring at her feet, she reflected how, although it was lovely to have Emma and Clancy to stay, their presence meant she had little time to herself. This was the first time she'd been alone since they all came back from Brisbane. And it had only come about because both Emma and Clancy had gone to *Kiddie Korner*, and Libby didn't have to be at the library today. She'd waved them off after breakfast with a sense of relief and made herself a second cup of tea, looking forward to a quiet day with nothing and no one to interrupt her.

She had finished her tea and closed her eyes to enjoy the relative silence when the ringing of her phone broke into her thoughts. Picking it up, Libby smiled with pleasure to see the call was from Bev at the local garden centre. A few months earlier, on a visit to *The Pandanus Garden Centre*, she'd admired a wooden bench seat. Unlike many she had seen, this one was made of ironbark sleepers, and the back was deep enough for a plaque of some sort. It was exactly what she wanted. Libby could imagine it sitting on the viewing platform which was set off the boardwalk opposite her gate with views of the beach and the ocean – a fitting memorial to Bernie, looking out onto his favourite view. She'd gained permission from the council to place it there and had been looking forward to its arrival.

The one she had seen had already been purchased, and Bev, who owned the centre, explained the benches were made to order by a local man. Charlie Bird was a retired schoolteacher who had taken this up as a hobby and only built the seats by request. It was several months since Libby had ordered the bench, but she already had the brass plaque engraved with the words, *For Bernie in memory of many happy years together*, and the years of his birth and death.

'Hello, Bev,' she said excitedly.

'Libby. I've just had a call from Charlie. Your bench seat is ready. He can deliver it for you today or bring it here for you to pick up, whichever suits you best.'

'Oh, here please.' Libby couldn't think how she'd manage to pick up the heavy wooden bench herself. 'Do I need to contact him?'

'I can do that. I see it's already paid for, and we have your address. Will you be home?'

'All day.' Libby was smiling when she finished the call, deciding to take a quick shower and dress before her order arrived. She wondered if Charlie – who she'd never met – would be able to attach the brass plaque for her, too. She wasn't good at those sorts of jobs. She missed Bernie doing them for her. She paused for a moment, a wave of grief engulfing her as she pictured his familiar face, the way his eyes crinkled when he smiled, the unruly strand of hair which always fell across his forehead, the one she loved to push back before planting a kiss on his lips. Then she forced herself to head for the shower.

Dressed in a pair of denim three-quarter pants and a tailored white blouse, Libby had almost given up hope when the doorbell rang. Opening the door, she saw a wiry grey-haired man standing there. Behind him was a ute, on the tray of which sat the varnished wooden bench she was waiting for. It looked wonderful.

'Mrs Walker?'

'That's me. You must be Charlie and you've brought my bench.' Libby pushed past him to go to the ute and stroked the wooden seat, before turning back to the bemused man. 'Sorry. I'm just so glad to see it. Thank you so much.'

Charlie scratched his head. 'I've delivered a lot of these, but I don't normally get this reaction.' He grinned. 'Where would you like it?'

'Out behind the house. There's a viewing platform leading off the boardwalk. Can you manage?' The bench was made of solid wood. It looked heavy.

'No worries. If you can make sure the doors and gate are wide open and keep out of the way, I'll have it in place for you in no time.'

'Of course.' Libby did as he asked.

He was right. It was a struggle, but Charlie had obviously done this many times, and before long the bench was sitting in the exact spot she'd imagined it. She stroked it again, wishing Bernie could be here to see it, to sit on it with her, to enjoy the view one more time. Now it would be others who'd sit there in his place.

Libby was so lost in her thoughts, she forgot Charlie was still there until he cleared his throat.

'Was there anything else?' he asked.

'There is one thing. The bench is a memorial to my late husband.' How she hated the phrase. 'I have a plaque which needs to be attached to the back of it. I wondered…'

'I can do that for you. Do you have screws and a screwdriver? I keep a few bits and pieces in the ute.'

'I have them.' The screws had come with the plaque, and she still had all of Bernie's old tools. Although she rarely used them – didn't know how or have the strength to use many of them – she was loath to throw or give them away.

Once the plaque was fixed in place, Libby farewelled Charlie and went inside to fetch her camera. She needed a photo to mark the occasion and wanted a better one than she could take with her phone. Even though she wasn't familiar with the camera Bernie had used to take his shots of the coastline in all its moods, it surely couldn't be too difficult. She thought of the exhibition they'd attended here before Bernie became so sick. Martin Cooper had been one of his heroes, and he'd been thrilled to see the announcement in the local paper, then to meet the man himself. One of Martin's coffee table books, containing shots of this very coastline, lay on the low table in the living room – a memento of the happy occasion, even though Bernie hadn't lived to enjoy the book which had been published after his death.

But when she tried to focus the camera, Libby discovered it wasn't going to be as easy as she'd imagined. First of all, she had trouble focussing; her eyes blurred with tears when she put her eye to the viewfinder. Then there were the settings on the camera. The expensive piece of equipment, bought to satisfy Bernie's exacting needs as well as his expertise developed over years, was more complicated than Libby had expected. She was on the point of giving up and returning inside to fetch her phone when she heard someone behind her.

'Need some help?'

Libby turned abruptly to see a tall man, his thick grey hair ruffled by the breeze, his eyes a shade of flint grey, like the pebbles which edged her garden. There were deeply etched lines on his face, a sign of time spent in the sun. He was dressed in a pair of jeans and a tee-shirt and looked vaguely familiar.

'Do I know you?' As soon as she spoke, Libby regretted the words. The stranger was trying to be helpful. 'Sorry, I mean…' She blushed and lowered the camera.

'I think we met on the beach. You were retrieving a young child and a dog.' His eyes crinkled in amusement.

'Oh, of course.' That was why he looked familiar, she thought, though on the beach he hadn't been wearing jeans and a tee-shirt. The image of a tanned, naked chest appeared in her mind's eye. She blushed again.

'Adam,' he said.

'Libby.'

'I'm renting the house up there for a few months.' He pointed to a house further up the boardwalk.

He must mean Grace Winter's place. Grace was in the same book club as Libby, and they worked together in the library. Only last year, she had formed a relationship with Ted Crawford and moved in with him. Libby knew she rented her home out to tourists, but this was the first one she'd met.

'You look as if you need help,' he said, gesturing to the camera.

'Oh!' Libby felt foolish. 'It's… it was my husband's camera. I'm afraid I'm not used to it. I wanted to…' She looked across at the bench.

'May I?' He held out his hand.

Reluctantly, Libby handed over the camera. 'The bench is in his memory,' she said. 'I just had it delivered and placed here overlooking…' Her voice broke.

Without speaking, Adam fiddled with the camera, then took a few shots before handing it back. 'That should do it. I have one not unlike it myself.'

'Thanks. It's kind of you.'

They stood for a few moments without speaking, gazing at the bench seat, then, gesturing towards the plaque, Adam asked, 'Your husband?'

Libby nodded.

'I'm sorry.'

She nodded again, never sure how to respond to people's condolences. It was difficult enough when they were offered by friends, people who'd known Bernie, known them as a couple. This man was a stranger.

'Can I offer you a cup of tea – as a thank you? It's the least I can do.' Libby spoke hurriedly, immediately regretting her words. What was she thinking of, inviting a stranger into her home?

Adam hesitated for a few moments, then pushed a hand through his hair as if embarrassed. 'Thanks,' he said.

They walked across the boardwalk into Libby's garden. To Libby's relief, Adam was content to remain on the deck while she went inside to make tea, berating herself for her impetuous invitation. But, once they were settled with cups of Earl Grey and a plate of brownies left over from a baking session with Clancy, she felt more at ease.

'Have you lived here long?' Adam asked in a gentle voice.

'We bought the house several years ago, mainly as a holiday home. We planned to retire here.'

Libby remembered the day they discovered the house as if it was yesterday.

*

'Look!' Libby clasped her husband's hand and pointed to the For Sale *sign in the front yard of the little beach cottage. 'It's perfect, Bernie.'*

'It certainly looks exactly like what we've been looking for, but let's wait to see inside before we get too excited.'

Libby smiled. Now Emma was grown and married, it was time for Libby and Bernie to consider their own lives. They'd been down this track before, searching for the perfect holiday cottage, one which could double as their retirement home in the not-too-distant future.

The past few weekends they'd travelled up and down the coast in search of the perfect spot, becoming more and more disheartened as they discovered faults with almost every place they visited.

Bellbird Bay was almost last on their list and, so far, the seaside town had met all their exacting criteria. It wasn't too big, too populated, and the developers hadn't yet discovered it. Also, it was within reasonable driving distance from Brisbane where they'd spent most of their married life, and where their daughter and granddaughter lived.

But, despite the town being everything they wanted in a holiday-cum-retirement home, so far, all the houses they'd seen had been a disaster.

However, Libby felt a frisson of excitement at the sight of this cottage, hardly more than a holiday shack, situated as it was in a narrow street whose houses backed onto the ocean – or at least onto the coastal pathway which flanked the ocean. She could imagine living here, early morning walks along the beach, sunset drinks on the back deck, lazy afternoons sitting outside with a good book while Bernie pottered around in the garden.

'Let's arrange to view it,' she said, a note of excitement in her voice.

Bernie hugged her tightly, forcing her to beg for breath.

*

She realised Adam was waiting for her to say more. 'Then my husband died.' The stark phrase told nothing of the months of suffering, the well of grief from which she was only now emerging. 'And I moved here by myself. The little girl you saw me with on the beach is my granddaughter, Clancy. She and my daughter are staying with me at the moment.'

Just then, Milo pushed his way out of the house to join them. He went straight to Adam and began sniffing at his ankles.

'Here, Milo,' Libby said, seeing Adam flinch. Surely he wasn't afraid of dogs? Milo wouldn't hurt a fly, but he was rather a large animal. 'He just wants to get to know you. He's really quite gentle,' she said with a smile.

'Right.' Adam put his hand down to warily pat Milo's head. The dog reacted by pushing his head into his hand.

'What about you?' Libby asked. 'What brings you to Bellbird Bay?'

'Strangely enough, a death brought me here, too, the death of a good friend.' Adam gazed out towards the ocean for a moment before continuing. 'Greg grew up here in Bellbird Bay, in a house not far from this one, actually. Before he died, he charged me with spreading his ashes in the ocean here on Christmas Eve. I promised I would.'

'I'm sorry for your loss, too. He must have been a good friend.'

'We went through a lot together.'

Libby had the impression there was more to it but could see Adam was having difficulty controlling his emotions, so decided to change the subject.

They had finished their tea and were chatting about the various events to be held in Bellbird Bay over the coming festive period when Emma and Clancy appeared in the kitchen doorway.

'Mum?' Emma looked from her mother to Adam, then back again.

'It's that man again, the one from the beach.' Clancy cowered against her mother's legs.

Milo, who had been lying at Libby's feet, rose to go over to greet Clancy, his tongue ticking her feet and making her squeal.

'Emma, this is Adam. He's renting a cottage belonging to a friend of mine and helped me out with your dad's camera. Adam, this is my daughter, Emma, and Clancy who you've already met.'

'What were you doing with Dad's camera?' Emma asked suspiciously, not moving from her spot in the doorway.

'The bench arrived – the one I told you I'd ordered. I wanted to take a photo of it, but the camera beat me until Adam arrived. We're just having a cup of tea.'

'I can see that.' Emma still didn't move.

'I should go.' Adam rose. 'Thanks for the tea. I'm glad I could be of some help. Good to meet you, Emma.' He nodded in her direction, and left, the gate swinging shut behind him.

'That was rude,' Libby said, when Adam was out of sight and hearing, and Emma and Clancy had joined her on the deck.

'Rude? I come home to find you entertaining a strange man. Dad's only been gone for… Mum!'

'Hardly entertaining, Em. Adam was very helpful, and the tea was my way of saying thank you.' Libby wondered why she felt she had to explain herself to her daughter.

'So you say.' Emma pursed her lips.

'How was your day? And how did you enjoy *Kiddie Korner*, Clancy?' Libby asked, realising Emma would continue to berate her if she didn't take charge of the conversation.

Clancy replied first. Now Adam had left, she was happily playing with Milo. 'I had fun, Grandma. I did a jigsaw and painted and played in the sandpit with Angie and…'

Libby smiled, glad Clancy was settling in. She looked at her daughter. 'Em?'

'It was good, Mum. Kate put me to work helping out with one of the younger groups. It was a bit odd at first, but I quite enjoyed it. It was pretty hectic. It took my mind off…' She stopped and looked at Clancy before Matt's name crossed her lips.

'So you'll both be going back?'

'Tomorrow. You're working then?'

'Yes. Why don't I make us both a cuppa? And I'm sure Clancy would like a glass of milk or juice.'

Clancy looked up at the sound of her name. 'Juice, please, Grandma, and are there any of our brownies left?'

'Let's go and see.' Libby rose, holding out her hand for the little girl to grasp.

Emma followed them into the house, but didn't stop in the kitchen, Instead, she went into the living room where Libby heard her rifling around in the bookcase. She sighed. What was her daughter up to now?

Libby had made two cups of lemon and ginger tea and poured a glass of juice for Clancy. She and her granddaughter were seated at the kitchen table with a plate of the remaining brownies when Emma reappeared. She was flourishing a book from Bernie's collection.

'I thought I recognised him,' she said, as if her suspicions were confirmed. 'This is him, isn't it? Even though it must have been taken years ago, he hasn't changed very much. The man you were gaily entertaining to tea is none other than Dad's favourite author. He's Adam Holland. What's a famous author like him doing here in Bellbird Bay?'

Ten

Adam hurried along the boardwalk, glad to leave the tense atmosphere which had arisen with the arrival of the daughter and granddaughter of the woman he'd only just met. He'd been enjoying talking with Libby – he didn't know her surname and been glad she hadn't asked for his. It had been restful to spend time with someone – a woman – who didn't immediately fawn over him because of his fame, fame he didn't feel he deserved and which brought him more torment than pleasure. He sometimes felt that even Yvette was more interested in his reputation than in him as a person.

The poor woman was still grieving. He recognised the signs and could empathise with her, even though his loss had been of a good friend, not a partner. There was something about her that sparked his interest, and they'd been getting along famously until her daughter arrived. He recognised the expression on the daughter's face. He'd seen it before, written about it, even. It was a mixture of suspicion and jealousy. The daughter – Emma was her name – no doubt wanted her mother to spend the rest of her life grieving for her dead husband. And, right now, Libby might imagine it's what she'd do. But she was still a young woman. She must be around Adam's age, in her mid to late fifties, and could live for another twenty to thirty years. That was a long time to be alone.

But wasn't he alone? He thrust the thought aside and settled down to a few hours of writing.

When he finally closed his laptop, he stretched his arms above his head and gave a sigh. Jay Bolton was proving to be a welcome relief from his usual type of hero, and Adam was recognising a lot of Greg in him, or Greg as he would have been if he'd been reporting crime instead of politics. Adam felt sure Greg would approve of his similarity to the fictional character and the setting on Queensland's Sunshine Coast.

Heading to the kitchen, he poured himself a coffee from the coffee percolator which always sat ready on the stove top. It was one he'd owned for years and served him well. He had no need of the fancy machines many of his friends had graduated to and swore by. If he wanted anything fancier, he'd go to a café – and he'd discovered there were plenty of those in Bellbird Bay.

He carried his coffee out to the deck and stared out at the view, the same view as the one from Libby's deck and from the viewing platform where the memorial bench to her husband now sat. He could see it from here if he leant over the fence.

Coffee finished, Adam felt restless. He'd met his word deadline for the day so, rather than returning to his desk, he set out to walk up the boardwalk in the direction of the headland. He hadn't gone in that direction before, preferring to make his way down toward the esplanade where he had breakfast every morning and where he was able to purchase the few essentials he needed to keep body and soul together.

Adam walked quickly and soon reached the rocky headland. The view from here was stupendous, the outcrop dividing two bays. On the far side, the ocean was much wilder than he was accustomed to seeing in the bay, and the sea was dotted with the dark heads of surfers waiting to catch a wave.

He was enjoying the view, when he became aware there was someone behind him. Turning quickly, he saw a thin, elderly woman wheeling a green bicycle. Her face, lined and brown from too many years in the sun, was peering at him from beneath a wide-brimmed straw hat.

'You'll be the new man in Grace Winter's place,' she said, her gaze scanning him from head to toe as if assessing him.

'How did...?'

The woman tapped her nose with one bony finger.

How old was *she?* She looked as if a gust of wind would blow her over, but there was something about her that forced Adam to pay attention.

'I get about. I know things. For example, I know you believe you're here on a mission, but you were always meant to come to Bellbird Bay. It's where you'll find your destiny.' She nodded twice as if confirming her words, then turned away to disappear through a gate in the shabby white fence.

For a few moments, Adam stared at the tall house into which the woman had disappeared, wondering if he'd imagined the entire exchange. The sign on the now closed gate said, *Headland View*. Did the woman live there – or was she, like him, a visitor to the town? Either way, her words had the effect of knocking him for six.

By the time he reached his back gate, it was growing dark, and strangely for him, the thought of the dark empty house sent shivers up his spine. Telling himself not to be stupid, he nevertheless bypassed the house and headed down the boardwalk to where the lights of the surf club were a welcome sight.

The same dark-haired young man who had served him on his previous visit was behind the bar. This time, Adam ordered calamari with chips and salad along with a beer to chase away the memory of the weird woman's words. He was about to pick up his beer and find a place to sit, when he heard the barman say, 'Your usual, Coop?'

Adam recognised the man who appeared at his side. It was the photographer, Martin Cooper.

'Thanks, Nate. Your mum's on her way. A white wine for her,' he said with a grin. Then he nodded at Adam.

Adam nodded back. Then Martin Cooper stared at him. 'Don't I know you?'

'I don't think so, but I know who you are. I'm an admirer of your work, have one of your coffee table books.'

Martin waved his hand in the air dismissively, indicating he didn't think much of the books, then stared at Adam again, before snapping his fingers. 'I know. You're the guy who's renting Grace Winter's place, the one who's Greg Holmes' friend.' His face became serious. 'The one who brought him home to Bellbird Bay.' He thrust out a hand. 'Growing up in Bellbird Bay, we all knew Greg.'

Adam shook the outstretched hand.

'On your own? Why don't you join us? My partner should be…' He looked around. 'Here she is.'

Martin was a tall man with faded blond hair. His partner was slim, attractive, her dark hair showing streaks of grey. When she reached them, she leant over the bar to receive a kiss on the cheek from the barman, who handed her a glass of white wine.

'Ailsa, this is Grace's new tenant…' He raised an eyebrow in Adam's direction.

'Adam.' They'd discover who he was soon enough. Adam wondered if Martin Cooper had similar feelings about his reputation. Hadn't there been some scandal a couple of years back? Adam had a vague recollection of Greg mentioning something about it. He hadn't paid much attention, more interested in the sales figures for his most recent release.

'Adam,' Martin repeated. 'You will join us?'

'Please do,' Ailsa said. 'We're meeting a couple of friends for dinner, but you'll be most welcome.'

Adam was about to refuse politely, when another couple came across the restaurant to join them, the man's long blond hair tied back in a ponytail, the tiny woman's a dark cloud on her shoulders.

'Hey, Will, Cleo,' Martin greeted them. 'This is Adam. He's joining us. He's the guy Eddie mentioned who's come to spread Greg Holmes' ashes.'

'Good man.' Will shook Adam's hand. 'Heard about Greg. Another good man gone too soon. Like Coop here, he left when he finished school, but *he* never came back.' He nudged his friend with his elbow.

There was obviously a story there.

Adam realised it was now too late to avoid joining them, so decided to give in to the inevitable and followed the four to a table on the deck overlooking the wide stretch of white sand, illuminated only by the moon and a spotlight on the edge of the club's roof.

During their meal, the two women chatted together, while Martin and Will regaled Adam with stories of Greg's youth.

'Of course, he was a couple of years above us at school,' Martin said, 'but he was always kind to us, unlike some of his mates who resented what we managed to accomplish in the surf.'

It turned out Martin had also come across Greg in a war zone, before he gave it up to focus on the political scene in the capital. 'You knew Greg then?' he asked Adam. 'Strange we never crossed paths, although Greg and I only met briefly. It was chaotic.'

Suddenly Will, who had been studying Adam carefully said. 'I know who you are. I'm not much of a reader but Owen – my son – gave me a book for Christmas, and it sucked me in. You're the author. Adam... Adam...'

'Adam Holland,' Cleo finished for him, evidently having been listening to their conversation.

So much for him remaining incognito.

To his surprise, Adam didn't feel as upset as he'd expected when Cleo said his name aloud, though he did glance quickly around to see if there was anyone else within earshot.

'Guilty as charged,' he said, forcing a smile.

'Know what it's like, mate. Guess you thought you'd stay under the radar up here, but once you're a household name there's no escape. Believe me. You just have to grin and bear it,' Martin said with a wry grin.

The woman who'd been introduced as Ailsa patted his arm, and Will grinned.

'How are you liking Bellbird Bay?' It was the dark-haired woman – Cleo.

'Very much,' Adam replied, glad to be on neutral territory. 'I've visited the house where Greg grew up, met a woman called Eddie.'

'Lovely lady,' Ailsa said. 'I met her through Bev, Martin's sister.'

'Twin sister.' Martin grimaced. 'Five minutes older and she never lets me forget it.'

'Don't you forget all the things she's done for you,' Ailsa reminded him.

'What else?' Cleo asked, clearly keen to close off this friendly banter.

'Just finding my way around the town,' Adam replied. 'I walked up to the headland this afternoon.' Then he remembered the strange woman he'd met there. 'There was this elderly woman,' he said, only to see all four start to laugh. 'What?'

'You met Ruby Sullivan. We've all been subject to Ruby's pronouncements from time to time. She didn't spook you, did she?' Ailsa asked.

'Well…' Adam remembered the woman's words.

'Trouble is, she's usually spot on.' Ailsa grinned.

But surely not this time? It was Greg's last wish which had brought him to Bellbird Bay, not some weird destiny over which he had no control. A shiver ran down Adam's spine.

'She's been around Bellbird Bay for what seems like for ever,' Will said. 'As long as I can remember, anyway. No one knows how old she is and, as far as we know, she and her family have always lived in that house which she now runs as a bed and breakfast. It's very popular.'

'And she makes the most delicious cakes,' Cleo added. 'We sell them at *The Pandanus Café.*'

'*The Pandanus Café?*' Adam hadn't come across it.

'It's the café part of *The Pandanus Garden Centre and Café,*' Ailsa explained. 'Martin's sister, Bev, owns both, and Cleo manages the café. You must visit and sample Ruby's cakes.'

'So all of you grew up here?'

'Will and I did,' Martin said. 'But Ailsa and Cleo are ring ins. Lucky for us.' He threw Ailsa a look filled with such naked love Adam was forced to avert his eyes. It made his forays into the romance field seem paltry by comparison. What must it be like to feel like that for another human being – and to have your feelings returned, he wondered, seeing the love in Ailsa's eyes as she returned Martin's gaze.

The conversation became more general as the others suggested places for Adam to visit, so many he'd have no time to write if he followed all of them. Then the talk turned to Christmas.

Adam hadn't given much thought as to how he'd celebrate the special day in the Christian calendar. If he'd been in Canberra, no doubt Yvette would have managed to persuade him into having lunch by Lake Burley Griffin in an expensive restaurant, after exchanging equally expensive gifts. But here, with no one to consider but himself, for Adam, it would be just another day, one in which he'd write, walk along the beach, perhaps take a swim, and no doubt be bombarded by calls and texts from Yvette.

It was a good evening, and Adam felt he'd found some friends here in Bellbird Bay when he finally farewelled the four and started back up the boardwalk. It was peaceful at this time of night. Most of the houses he passed were in darkness, but he noted a glimmer of light shining through the curtains of the house belonging to the woman he'd met that afternoon. On an impulse, he stepped onto the viewing platform to gaze at the bench seat with its plaque in memory of Libby's husband – another reminder that for some, love could be all-encompassing.

Adam turned to face the ocean, now shrouded in darkness. In the distance, on the horizon, he could see the lights of what he assumed was a ship at anchor. A sudden gust of wind forced him to wrap his arms around himself. Then he returned to the boardwalk to continue his walk home.

Eleven

Emma was sitting in the kitchen crying when Libby came home from work, and Clancy was nowhere in sight.

'Where's Clancy?' she asked, as Milo rose from his favourite spot by the window to greet her, his tongue hanging out to show his delight she was home.

'I'm not sure. She went to her room with a book.' Emma looked so distraught, her eyes red, her face blotchy, Libby gathered her into a hug. 'What's happened?'

'It's Matt,' she sobbed.

Only then, Libby saw the mobile phone gripped tightly in her daughter's hand. 'He called?'

Emma nodded. 'He... he wants to see Clancy, wants her with him and his slut for Christmas.'

'Well, that's not going to happen.' Libby felt a burst of anger threaten to break through her usually calm manner.

'But Mum... He says he's entitled to access. What if...?'

'He walked out on you and Clancy. No court's going to allow him to have her for the holiday,' Libby said, sounding more confident than she felt. She had no idea what the family court would or wouldn't permit. But right now, she had to calm Emma down for her own sake and for Clancy's. 'Now why don't I make us both a cup of tea and you can tell me exactly what he said?'

Emma nodded and rubbed her eyes, but she had stopped crying.

'I'll just check on Clancy.' Libby went through to the bedroom where she found her granddaughter sitting cross-legged on the floor, reading aloud from *The Cat in The Hat*. She gave a sigh of relief. At least Clancy hadn't seen her mother in this state.

'Hi, Grandma.' The little girl stopped mid-sentence and looked up. Is it teatime? I'm hungry.'

Libby smiled at the resilience of the young. 'I'm about to make tea for Mummy and me. Would you like some warm milk with honey?'

'Yes, please.' Clancy carefully closed her book and got up to take Libby's hand. 'Do you have any of those special biscuits I like?' she asked, as they made their way back to the kitchen.

By the time they got there, Libby was pleased to see Emma had made an effort to pull herself together and had already filled and turned on the electric jug.

'Thanks, sweetheart,' she said, releasing Clancy's hand.

Clancy immediately made for Milo who, seeing her arrive, had risen to his feet again.

Libby waited until Clancy had finished her milk, eaten one of the iced vovos which had become her favourite treat, and disappeared outside with Milo and a ball. Then she made herself and Emma a second cup of camomile tea and turned to her daughter. 'Now, tell me exactly what Matt said.'

Emma pulled out a tissue again and, through a torrent of tears, during which Libby had trouble making out the words, managed to say, 'He said she's his daughter too and he has a right to see her. He and April are planning to spend Christmas and New Year in Fiji and they want to take Clancy with them. He can't, can he?' She gazed pleadingly at Libby, searching her face for an answer.

'I'm pretty sure he can't. Wouldn't she need a passport?'

'She has one. Remember we went to New Zealand to visit Matt's folks when she was just a baby. It's still in the house.' She bit her lip.

'We should consult a lawyer.' Libby frowned. She didn't have a lawyer in Bellbird Bay. Don Townsend, who had been her and Bernie's solicitor, was in Brisbane, and she wasn't sure he dealt with family law. She'd known Emma would have to go down that route one day but hadn't expected it to be so soon. 'Let me see what I can do,' she said to pacify Emma. 'I'll check my contacts.'

'Thanks, Mum.' Emma sounded relieved, but Libby's mind was

going round in circles. *Had she promised Emma more than she could deliver?*

'Why don't you take Clancy down to the beach while I make some calls?'

'Yes, please, Mummy,' Clancy said, appearing in the doorway.

'I suppose,' Emma said, but rose and slipped her feet into her sandals which were sitting by the door. 'Come on, Clancy.'

'Can Milo come, too?'

The dog gave a short bark at the sound of his name and wagged his tail.

'Okay.'

Libby took his lead from the hook by the door and handed it to her daughter. 'The fresh air will do you both good. Don't hurry back.'

Alone again, Libby stared at her phone wondering if it had been a mistake to offer to help Emma. She really should be doing this herself. But, since Matt's betrayal, her normally bright and independent daughter had become more needy. She took a deep breath, searched for Don Townsend's name on her contact list and pressed to connect the call.

It had been a relief to speak with her and Bernie's old friend, even though the sound of his voice reminded her of their last meeting – that dreadful time in his office when he had to explain Bernie's will to her. She had been the one to break down on that occasion. Today, he was in an ebullient mood, eager to hear how she was enjoying life in Bellbird Bay. He became more serious when he heard of Emma's plight.

Libby could almost hear his thought processes, but in reality it was the clicking of his keyboard as he searched for someone who could help.

'Got it!' he said at last. 'There's a family lawyer you can contact who should be able to help. Sharon Smith works out of an office close to where you are. I'll email you her information. Do you still have the same email address?'

'I do. Thanks, Don.'

'Not a problem. And be sure to get in touch when you're in Brisbane. Pam and I would love to see you. It's been too long.'

'I will.' But as Libby ended the call, she knew she wouldn't be contacting them. Don had been Bernie's friend. They'd played golf together. She and Pam had never had much in common, only enduring each other's company because of their husbands. Pam was one of the many ladies-who-lunch Libby had come across and usually tried to avoid. Thank goodness there weren't many like her in Bellbird Bay. She thought of the friends she'd made here and gave a sigh of pleasure.

Don's email came through almost immediately and, by the time Emma and Clancy came home, Emma looking a little brighter, and Clancy with a handful of shells and chattering about what they'd seen on the beach, Libby had arranged an appointment for her daughter with Sharon Smith in two days' time.

Twelve

The discussion in the surf club about Christmas stuck in Adam's mind. It was still several weeks away, but he found himself plagued with memories of Christmases past, especially those of his childhood. His mother had always loved to celebrate. For weeks beforehand, their house had been redolent with the scent of Christmas pudding, Christmas cake, and all sorts of other offerings designed to make the day special. It had been his dad's job to source the tree. And, as soon as he was deemed old enough, Adam had joined him to search for exactly the right one – with evenly spaced and which would be tall enough to reach the ceiling without actually touching it. Then there was the delight of decorating the tree with ornaments gathered over the years and carefully packed in their special box, only to be taken out once a year. He wondered what had happened to them. He hadn't seen them since his mother left, and Christmas had never been the same since then, either.

It was all a far cry from the bare rooms he presently called home. In Canberra, there had been the plethora of social events leading up to the holiday, gatherings that even Adam with his hatred of such occasions, was unable to avoid.

He stared around him in despair. Surely he could do something to relieve the anonymity of the place? The owner had rented it furnished but while comfortable, there were none of the personal items that made a house into a home.

He didn't want a Christmas tree, that would be going too far with no one to enjoy it other than himself. But Adam remembered the poinsettias his mother loved to buy each year and place on the sideboard, saying how their red and green foliage reminded her of home. Adam had been twelve before he realised she was referring to the small town in the south of England where she'd grown up and left in her early twenties, never to return. He'd visited it during his gap year, when he and a mate had done the European trip many young Australians yearned for, before starting university. The small country town with its narrow streets and equally small houses hadn't felt like home to him, and there were no relatives left there. He'd taken some photographs and been glad to leave it for the bright lights of London.

Now the idea of a poinsettia fired him with the desire to attempt to recapture at least some of the happy childhood Christmases he remembered, before the last one when everything fell apart. At the surf club, hadn't there been talk of a garden centre owned by Martin's sister and where Cleo worked? Adam racked his brain. It had been the name of a tree. He opened his phone and googled Bellbird Bay Garden Centre. There it was. *The Pandanus Garden Centre and Café.*

Half an hour later, Adam had entered the address of the garden centre into the satnav in his Volvo and was on his way.

Adam whistled under his breath when he drove through the arched entrance which proclaimed it was *The Pandanus Garden Centre and Café* and into the parking lot. It was much larger and more impressive than he expected. Martin's sister must be quite a woman to have established something like this in Bellbird Bay. Were there really enough dedicated gardeners in this small town to keep a place this size in business?

When he walked through the shop into the garden centre proper, he could see there were. The place was bustling with people, all seemingly intent on filling their trolleys with a mix of plants, potting mix and decorative planters.

He wandered around admiring the displays before catching sight of a shelf of poinsettias designed to be given as gifts, sitting in white pots which set off their colourful foliage. With no need for repotting, they were exactly what he wanted. He picked one up and took it to the checkout. Then, curious to see more of the place, he caught sight of the sign for *The Pandanus Café* almost hidden by a hedge of blue flowers he didn't recognise. He was no gardener.

The idea of coffee was appealing, so he headed through the archway to discover small tables had been artistically placed among a series of low bushes and towering palm trees. In its centre was the large pandanus tree from which the place no doubt got its name. Taking a seat, he picked up a menu, remembering what Cleo had said about the cakes baked by the weird old woman he'd met on the headland.

Ordering a long black and a slice of the delicious sounding pear frangipani, Adam settled back to check his emails on his phone, frowning at the sight of one from Julian reminding him to sign and return the contract about the television deal and asking again what he was working on, and yet another from Yvette which he read and deleted. It was more of the same. She wanted to join him in Bellbird Bay for Christmas. He knew he should call her but couldn't face talking with her right now, hearing her pleas, her disappointment. He promised himself he'd do it sometime later. He was working out how to reply to Julian when he heard a small voice say, 'Can I have a milkshake, Grandma?'

The voice sounded familiar and looking up, Adam saw Libby and her granddaughter entering the café

She looked around and their eyes met.

Without thinking, Adam half-rose. 'We meet again. Why don't you join me? It seems to me I owe you a coffee, and I have it on good authority the cakes here are delicious. They serve milkshakes, too,' he said to the little girl who was keeping a firm grip of her grandmother's hand.

Libby appeared flustered, her eyes darting around the café before meeting his again. 'Thanks, it's kind of you,' she said. 'We'd like that, wouldn't we, Clancy?'

The little girl didn't seem so sure but took a seat anyway.

'Your daughter not with you today?' Adam asked, to ensure the woman who'd glowered at him disapprovingly wasn't going to suddenly appear.

'No, she's working today.'

'She lives with you?' Adam had got the impression the daughter and granddaughter were only visiting.

'No. It's complicated.' Libby sighed.

'Most things are,' Adam agreed. He had no desire to inquire any further into Libby's personal life. It was none of his business. He didn't even know why he'd asked her to join him. The last thing he needed in his life right now was the complication of another woman, and this one was grieving for her late husband – not his usual type at all.

A waitress appeared, and Libby ordered a cup of lemon and ginger tea for herself and a strawberry milkshake for Clancy, then, at Adam's insistence – and to Clancy's delight – two slices of strawberry cheesecake.

'Preparing for Christmas?' Libby asked, gesturing to the poinsettia sitting on one of the chairs. 'I always feel it's coming closer when I see them on display. I must get one, too.'

'You come here a lot?' Adam cursed himself for such a trite remark. He sounded like a teenager trying to pick up a girl in a dance hall. 'I mean…' he blustered, '…it's a lovely centre and café.' What was wrong with him? He was as tongue-tied as a young boy on his first date.

'Isn't it?' Libby looked around with enjoyment. 'Visitors are always surprised to see such a substantial garden centre here. Bev has done a wonderful job.'

'I met her brother,' Adam found himself saying.

'Martin.' Libby nodded. 'Another native of Bellbird Bay who made good. The place is full of them. Bernie and I were surprised, too, when we bought here.' Her eyes clouded, and she looked uncomfortable. Then she seemed to pull herself together. 'I must apologise. I didn't recognise you the other day. Bernie loved your novels. He was a big fan.'

Adam flinched. He tried to put on his professional smile, the one he'd donned for Harry in the bookshop. But this time, it didn't work.

'You should be proud of them.' It was as if Libby could see into his mind.

'I am, but… I'm not good at this.' He waved a hand in the air. 'I'm not one of those authors who enjoy praise and recognition.' He dragged a hand through his hair, to see a sympathetic expression on Libby's face.

Their order arrived, and they were kept occupied by Clancy's chatter. When Clancy moved off to examine a Christmas display in one corner of the café – a grotto complete with reindeer and sleigh all made from twigs, Adam ordered another coffee for himself and tea for Libby.

'Sometimes it helps to talk to a stranger,' Libby said encouragingly.

'No, I...' But somehow, Adam found himself unburdening himself, telling her about Greg's last wish, his increasing boredom with the Canberra social scene, his political thrillers, the television deal, and the new direction his writing was taking.

'Sorry,' he said, dragging his hand through his hair again, 'I shouldn't have dumped on you like this.'

'It's fine,' she said, placing a hand lightly on his. 'It seems to me you needed to tell someone. I'm glad I was here for you.'

The strange thing was, having got it all off his chest, he did feel better. 'Thanks,' he said, 'I'm glad, too.'

'Maybe it was meant to be,' Libby said, chuckling.

Clancy ran back over to pull on her grandmother's hand, and with a wave of her hand and a smile from Libby, they left.

Adam stared after them, Libby's last words going around and around in his head. They were so similar to what the weird woman had said, though hadn't she mentioned something about destiny. What was it about this place?

But for some reason, he felt content, more content than he had in ages. Content and optimistic that everything was going to get better.

Thirteen

'We went to this place where there were lots of flowers, and a Christmas grotto and I had a milkshake and a strawberry cake, and that man from the beach was there again,' Clancy started chattering as soon as Emma arrived home.

'Mum?' Emma stared at Libby.

'We went to the garden centre. I wanted to pick up some punnets of small flowering plants for the front path. And we went to the café. *The Pandanus Café* is part of the garden centre, and they do lovely teas, coffee and cakes.'

'And milkshakes, Grandma,' Clancy interrupted.

'Yes, sweetie, milkshakes too. Adam Holland was there, and we joined him. It was no big deal.' Libby wondered again why she felt she had to explain herself to her daughter.

Emma pursed her lips. 'I don't think you should encourage him, Mum.'

Encourage? What on earth was Emma thinking?

'We had tea. We chatted. It would have been rude to refuse.' And it had been very pleasant to chat with someone who knew nothing about her.

'I just think that Dad…' Emma began.

'Your dad would be delighted to know I'd met one of his favourite authors,' she said, trying to stifle the anger building up in her.

'You're not going to see him again, are you?'

Libby took a deep breath before replying. 'Bellbird Bay is a small town, and he's living a little way up the boardwalk from here. It's highly likely we'll bump into each other again – like we did today. Do you want me to ignore him? To ignore every man I meet because you have some weird idea about me and Dad's memory? You know I haven't forgotten him. I never will. The bench seat out there is testament to that.' She pointed out to the viewing platform where a pair of seagulls were christening the seat. 'But it doesn't mean I have to become a hermit.'

Emma stared at her mother for a few moments, then turned on her heel and walked out without saying another word.

Libby grasped the back of a chair for support and exhaled. She could scarcely believe she'd spoken to her daughter like that. Emma was still upset about Matt. She'd spoken without thinking. Libby should follow her, apologise. But she didn't. The altercation had disturbed her, but it had strengthened her resolve. If she met Adam Holland again, she'd speak with him, she might even invite him for tea again. In the meantime, she went into the living room, to the bookcase and took one of his novels from the shelf. It was high time she sampled his writing.

*

Next morning, Libby had trouble wakening. She'd stayed up late reading Adam's book, the first in his political series. She had only intended to read a few pages, to discover what his writing was like, why Bernie had been so engaged in the books. But the writing was so good, she found herself sucked into the plot, unable to put the book down. It had been well after midnight before her eyes began to close. No wonder he was such a popular author, and no wonder there was to be a television series made. She could picture one of her favourite actors in the leading role.

But she had to get up. She could already hear Emma and Clancy in the kitchen. As usual, Emma had the radio on, and Clancy was singing loudly along to the Wiggles tune which was playing. The tantalising fragrance of coffee was wafting through the hallway, making Libby realise a caffeine hit was exactly what she needed this morning to bring her fully awake.

A cool shower helped. Then, dressed in a blue and white striped summer dress, she joined her daughter and granddaughter in the kitchen.

'Tea, Mum? You did remember I'm seeing that solicitor this morning?' Emma sounded tense.

'Of course, darling. Good morning.' She kissed her daughter on the cheek. 'Morning, sweetheart,' she said, dropping a kiss on Clancy's head. The little girl didn't appear to notice, intent on spooning up the Coco Pops from one of the sachets in the Kellogg's Fun Pack Libby had bought, much to Emma's disapproval. There didn't seem to be much Libby did these days without earning her daughter's disapproval. But she *had* arranged the appointment with the solicitor. 'I'll have coffee this morning,' she said. 'I didn't sleep well.'

Emma raised her eyebrows but said nothing as she poured Libby a mug of coffee.

'Thanks, honey.' Libby helped herself to toast, spreading it liberally with her favourite fig and ginger jam, and took a gulp of coffee. The hot liquid immediately took effect, sending a jolt through her body and providing her with the energy she craved and would need to get her through the day. She didn't know anything about this Sharon Smith, but Don had recommended her, and she trusted his judgement.

Libby had agreed to accompany Emma to town and, once they had located the solicitor's office, she hugged her daughter, saying, 'Good luck, Em. I'm sure it will be fine. Clancy and I will go to the park.' She pointed to a cluster of trees at the end of the street. 'Meet us there when you're finished. Okay, Clancy?'

'Yes please, Grandma.' Clancy took Libby's hand and started to pull her in the direction on the park.

'Thanks. Mum.' The colour drained from Emma's face, reminding Libby of how, as a child, Emma had always become nervous before important events, even becoming physically sick once, before her performance as the lead in a school play.

'I'm sure it'll be fine,' she repeated. 'Just explain what happened, and what Matt wants to do.'

As she left Emma to push open the heavy glass door, Libby hoped she was right. There were such dreadful tales of fathers abducting their children. But, although Libby had no great liking for Matt, she didn't imagine he intended anything of the sort. She looked down at the happy little girl, skipping along beside her and vowed nothing would ever happen to her if she could prevent it.

The park, which Libby hadn't visited before, proved to be a child's delight with not only swings but a slide, climbing net, rope climbing frame and an old-fashioned merry-go-round. There were also a number of shade trees including one enormous Moreton Bay Fig, its branches providing a green canopy under which several young mothers were sitting on rugs or blankets while their babies crawled around on the grass.

Clancy immediately made a beeline for the swings, calling for Libby to push her, which she did. Then, tiring of this activity, the little girl hared off to sample the other pieces of equipment, leaving Libby to find a seat in the shade from where she could keep an eye on her granddaughter.

It was pleasant watching the children enjoy themselves, seeing young mothers helping those younger than Clancy, and letting her cares drift away. But they didn't go entirely. The image of Emma sitting in the solicitor's office was one which filled her with trepidation. How dare Matt make such a demand, but what could you expect from a man who walked out on his wife and daughter without any warning? He clearly had no thought for anyone but himself. Libby was afraid Emma had a difficult time ahead as she navigated the inevitable divorce proceedings.

Then her thoughts turned to Adam Holland, to the man who had appeared in her life so unexpectedly. There was something about him that fascinated her, even more so now she was reading his novel. It wasn't her usual genre, preferring as she did to read women's fiction or historical family sagas but, to her surprise, she had immediately been drawn into the political intrigue he had become famous for. She wondered when she would see him again, inevitable in such a small town, as she'd told Emma.

Her thoughts stalled as she remembered her daughter's reaction to her and Clancy having tea with him. She had no intention of forming a relationship, which was what Emma was clearly afraid of. But would it be so strange if she did meet someone – not today, or even this year, but sometime in the future? She still missed Bernie terribly, missed him to chat to, and in her bed which seemed so big and empty without him to cuddle up to. But the thought of being alone for the rest of her life filled her with dread.

She was pulled out of her thoughts by Clancy running up to her shouting, 'Here's Mummy!' and, looking up, Libby saw Emma walking towards her. She rose to meet her daughter, relieved to see her smiling.

'It went well?' she asked.

Emma nodded. 'Can we have tea somewhere and I'll tell you what she said?'

'Sure. There's a café in the next block.'

The three walked along till they came to *The Greedy Gecko*, Clancy laughing at the name. She was familiar with the harmless small lizards which found their way into their Brisbane home to climb up the walls and were also common here on the coast.

Once they were seated and had ordered cups of green tea for Libby and Emma and a banana smoothie for Clancy, Libby said, 'Well?'

'She was lovely,' Emma said, smiling, 'so easy to talk to. You were right about one thing.' She threw a glance in Clancy's direction to ensure she wasn't listening, but the girl was engrossed in a colouring-in sheet she'd been given by the waitress who took their order. 'Matt can't take her overseas without my permission. We could undergo something she called a family dispute resolution, and she could help with that – but given it's only a few weeks till Christmas, she doubts it could all be organised in time.' Then Emma's lips tightened. 'She did say I needed to talk with him about it, and suggested Matt and I get together to discuss what she called a parenting plan.' Her eyes moistened. 'Oh, Mum, it all sounds so clinical. It's our daughter were talking about, not a piece of property.' She stroked Clancy's head, but the little girl shook off her mother's hand.

'Well, it's good news for Christmas, at least,' Libby said, trying to sound reassuring. She'd known it would come to something like this. Children were often used as pawns in separation and divorce. It wasn't fair. She looked at Clancy's small head bent over the picture which depicted a jovial Father Christmas giving out gifts under a towering Christmas tree, completely unaware of the dispute which was about to erupt over her. She wished she could spirit her and Emma away, far away from Matt and the woman he'd chosen to shack up with in preference to her daughter.

Their teas came with tiny discs of shortbread which neither Libby nor Emma had a taste for, but Clancy was delighted to receive. Then, in between slurps of her smoothie, Clancy regaled her mother with her exploits at the park, an account which lasted until they were all finished their drinks.

'Sounds like you and Grandma had fun,' Emma said.

'Yes.' Then, out of the blue, Clancy asked, 'Where's Daddy? Does he still have to work? Will he be here for Christmas?'

Emma gazed at her mother as if seeking her help. Her mouth opened and shut, no words coming out.

'Maybe we'll need to ask him,' Libby replied, her eyes meeting Emma's over Clancy's head. 'Would you like that?'

'He's always there for Christmas to put out the carrots and whisky for Santa,' she said in such a matter-of-fact manner Libby almost choked. 'Who'll do that if he's not here? And I want to show him the park and the beach and your house, Grandma.' She smiled winsomely at Libby as if having suddenly decided to include her home in the sights of Bellbird Bay.

'I'll pay, Mum.' Emma slipped out of her seat and made her way to the counter, leaving Libby to deal with Clancy's questions.

'Well, sweetheart,' Libby began, 'your daddy's very busy right now. He may not be able to spend Christmas with us. But we can still make it a special time. I promise to put out the carrots and whisky for Santa, and maybe we can have a beach picnic. What do you say?'

'Maybe.'

But Libby saw her drooping lip and knew her granddaughter wasn't going to be so easily satisfied.

Fourteen

When Adam awoke the morning after his meeting with Libby, he was fired up to continue with his new book. The previous day, after returning from the garden centre and placing the poinsettia on the dining room table, he'd spent the afternoon writing. It had turned dark when he finished for the day, closing his laptop with a sigh and stretching his arms above his head. He'd left his hero learning about a third corpse which had been discovered on the beach. Now he needed to help him find some way of getting closer to the investigation. He'd been deliberating on whether Jay could form an alliance with the widow of one of the victims but was aware he might be transferring his own desire to see more of Libby to his character.

But first, he needed coffee and breakfast. A brisk walk down the boardwalk to the esplanade and a breakfast of scrambled eggs and bacon with his long black at *The Bay Café* set him up for the day. As he walked home at a more leisurely pace, Adam was half-hoping to see Libby walking her dog. But today, there was no sign of her. What was he thinking? He had no room for another woman in his life. He already had Yvette, who he still had to decide how to deal with. Libby was still grieving – and had her daughter's attitude to cope with. She wouldn't be interested in him.

Having settled the matter in his own mind, if not to his satisfaction, Adam was in a jubilant mood when he sat down to write, the words flowing freely as he set up difficult situations for his hero. He was enjoying writing this novel, using the beach he could clearly see from his window as the setting.

After a productive morning with only a brief break for a snack as his lunch, Adam lifted his eyes from the keyboard for a moment to see a dog running along the beach. The flailing tail looked familiar and, when he rose to get a better look, he could see the dog was accompanied by Libby and her granddaughter. With a regretful glance at the scene in which Jay Bolton had decided to seek out an interview with the brother of the latest victim against the directive of the detective in charge of the case, Adam slid his feet into a pair of sandals and headed out.

He reached the foot of the steps leading down to the beach just as Libby was walking back, Clancy and Milo running ahead of her and splashing in the shallow water.

'Oh!' Libby stopped in her tracks, clearly surprised to see him. 'Not writing today?'

'Taking a break. All work and no play, you know.' Adam smiled. Now he had reconnected with Libby, he was unsure what to say. 'Your daughter working again?' he asked after a pause.

Libby's eyes clouded over.

'Problems?'

'Yes and no.' She hesitated as if reluctant to say more then, 'Her husband left her and Clancy. Walked out with no warning. He's met someone else. That's why they're staying with me.' She tightened her lips, her eyes going to where Clancy and the dog were still playing in the water, splashing each other. Adam could hear the little girl giggling. 'Now he wants to take Clancy to Fiji for Christmas with him and his new partner.'

'Can he do that?' Adam didn't know much about the law but was pretty sure the permission of both parents was required. He seemed to remember reading about a case that...

'Not easily. Emma spoke with a lawyer this morning. It seems she needs to agree, and she's been advised to talk to him and to set up a parenting agreement. I'm not sure what it entails, but...' She bit her lip. 'She's calling Matt now. It's why we're on the beach. It's all such a mess. Clancy misses her dad; she can't understand why he's not here with us.'

Just then, Clancy and Milo came running back to them, the large dog sniffing around Adam's ankles, his paws digging up the wet sand under his feet. Adam flinched. *What was it about this dog, or was it something about him that attracted the creature?*

'Here, Milo,' Libby called, clearly seeing his discomfort. 'Milo must like you. He's a friendly dog, but he seems even more so when you're around.'

'Hmm.' Adam wasn't so sure it was friendliness that prompted the dog's behaviour.

'What about you?' Libby asked. 'Is your writing going well? And you mentioned a television deal.'

'It's going very well.' Looking at Libby, the sun forming a halo around her hair, he was struck how he'd incorporated her looks into the description of the woman Jay was becoming involved with. He really needed to keep his real life separate from his fiction. It wasn't something he'd had any challenges with before, even though he lived in the political environment he wrote about. 'As to the television deal.' He sighed. 'I signed the contract. Now it's up to the production company. I really don't want to be involved.' Julian thought he was mad, telling him most authors would be thrilled at the prospect of attending planning sessions, speaking with the directors and producers, even attending the shoots. Adam could imagine nothing worse than watching as his words were mangled into something he didn't recognise.

'Here we are,' Libby said, as they reached the foot of the steps leading up to her deck and the viewing platform. 'I'd ask you in for tea again, but...' She gave a wary glance up at the house.

'I understand. Why don't I make tea for us this time? Unless your daughter is expecting you back now.'

'I don't know.' Libby's forehead creased, then she nodded as if deciding. 'Why not? Milo, too?'

'Milo, too,' Adam agreed, as the dog gazed up at him with a pleading look. Maybe he could even get used to the animal.

Adam opened the door with a flourish and Milo ran in, sniffing, Clancy following. Libby took her time, but they were in the living room before Adam remembered he hadn't taken time to tidy the place before rushing down to the beach. As usual for him, the floor around his desk was strewn with papers, the laptop still open, and a couple of empty mugs sitting beside it, testament to the coffee he'd drunk that day.

'Sorry.' He dragged a hand through his hair. 'I've been using this room as a study. The view... Come through to the kitchen and I'll put the jug on. You prefer tea to coffee?' he asked, remembering the tea Libby had served him. It had been some sort of scented stuff. 'I only have very basic teabags, I'm afraid.'

'That'll be fine. Clancy will drink milk or juice if you have it, and maybe some water for Milo.'

'Right.' Adam set about making tea, filling a glass with orange juice and pouring water into a bowl on the floor which Milo immediately began lapping up noisily.

'I have biscuits somewhere,' he muttered, fossicking in the pantry to find the packet of Tim Tams, an impulsive purchase made on his last trip to the grocery store.

When they were seated companionably on the deck, Clancy and Milo happily engaged in a game with a ball they'd been playing with on the beach, Adam said, 'Your daughter doesn't appear to approve of me.'

Libby put down the cup she'd been clasping in both hands and sighed. 'No, I'm afraid she sees you as a threat.'

'A threat?' Adam asked, knowing perfectly well the source of the woman's concern.

'She was close to her dad and can't bear the thought I might...' She blushed. 'Not that I imagine... but Emma is very possessive of his memory. She doesn't seem to realise I need to make new friends here in Bellbird Bay.'

'I'm sure you've made friends in the time you've been here.' Adam pretended to misunderstand.

'Of course. Eddie, who lives next door, has been a wonderful support, and Grace – your landlady – and a few others I've met through working at the library and a book club I belong to. But she hates the idea I might have male friends.' She picked up her cup again, seeming eager to change the subject. 'I've been reading one of your books. We have a shelf full of them. As I think I said, my husband was a big fan, but I hadn't read any.'

'Oh!' Adam wasn't sure how he felt about Libby reading his novels. There was so much of himself in them. 'And...?' He held his breath waiting for her reply, not sure why it meant so much to him.

'I loved it. I have to say I didn't expect to. It's not my usual choice. I only picked it up out of curiosity. But I loved your main character, the way the plot unfolded. I couldn't put it down.'

Adam exhaled. 'I'm so glad. They're not for everyone, but a lot of people seem to enjoy them.'

'I can see why.' She smiled.

Adam felt a rush of emotion, not the embarrassment he normally experienced when a reader effused about his books, the wish the floor would open up and swallow him. But Libby wasn't offering gratuitous or extravagant praise. She was simply stating a fact, so why did it affect him in this way?

Fortunately, Milo chose that moment to decide it was time to investigate Adam's toes again, and his silence hopefully went unnoticed as Libby said it was time for them to leave.

Adam watched the trio walk down the boardwalk, Clancy holding her grandma's hand and skipping along, Milo ambling beside them. Anyone watching would assume they hadn't a care in the world. Adam knew better. He was glad Libby had confided in him. He wished there was something he could do to help, but he was completely out of his depth where family law was concerned. All he could do was be there to offer an ear when she needed one.

Fifteen

Emma was pacing up and down on the deck, a pinched expression on her face when Libby returned.

'Where have you been?' she asked. 'You weren't on the beach.'

'We had tea with the nice man,' Clancy said helpfully. 'And he had Tim Tams.'

'Mum!'

'We met Adam Holland on the beach, and he invited us back for tea,' Libby said. 'Clancy, why don't you go and turn on the television while Mummy and I have a talk. I think Play School will be on.' Clancy disappeared, Milo following.

'How did your call go?' Libby asked Emma, choosing to ignore her glare at the mention of Adam Holland's name. She sat down and patted the chair next to her.

Emma reluctantly took a seat. 'We spoke,' she said. 'I told him what Sharon said. He wasn't impressed, but he's agreed we need to talk face-to-face, and *I've* agreed he can see Clancy. He's coming up to Bellbird Bay on the weekend. I asked him not to bring April, but... Oh, Mum, I don't know what I'm going to say to him, and I don't know how I'm going to tell Clancy.'

'It's always best to tell the truth,' Libby said, placing her hand on Emma's arm. 'Clancy isn't a baby. She'll be starting school next year. She's old enough to understand grownups can sometimes quarrel. The story of him having to work wasn't going to wash for ever.'

'I suppose not, but what if...?'

'Let's deal with what is. Matt will be here on the weekend. He'll spend time with Clancy, talk with you, and hopefully the pair of you can resolve things to suit both of you – and Clancy.'

'Mmm.'

Libby could see Emma wasn't entirely satisfied, but she was looking brighter than she had when Libby got back.

'Now, why don't we go out to dinner? It'll help cheer you up. I'm not in the mood to cook and I don't think you are, either.'

'Where will we go?'

Glad her daughter was at least responding, Libby thought quickly. She rarely went out in the evening, apart from her regular book club and the odd dinner at friends' homes. It had been different when Bernie was alive, but while she felt comfortable going to a café for coffee or lunch, the prospect of sitting alone in a restaurant in the evening, surrounded by couples and families, was an experience she'd rather do without.

'What about the surf club?' she asked at last. 'We can walk down the boardwalk. They start serving dinner at half five. I went there a few times with your dad when we came up for weekends and I remember they have a children's menu.'

'Sounds good, Mum.' Emma opened her phone and started typing. 'Here it is. You're right. They do have a children's menu. Clancy will like it.'

Glad to have made one suggestion her daughter agreed with, Libby went to shower and change. When she returned to the kitchen, Emma and Clancy had changed too, and the little girl was hopping excitedly from one foot to the other.

'Mummy says we're going out to dinner, Grandma. Can Milo come, too?'

'I'm afraid not, but he can stay here and guard the house for us. Do you want to help me put his dinner into his bowl before we leave?'

'Yes, please.'

Libby watched as Clancy carefully filled Milo's bowl with food, then she filled his other bowl with water. 'We can go now,' she said with a smile.

It was a lovely evening and as they walked down the boardwalk, a gentle breeze ruffling their hair, Clancy skipping along between them, it was almost possible for Libby to forget her worries. This was why she had moved to Bellbird Bay, why she and Bernie had chosen it for their retirement.

Emma caught her mood. 'It's difficult to believe I spent the morning with a solicitor and the afternoon on the phone to Matt,' she said. 'I wish I could magic him away and Clancy and I could stay here for ever. But I can't, can I? He'll be here on the weekend.'

'Daddy's coming here?' The excitement in Clancy's voice was unmistakable.

Emma grimaced at Libby over her daughter's head. 'Little ears,' she murmured. In a louder voice she said, 'Yes, sweetie, but he won't be staying with us and Grandma. I'll tell you all about it tomorrow,' she promised, as Clancy opened her mouth to object.

'Here we are,' Libby said, glad they'd arrived at the surf club. 'I have a membership card somewhere. Your dad insisted we join, and I automatically renewed even though I had no idea if I'd ever come again. It's a nice club,' she said, leading the way in and up the stairs to the restaurant.

They had just reached the top of the stairs when a voice said, 'Libby! And this must be your daughter and granddaughter.'

Looking around, Libby saw her friend, Grace Winter. She immediately felt guilty. Apart from seeing her at book club, she'd practically ignored Grace since Emma and Clancy arrived. Although they both worked in the library, their shifts hadn't coincided, and they hadn't met for their usual coffee. 'Grace, lovely to see you, too.' She looked beyond Grace to where Ted Crawford, her partner, was standing with a young couple and a small child. 'Your daughter?' she asked. She knew Grace's daughter had a young child and was living with Ted's son – who wasn't the father. It had been a source of gossip at the time but had soon died down.

'Yes, this is Mel and young Isla – and Ted's son, Aaron, and grandson, Zack,' she added as a teenager bowled up with a grin.

'This is Emma and Clancy,' Libby said, seeing Clancy immediately fascinated with Isla who must be around eighteen months. 'Em, this is my friend, Grace and her partner, Ted.'

Emma smiled politely.

'When are we going to eat, Dad?' Zack asked.

'Sorry, Libby. Zack's a bottomless pit. Aaron was the same at his age. Why don't you join us for dinner?' Ted asked.

Libby could see Emma eyeing Mel and Aaron with what looked like envy. They were standing hand-in-hand and were the epitome of young love. It wasn't so long ago she and Matt had been exactly like that.

'I don't think…' she began.

'Oh, please do,' Grace said. 'We haven't seen much of each other recently and I'd love to catch up.'

'Well…' Libby looked at Emma.

'Okay by me, Mum.'

'Thanks, Grace, Ted. It's kind of you.' And it would prevent her and Emma spending their meal thinking about Matt's arrival at the weekend.

When the group finally found a table and sat down, Libby was pleased she, Grace and Ted were seated at one end of the table, with the younger members of the party together at the other and the children in between. It was a relief to be at a distance from Emma, making her realise how much her daughter's company stressed her. Glancing along the table she could see Emma chatting to Mel, and Clancy trying to look very grown up beside Zack who appeared to be humouring the little girl.

'You can relax. They're both fine.'

Libby looked into her friend's eyes which were full of concern. 'Does it show?' she asked.

'I don't expect anyone else would notice. But I have two daughters and know how we mothers worry about them. It's good Emma and Mel seem to be hitting it off. Mel needs friends, too. She had a hard time last year, before she and Aaron got together. I sometimes have to pinch myself it all turned out so well and I'm a grandmother to two lovely little girls. I'm so grateful Isla is here as my other granddaughter lives in Sydney. *Your* granddaughter seems lovely.'

'She is.' Libby smiled, then her smile faded. 'Her dad's coming to Bellbird Bay on the weekend. He and Emma have a few things to sort out. I'm not looking forward to telling Clancy her dad won't be coming home, and she'll be celebrating Christmas without him.'

Grace's eyes widened. 'Oh, my dear. I'm sorry. I didn't realise.'

'It's the old story, Grace. He found a younger model. But he wants to take Clancy off to Fiji with them for Christmas. It's not on.'

'I can see why you're worried. I'm surprised his new squeeze wants to be lumbered with a child. Sorry, that came out wrong, but you know what I mean. Most young women who get their hooks into someone else's husband don't want the trouble of his child – especially on a tropical island holiday.'

'You mean she may not be on board with his wanting to have Clancy with them? I hadn't thought of that.' Suddenly Libby felt brighter.

'And I hear you've met my new tenant,' Grace continued.

Libby blushed. 'How did you know?'

'This is Bellbird Bay. You should know how difficult it is to keep anything secret.' Then Grace relented. 'Ted saw you walking up the boardwalk with him. You had your granddaughter and Milo with you, so I'm not suggesting anything untoward. Are you a fan of his books?'

'No… yes. Bernie was. We have them all at home. I've only read one – and I did enjoy it.'

'You sound surprised.'

'I was. Not my usual type of read.' Libby was glad Grace had moved on to Adam's books rather than the man himself. But her relief was short-lived.

'What's he like? I haven't met him. I rent the house out through Beth from *Bellbird Realty* and recognised the name. Ted loves his books, too.'

Libby pondered for a few moments before replying, remembering the gentle, sometimes taciturn man whose company she was beginning to enjoy. 'He's nice,' she said, a warm feeling engulfing her at the thought of the kindness in his eyes, the way his face lit up when he smiled. 'He's nothing like what you might expect from an author of his standing. He seems determined to avoid the limelight. I think he hoped no one here would recognise him. I didn't, until Emma saw his likeness on one of the books in Bernie's collection.'

'So, no chance of a library talk?'

'I'd say not. Adam…' Libby felt awkward referring to him by name, '…wants to stay under the radar.'

'Hmm, difficult to do here.'

'Mmm.'

'Grandma.' Clancy appeared at Libby's elbow.

When she had dealt with her granddaughter's request, Libby turned back to Grace, and their ensuing conversation took a different tack. To Libby's relief, there was no more mention of Adam Holland.

But as they walked home up the boardwalk, Libby's thoughts were all over the place. Ted had seen her and Adam together. He'd told Grace. How many other people in Bellbird Bay were aware she had made friends with the author? And did it really matter? Was she too worried about her daughter's feelings to have a life of her own? 'How did you enjoy the evening, Em?' she asked, when they arrived back at the house.

'It was good, Mum. I like Mel. She works in the gallery near the café we went to the other day. We're going to catch up for coffee. She was telling me her mother and Ted only met just over a year ago. Her dad's dead, too.'

'That's right, honey.' Was Emma making a comparison between Grace meeting Ted and Libby meeting Adam? Surely not. There was no likelihood of her and Adam forming a relationship. But she couldn't suppress the thrill she felt as the thought took root.

Sixteen

Adam determined to put Libby Walker out of his mind and focus on his writing and his promise to Greg. There were still a few weeks to go till Christmas Eve, and he wanted to check out Bellbird Bay more before then. Greg hadn't been specific as to where he wanted his ashes scattered, only saying the beach at Bellbird Bay, but, already, Adam could see the main beach by the surf club was too busy for such a tribute.

After a morning spent getting his hero out of a tricky situation, he headed out to explore the coastline outside town, hoping he could find a peaceful spot to lay his old friend to rest.

For the first few kilometres, he was disappointed, seeing how the road fell away to a steep incline and rocky outcrops. Then, just as he was giving up hope and about to turn around, he came upon the most beautiful bay. Stopping the car, he got out and stood on top of a grassy slope gazing down at the stretch of perfect white sand anchored between two hornlike promontories. The water in the bay sparkled and glistened in the sun, and the entire area was a peaceful oasis, the waves lapping gently on the shore.

He walked down the steep, narrow pathway which appeared to be the only means of accessing the beach.

Once there, he sat down on the sand, gazed out at the ocean and let the ambiance of the place wash over him. He'd found what he was looking for. He could almost hear Greg's voice in the breeze telling him this was where he wanted to end up. Adam didn't know how long he sat there but eventually his knees began to ache and he became aware of the cries of the seagulls swooping overhead. He rose and walked down to the edge of the water which was so clear he was tempted to throw off his clothes and leap in. But he didn't want to defile the unspoiled atmosphere of this place. There was almost a sacred feel about it. Turning, he made his way back up to his car.

Adam realised he must have spent longer at the beach than he thought. By the time he drove back into Bellbird Bay, it was late afternoon, and he was beginning to feel peckish. Disinclined to cook dinner for himself and feeling like company, he parked by the surf club.

When he reached the top of the stairs, he saw one of the guys he'd met there on a previous visit. Tonight, Will Rankin was accompanied by a younger version of himself. Adam hesitated, but Will saw him and waved him over to join them.

'Good to see you again, Adam,' Will said. 'This is my son, Owen. Owen, this is Adam Holland. He wrote the book you gave me last Christmas.'

'Wow!' Owen said, shaking Adam's hand. 'I love your books. I've never met a real writer before. What are you doing in Bellbird Bay?'

'Sorry,' Will said. 'No tact.' But he chuckled. 'Adam's here to honour an old friend. We all knew Greg, but he was a bit older than us and didn't hang around after he left school. Been seeing a bit of the countryside, Adam?'

'I'll have a Four X, thanks,' he said to the same dark-haired barman as before. 'Went for a drive today and discovered the most amazing, deserted beach. Pristine white sand, clear water, such a sense of peace. Sorry,' he said, aware he was babbling, 'but it got to me. I think Greg would have liked it for his final resting place.'

'That'd be Dolphin Beach.' Will nodded. 'It's a beaut spot. We managed to save it from the developers not too long ago.'

'Really?' Adam paid for his beer and took a gulp. He couldn't imagine anyone wanting to build on what had seemed to him a sacred place.

'It's a long story, but we did it. Discovered a herd of dugongs in the bay and…' He spread his hands.

'What are you writing now?' Owen asked, seemingly fascinated by

Adam who, to his surprise, wasn't fazed by the young man's interest. 'Is there another Phil Hanlon book in the works?' he asked, referring to the hero of Adam's political thrillers.

Adam took another gulp of beer before replying, not sure what made him say what he did. 'Actually, I'm working on something different. My new book is set in a fictional town not unlike Bellbird Bay, and my new protagonist is a journalist with a nose for crime.' He waited with bated breath. Owen had called himself a fan. What would his reaction be?

'That sounds awesome. When will we be able to read it?' Owen's voice was filled with enthusiasm.

Adam gave a sigh of relief. He hoped his agent would have the same reaction. He knew he couldn't hold out on him for much longer. 'Not for a while yet,' he replied. 'But I'm glad you like the idea.'

Owen opened his mouth to speak again, but Will put a restraining hand on his arm. 'That's enough, Owen. Adam didn't come here to face an inquisition. Let the man enjoy his beer in peace.'

'Okay, Dad. Sorry, Adam.' He turned away to talk to the barman.

'Sorry about that, Adam. Sometimes he doesn't know when to shut up. We're not all so inquisitive. Sorry I can't eat with you tonight. Have to get home to Cleo.'

Adam saw how Will's face softened when he mentioned his partner's name. He wondered what it would be like to have someone waiting for him at home, instead of going back to an empty house. He was so caught up in his musing, he wasn't aware of Will speaking to him again until he saw a couple walking towards them. They were older, the man with a thatch of thick white hair and the woman with silvery tendrils waving around her face.

'Adam, meet Ted Crawford and Grace Winter. I believe she's your landlady.'

'How lovely to meet you at last,' Grace said, shaking Adam's hand. 'I've heard a lot about you.'

'I'm enjoying staying in your lovely house.' What did one say to the owner of one's rental, and what had she heard about him – and from whom?

'I love it, too. I came here after my husband died – and I met Ted.' She gazed lovingly at the man by her side.

Adam shuffled his feet, embarrassed yet again by a show of affection. What was it about this place? Everyone seemed to be part of a loved-up couple. Except Libby Walker and her daughter, he reminded himself.

'Good to meet you.' It was Ted's turn to shake Adam's hand. 'I'm a big fan. I have all your books. Can't wait for the next one.'

'Sorry, folks, I have to go,' Will said, and walked off, leaving the three together. Owen was still fully occupied chatting to the barman.

'Are you here for dinner on your own? Would you like to join us?' Grace asked.

Much as Adam was tempted to refuse, it would have been rude to ignore the overture of friendship from his landlady. 'Thanks,' he said. 'Good of you.'

'How are you finding Bellbird Bay?' Grace asked, when they were seated by the full-length window looking out onto the ocean.

'Very friendly,' Adam said without thinking.

'It's like any other small town,' Grace said. 'I came here from a small country town in New South Wales and found lots of similarities. You're a city dweller?'

'Canberra for most of my life, after racketing around the world.'

'I used to read your political columns – before you turned to writing thrillers. Followed them avidly and, even though I love your books, I miss your political insights,' Ted said. 'Though I can imagine it was a bit stressful in what they like to refer to as the Canberra bubble.'

'You're not wrong. What about yourself?'

'I practiced law in Brisbane. I grew up here and came back when I retired. Should have done it earlier but life got in the way, as it does.'

Adam nodded. He knew all about that. Here in Bellbird Bay, for the first time in years, maybe ever, he was finding time to relax.

'Do you surf?' Ted asked.

Adam shook his head. He'd seen the groups of surfers out in the ocean each morning, some seemingly staying there all day. And he knew Will Rankin ran the local surf school. 'You?'

Grace laughed. 'Ted is one of the local heroes, first to win the local surf championships three years in a row, and you may have noticed him featured on the mural as you came up the stairs.'

So this was the man on the mural he'd wondered about.

'But not the only one anymore,' Ted said with a grin. 'Young Owen there did it last year, too.' He gestured across to Will's son at the bar. 'He designs boards now. A fine young man.'

During their meal, the conversation continued about local events and Christmas plans – Adam had none but Grace and Ted had a big, blended family and were planning a week-long get-together.

Then, out of the blue, Grace said, 'I hear you've been seeing a bit of Libby Walker.'

What the...? Adam almost choked. 'How did...?'

Grace tapped her nose. 'Small town.'

Ted chuckled. 'Not so strange, Adam. It's hard to keep things secret in Bellbird Bay, as Grace and I discovered when we became friends.'

'She's a lovely lady,' Grace said.

'Mmm,' Adam muttered, looking down at his empty plate and wondering how soon he could leave.

'She was very complimentary about you, too.'

Adam's heart leapt. *She was?* So perhaps she could overcome her daughter's disapproval. Perhaps, if he moved cautiously, there was a way they could be friends – even more than friends.

When he left the surf club to drive home, Adam felt more optimistic than he had in a long time.

Seventeen

On Saturday morning, Emma was rushing around like a mad thing, only to collapse in a heap on a chair in the kitchen while Libby prepared breakfast.

'When will we see Daddy?' Clancy asked, as she slurped up her cereal. To her disappointment, the fun pack Libby had bought was finished, and Emma had insisted they buy the Weet-Bix Clancy ate at home. Although Emma had already explained Matt wouldn't be staying with them, and wouldn't be with them for Christmas, Libby could see from Clancy's expression she hoped to change her dad's mind.

'Eat your breakfast,' Emma said, ignoring the question. Matt had called when he arrived the evening before. He was staying at *Headland View* B&B and had promised to walk down after breakfast.

Libby looked at her daughter. This morning, Emma had made more of an effort than usual. She was wearing a pair of smart jeans and a pale lemon linen shirt and was fully made up. But her makeup did little to disguise the new lines around her eyes and mouth. Libby felt a flare of anger at what Matt had done to her formally happy daughter.

'He'll be here, soon,' Libby said to comfort her granddaughter, while dreading her son-in-law's arrival.

Libby was loading the dishwasher, and Emma was on her second cup of coffee when Clancy, who had been standing at the window, her eyes fixed on the boardwalk, yelled, 'Daddy's here!' and flew out the open door and into Matt's arms.

'It's going to be fine,' Libby said, as Emma grasped her hand tightly. 'He can't do anything here. At least he's on his own.' She knew Emma's worst fear was that Matt would have brought April with him, but, if he had, he'd left her behind at their accommodation.

'Thanks, Mum.' Emma rose to greet the man who walked inside, Clancy hanging onto his arm.

'Can we go to the beach now?' Clancy asked, her eyes going from her mum to her dad and back again.

Emma glanced helplessly at Libby.

'Maybe we can go to the beach while your mummy and daddy...' Libby began.

'No!' Clancy said loudly, keeping a firm grip on Matt. 'We can all go to the beach.'

Seeing it would be impossible to extricate the girl from her dad, Libby nodded to Emma, who appeared confused at this unexpected turn of events. When they'd discussed things the previous evening, it had been decided Libby would take Clancy to the beach with Milo and leave Emma and Matt to have their conversation in the house. They'd not counted on Clancy's delight in seeing her dad again.

'I'll just...' Emma disappeared into the hallway, and Libby heard the bathroom door close.

She could imagine how Emma was feeling. 'Hello, Matt,' she said, trying to maintain a neutral tone. There was no sense in telling him what she thought of his odious behaviour, with Clancy so thrilled to see him. 'You made it to Bellbird Bay?'

'As you see. It's a nice place you have here.'

'Thanks.' Libby had forgotten he'd never been here before, always working on the few weekends when Emma had driven up the coast with her mum and dad. For a moment, Libby wondered if it had been more than work that had kept him away – even then. Then she stifled the thought. As a realtor, weekends were his busiest time. But this was a weekend, and he was here.

'I was able to offload my open houses this weekend,' Matt said sheepishly, clearly reading her mind. 'I told the boss I had urgent personal business to take care of, and, yes, I came up alone, if you were wondering.'

Libby nodded, unable to risk speaking.

'I'm ready.' Emma reappeared, having pulled her hair back into a low ponytail. She had donned a pair of sunglasses and was carrying a hat. 'Shall we go?'

'Milo?' Clancy asked

'Not this time, sweetheart. He can stay with me,' Libby said.

She watched the trio set off, past the viewing platform and down the steps. From here, they looked like any other happy family off for a morning on the beach. How she wished she could roll back time. When they were out of sight, she fetched her own hat and called to Milo, intending to walk down to the esplanade and perhaps have coffee there. She needed to do something to occupy herself, to avoid wondering what was happening between Emma and Matt.

She didn't get very far. As she was passing the house next door, she heard her name being called and, looking over the fence, saw her neighbour, Eddie, in the garden.

'On your own this morning? I'm about to make a cuppa. Join me?'

Libby didn't hesitate. Apart from the odd conversation over the fence, she hadn't spent time with Eddie since Emma and Clancy arrived. She was another friend she'd been neglecting. A tiny voice in her head she tried to ignore reminded her she'd seen more of Adam Holland than her old friends lately.

'Thanks, Eddie.' A dose of Eddie's good common sense was exactly what she needed. She opened the gate, and Milo bounded in, aware Eddie always had treats for him.

Once seated on the bench outside Eddie's window with a cup of peppermint tea, Milo lying contentedly at their feet chewing on a dog biscuit which he held between his front paws, Libby gave a sigh of relief.

'I saw your daughter on her way down to the beach. Was that her husband? Are they back together?' Eddie asked.

'I wish.' Libby heaved another sigh. 'They need to discuss Clancy and Christmas, though I'm not sure how they're going to manage it with her there, too. But there's nothing I can do about it, Eddie. Dogs are a lot easier to deal with than children.' She looked down affectionately at Milo crunching on his treat.

'About that. I have something to show you.' Eddie took out her phone, scrolling till she found what she was looking for. Then she held it out to Libby.

Libby peered at the photo. It was of a tiny golden pup. 'You're not…?' She raised her head to smile at her friend.

'I took your advice. She's a Labrador and I pick her up just after Christmas. Isn't she a beauty?'

'She certainly is. Oh, I'm so pleased for you. She'll be such good company.' Libby handed back the phone.

'It was after having Milo for you when you were in Brisbane. The house felt empty when I gave him back. Almost as empty as it felt when Paula went.' She paused and blinked away a tear. 'Anyway, I started looking around and found this litter.' Eddie smiled at the photo again before putting the phone back in her pocket. 'Now, what have you been up to? Did I hear you've met the author who's staying at Grace Winter's place?'

'Yes.' Libby blushed. She'd been right. She'd made herself the target of gossip.

'He came here, you know, visiting his friend's old home. Said he was in Bellbird Bay to fulfil a promise to his friend, but it seems like he's on some sort of a pilgrimage, visiting his friend's old haunts. They must have been close.' Her eyes slid to where the photo of her and her partner was on display.

Libby's gut clenched. Did Eddie mean…? Surely not. But Adam had given her no indication he was interested in her as a woman. Maybe she'd got it all wrong. Maybe Emma had nothing to worry about.

There was no sign of Emma, Matt and Clancy when Libby rose to leave, so she continued down to the esplanade. But her mind was in a whirl. How could she have so misjudged things? Adam Holland was only being polite. She tried to find the funny side, but all she felt was a profound sense of disappointment.

Eighteen

Emma and Clancy were already home when Libby returned from the esplanade, and Clancy was eager to tell her grandmother about the wonderful time she'd had with her dad. Emma didn't look happy.

'How did it go?' Libby asked, when Clancy had disappeared outside with Milo, happy to see the dog again.

'It didn't.' Emma's face tightened. 'Matt barely spoke to me; he was so busy with Clancy – and she loved being with her dad again. It's not fair!' she blurted out. 'What he's doing to her, pretending everything's fine when he knows full well he's not coming back to us.'

Libby's heart sank, but she hadn't really expected them to be able to talk when Clancy was with them. 'So?' she asked.

'I've said Clancy can spend the afternoon with him, and he and I are going to meet for dinner tonight. I'll wait till Clancy is in bed, so she doesn't want to come, too. You don't mind, do you, Mum?'

'Of course not. I hope you can come to some sort of solution, one which doesn't hurt Clancy too much.' Though what solution could there be, other than one in which Clancy was shunted between her parents like a parcel? Libby's heart bled for the little girl who had no idea her life was about to change for ever.

'Oh, Mum, I don't know. Clancy loves her dad. I hate to see her suffer, but…' she tightened her lips, '…I don't intend to give in to his demands.'

'Em…' Libby began, then seeing the mulish expression on her daughter's face, bit her tongue.

'I don't want to hear any of your platitudes,' Emma said, 'about how we need to think of Clancy, not ourselves. It's my life, Mum. You and Dad were happily married for years. You can't possibly understand what I'm going through.' She stormed out, leaving Libby staring after her, shocked at her outburst.

Libby and Bernie's marriage hadn't always been a bed of roses. They'd had their ups and downs. But they'd always managed to find a resolution to their disagreements. Libby had followed her mother's advice never to let the sun go down on a quarrel and it had worked, even if sometimes they had made up in bed. But Emma was right about one thing. Bernie had never been unfaithful.

The door burst open, and Clancy ran in, followed by Milo.

Her granddaughter's 'I'm hungry, Grandma,' forced Libby back to the present.

Checking the time, she realised it was past lunchtime. 'Why don't you wash your hands while I fix lunch?' she said, opening the fridge.

By the time she had made a lunch of chicken, tomato and lettuce, sandwiched between slices of soy and linseed bread, Clancy was back, and a subdued Emma appeared, too.

'Sorry, Mum. You caught the tail-end of my anger with Matt,' she whispered. 'Lunch looks good. Thanks.' She gave Libby an apologetic smile.

*

After an afternoon of Emma wandering around the house, unable to settle to anything, Libby was glad to see her go off with Matt. She'd found it difficult to make polite conversation with him while Emma fetched her bag but managed to put her personal feelings aside for Clancy's sake. There was no sense in antagonising him. She did want the best for her granddaughter, even if it meant Emma didn't get things all her own way.

They had no sooner left, than Libby heard her granddaughter call from the bedroom.

'Can I have a story, Grandma?' she asked, when Libby popped her head in.

Half an hour and three stories later – all from Clancy's new Dr Seuss books – the little girl's eyelids began to close. Libby dropped a kiss on her forehead, pulled the covers up to her chin and tip-toed out.

Back in the kitchen, she made herself a cup of camomile tea and took it out to the deck. She loved the view at this time of night. The sky glowed shades of pink and gold in the setting sun, and the only sound was the waves pounding on the shore. As she sat there clasping her cup in both hands, she reviewed the events of her day. First there was the bombshell from Eddie about Adam Holland. It wasn't what she'd said, but the implication of her glance towards the photo of her and Paula. Had Libby mistaken her meaning?

Libby shrugged away the disappointment which had enveloped her when she left her friend. She had more to think about than a man she'd only met recently. She was still grieving for Bernie and there was Emma's situation to consider.

They still hadn't told Clancy her dad had left them. And the little girl had come back from her afternoon with Matt full of the excitement and asking, 'Why can't Daddy stay here with us?'

Emma had made some excuse, but Libby knew they had to tell her soon. Perhaps Emma and Matt could do it together. She sighed. Regardless of how they sugar-coated it, Clancy would be hurt.

Libby finished her tea, picked up another of Adam Holland's books from the shelf and headed for bed, knowing she'd be asleep long before Emma returned.

*

When Emma appeared in the kitchen next morning, Libby and Clancy were enjoying boiled eggs with toast and vegemite for breakfast, and Milo was lying below the table in the hope of catching any morsels which dropped to the floor, despite having already been fed.

'Morning, darling,' Libby said, giving her daughter a wary glance.

'Morning, Mum.' Emma dropped a kiss on Clancy's head and ruffled her daughter's hair.

Clancy shook away her mother's hand. 'When is Daddy coming?' she asked.

Emma winced before replying, 'He said he'd be here at half-nine. We'll be out all day, Mum,' she said to Libby. 'Matt's organising a picnic lunch for us.'

'Sounds lovely.' Libby wondered how Emma's talk with Matt had gone, if they'd managed to resolve anything. Her daughter's expression gave no indication of what had transpired, but surely the fact they were spending the day together was a good sign? She longed to ask Emma what had been discussed but with Clancy there, there was no opportunity to do so.

Libby hoped the day would go well. It would be a relief to have a whole day to herself. She planned to have a swim, laze on the beach with a book, then perhaps go out to lunch. She had grown unaccustomed to having time alone since Emma and Clancy arrived. And she needed to reserve her strength for Emma's return.

As soon as they left, and the breakfast dishes were in the dishwasher, Libby, accompanied by an excited Milo, headed for the beach. On the way she stopped on the viewing platform to run her hand over the brass plaque, close her eyes and have a few words with Bernie. She'd discovered it calmed her to do this each time she passed the bench, though what anyone watching might think, she couldn't imagine.

Fortunately, this part of the beach was designated as a dog beach, which meant Milo could roam untethered, even though he tended to stay by her side, lying on her towel to guard her belongings when she ran into the waves for her swim.

It was a glorious morning, and soon became too hot to be enjoyable as the sand started to burn her feet. It was time to return home for a shower and to change into something more suitable for lunch than her swimsuit and the loose wrap-around cover-up she'd slipped on when she came out of the water.

Feeling refreshed and wearing a garishly coloured sundress she'd splurged on from the local boutique, *Birds of a Feather*, Libby ensured Milo had plenty of water before telling him to guard the house, while she set off down the boardwalk.

She stopped outside *The Bay Café* to read the blackboard menu then, after choosing an outside table, ordered a small quiche with salad and a mug of peppermint tea. She didn't notice the occupant of a nearby table until she heard a familiar voice say her name. Turning sharply, she saw Adam Holland smiling at her. Her heart gave an unexpected lurch.

'Looks like we're the only ones here. May I join you?' he asked, closing the newspaper he'd been reading.

Libby noticed it was the weekend version of the Courier Mail, reminding her she'd intended to buy her own copy on the way here. When eating alone, she always tried to bring along something to read. It made her feel less exposed, somehow. But her mind had been on Emma and Matt, wondering how things were going with them, and she'd completely forgotten about the paper.

Seeming to notice her hesitation, Adam paused.

Libby blushed, shocked by her reaction to seeing him here. 'Of course,' she said.

Picking up his coffee and folding his paper, he joined her. 'On your own today?'

Libby nodded, assuming he was talking about Emma and Clancy, then, seeing him peer under the table, she realised he was referring to Milo. She chuckled. 'You don't like dogs, or is there something about Milo? He may be large but he's really a gentle creature.'

Adam rubbed his chin. 'I've never had much to do with them – and Milo is so very friendly. I guess I could get used to him. Have you ordered?'

'Yes,' Libby said as a waitress appeared with her lunch. 'Are you eating here or just…?' She gestured to his half-empty mug of coffee.

'I had a rather late breakfast. I come here every morning. It makes a good start to the day, but today I'm later than usual. I'm guessing this is your lunch?'

'It is.' Libby wondered if he'd leave now. There was nothing to keep him. But he ordered another coffee, apparently intending to stay while she ate. To her surprise, she felt a warmth envelope her at the prospect of his company. She knew Emma would disapprove and somehow, the thought gave an added whiff of pleasure to their meeting.

Adam proved to be an interesting companion confirming her earlier opinion of him. He appeared unaware of the effect his presence had on her, and she strove to keep it that way. Perhaps she was imagining it. After all, he was the first attractive man she'd spent any time with since Bernie's death. What did it matter if he wasn't interested in women? He was good company, and she was satisfied with that.

'Your friend… you were close?' she asked.

'Greg? We met when we were both reporting on the war in Iraq. It was a hothouse situation where people became closer than they would have otherwise. Then, when we both returned home, we met up again covering political news in Canberra. It was…' Adam frowned as his phone pinged and he checked the screen.

'Bad news?'

'No, it…' He dragged a hand through his hair. 'I've been seeing someone in Canberra and… I guess I may have led her to believe our relationship was going somewhere, Heck, Libby, I don't know how to tell her. Now she's agitating to come up here for Christmas, and I don't know what to do.' He took a gulp of coffee. 'Sorry to subject you to the vagaries of my messy life.

She? A thrill rippled through Libby, So, he wasn't gay? His next words dispelled any hopes she might have cherished.

'I've always avoided commitment. I suppose it says something about me.' Adam sighed. Then Libby's heart rose as he continued, 'But I've enjoyed our meetings, our chats. It's made me wonder if there's been something missing in my life, if I've been too determined to stay independent that I've allowed myself to become too insular. I know you're still grieving for your husband and your daughter disapproves of me and…' he chuckled, '…there's the matter of your dog, but I would like to get to know you better, to become friends.' He gazed at Libby, his eyes seeming to bore right through her, into her soul.

Libby swallowed and clasped her hands tightly to stem the tremors of pleasure threatening to consume her. 'I'd like that,' she said.

Nineteen

It had rained for the past two days, heavy soaking rain. Adam hadn't ventured out, content to watch the raging sea from his window, amazed at the surfers who braved the elements to risk their lives in the swell, and mesmerised by the sheets of foam forming on the beach.

To his disappointment, there had been no opportunity to see Libby Walker again. After meeting her in *The Bay Café*, he was eager to continue their friendship even if that's all it could be for now. He had only planned to be here for the summer but was in no rush to return to Canberra. Perhaps he'd extend his stay. He could work here just as well as he could in his apartment in the capital – maybe even better. And there was no Yvette or her like to distract him with invitations and pleadings for company.

It had been good writing weather, and Adam was well on the way to finishing his first draft, with ideas for a second and third book in the series. He was making himself a mug of coffee and feeling pleased with his efforts when his phone rang, and he saw Julian's number on the screen. Cursing mildly, having hoped to escape his agent's clutches until after Christmas, he accepted the call.

When the call finished, Adam dragged a hand through his hair and stared into space. Julian had been adamant they needed to meet. Either Adam had to go to Canberra or Julian would come to Bellbird Bay. It had been a difficult conversation – Adam still hadn't revealed his new direction – but the result was Julian would book a flight and arrive in Bellbird Bay on Saturday, prepared to stay the weekend.

Adam clasped his mug of coffee and gazed out the window, thoughts about Greg and the things they'd shared swirling through his head. If it hadn't been for Greg, for his death, he'd never have come to Bellbird Bay, never have met Libby Walker. He'd eschewed commitment, remembering the man his father had been, the challenges his mother had faced, the man he didn't want to emulate. But there was something about Libby Walker that tugged at his heartstrings.

His phone rang again. This time, it was Yvette's number on the screen. Tempted to ignore it, Adam knew he owed it to himself and Yvette to be honest. He pressed to accept the call.

'Hi Yvette.' He held the phone at arm's length as a barrage of invective assaulted his ears, all of it justified, he reflected. He'd treated her badly and deserved her anger.

Adam waited till Yvette took a breath. 'I'm sorry. You're right. I've acted abominably,' he admitted. 'I don't deserve your forgiveness. You're better off without me.'

'But, Adam, we're good together. Think of…'

Adam listened while Yvette listed all the events they'd attended together, the drinks parties she'd hosted, with him a reluctant participant, and felt ashamed he'd allowed their relationship to progress so far and to last so long. He'd been fooling himself – and her – that there could be a future for them. But what sort of future would it be? How could he spend the rest of his life pretending to be someone he wasn't, trying to fit into Yvette's hectic social scene, a puppet in her busy life?

It had taken his friend's death and a deathbed promise for Adam to see the charade of the life he was leading. Here in Bellbird Bay, he'd found a sense of renewal – and he'd met a woman unlike those he normally hung around with, a woman he could respect, a woman he could even fall in love with.

Adam was so shaken up by the shock of this realisation, he almost missed Yvette's final flare of temper.

'I've had it with you, Adam Holland. Don't expect me to be waiting for you when you finally decide to return to Canberra with your tail between your legs. If your old friend and your promise to him mean more than I do, you can forget me, forget you ever knew me.'

'Yvette…' But Adam's words fell on deaf ears. Yvette had already hung up. Stunned, Adam stared at his phone. While he'd been trying to screw up the courage to end things with Yvette, to find the right time, the right words, she'd beaten him to it.

A flurry of rain burst against the window reminding Adam where he was. He sat down at his laptop to reread the chapters he'd written that morning. It was good, better than good. He thought it was his best work. He could only hope Julian was of the same opinion.

*

The sky cleared after lunch, allowing Adam to eat his ham sandwich on the deck. But it clouded over again as the rain began to pelt down heavier than before. Adam rose to ensure the sliding glass door was firmly closed, only to see the bedraggled figures of a woman and dog making their way down the boardwalk, struggling to remain upright in the heavy downpour.

It was Libby and Milo. They'd be soaked through before they reached Libby's front gate. Without thinking, Adam slid open the door and stepped out. 'Come in here!' he yelled, ignoring the fact he was not only inviting Libby inside but also her dog which would drip all over his floor and no doubt decide to shake himself there, too.

In the confusion of getting the pair into the kitchen, Adam scarcely noticed how wet he got himself or that Milo considerately shook himself before coming inside.

'You're soaked,' he said to Libby, seeing the rain dripping from her face, her shoes and jacket soaked through. 'What were you thinking?'

'There was a break in the weather. Milo hasn't been out for days. I thought we could make it up to the headland and back before the rain came on again.' She smiled, and Adam noticed how the rain had turned her normally carefully styled hair into a mass of curls, and the raindrops were shimmering on her eyelashes.

He had the strongest urge to take her in his arms and kiss the raindrops away. Instead, he said, 'What you need is a hot shower and a hot drink. Bathroom's that way,' he pointed. 'You'll find a robe on the back of the door. I'll hang up your jacket to let it dry. I'm not sure about your shoes.' He looked sadly at the canvas loafers Libby was wearing.

'Thanks. I'm afraid you may be right about the shoes. I should have had more sense. Will Milo be right?' She glanced to where Milo had settled himself just inside the door, making a wet patch on the floor but taking up very little space for such a large animal.

'He's fine,' Adam surprised himself by saying. 'I'll make the tea while you're in the shower.'

Libby disappeared.

For a few moments, Adam was transfixed picturing Libby, naked, in his shower. Then he gave himself a shake and filled the electric jug. Hearing a sound behind him, Adam turned to see Milo studying him. It was as if the dog could read his mind. Telling himself not to be stupid, that he was imagining things, Adam filled a bowl with water and placed it beside Milo, who looked up gratefully before lapping the water, sending droplets all over the floor.

He felt a twinge of disappointment when Libby returned, dressed again in the navy capris and white shirt she'd been wearing under her jacket. For some reason he'd expected to see her slight figure dwarfed by his large, blue, striped towelling robe. He'd imagined taking her in his arms, the feeling of her soft body against his, imagined loosening the robe to discover...

'Is everything all right?' Libby was gazing at him, a concerned expression on her face.

'Sure. The water's boiling. I bought some herbal tea after last time. Peppermint or camomile?'

'Peppermint, thanks. And you gave Milo water. Thanks for that.' She walked over to stare out the window. The rain was still pouring down.

'Will your daughter be expecting you home?'

Libby checked the time. 'She and Clancy are at *Kiddie Korner* today. They'll be back soon. I should text her. She might be waiting till the rain eases but will worry if she comes home to an empty house.' She took out her phone and texted a few words.

'What did you say?'

'Only that I was sheltering from the rain at a friend's house.'

'You didn't say which friend?' Adam raised an eyebrow.

'No.' Libby blushed, the pink tinge on her cheeks making her look even more attractive. A smile played across her lips. 'She doesn't need to know. She has enough to worry her at the moment.'

'How is the situation with her husband? You said they were talking things through to find a solution.' Adam handed Libby a mug of tea.

She curled up on a chair and clasped the mug in both hands before replying. 'It's not good. Matt spent time with both of them while he was here, making Clancy think everything was as usual, though she couldn't understand why her dad wasn't staying with us. Emma hasn't said much about what they discussed. All I could get out of her was that he'd agreed not to persist with the idea of taking Clancy to Fiji for Christmas – I suspect the new woman in his life might have something to do with that – and they plan to meet again early in January to work out custody arrangements. Emma is intending to go back to Brisbane then, too, so I suppose there will be a discussion about the house. She can't possibly keep up the mortgage on her own, even if she does get a teaching job. Sorry,' she looked up apologetically, 'I'm dumping my family worries on you again.' She gave a wry smile.

'Not at all. I did ask. And I'm sorry it still seems to be up in the air. At least you'll have Christmas together.'

'Yes, and I plan to make it memorable for Clancy's sake.' Milo uttered a low sound and Libby looked over at him with an affectionate smile. She took a sip of her tea. 'What are your Christmas plans?'

'Me?' Adam chuckled. 'I don't have any. Christmas Day will be like any other day for me. I expect I'll have a swim, then get on with my writing.' He frowned. The mention of his writing reminded him of Julian's call and the prospect of his agent arriving in Bellbird Bay in a few days' time.

'It bothers you?' Libby enquired gently.

'No, I enjoy my own company. It's….' He sighed. 'My agent is arriving on the weekend.'

'And why is that bad?'

Adam drew a hand through his hair. 'He doesn't know what I'm writing. He's expecting me to produce another in my series of political thrillers, and I'm not sure how he'll react to my change of direction.'

Libby didn't respond immediately.

Adam thought how cosy it was sitting here drinking tea with her in his kitchen. Even Milo's presence didn't detract from the pleasure he experienced in her company.

When Libby did speak, her words were encouraging. 'You're a good writer. Surely anything you write will make him happy?'

'I wish I had your confidence. But I don't intend to change, even if he hates the book.'

'What will you do if he does?'

Her question surprised Adam. Till now, he'd never met a woman who appeared this interested in his work. Yvette – and all those who'd preceded her – liked the fact he was a well-known author, enjoyed basking in his popularity. But he couldn't think of one of them who'd actually asked him about his writing.

He rubbed his chin. 'I'm not sure. But I sure as hell won't change the book.'

'Good for you.' Libby glanced out the window. 'Look, the rain's easing. I should grab my jacket and make a run for it.'

Seeming to understand his mistress's words, Milo chose that moment to stretch out and let out a low growl. He rose to his feet, moving towards Libby, his tail flailing and threatening to dislodge a sheaf of papers from the table.

Adam caught them just in time. He really should try to be tidier. But when it was just him, there was no need. He supposed he should make an effort before Julian arrived.

'Thanks for rescuing me and for the tea and conversation. I enjoyed it. And I'm glad Milo behaved himself.' Libby chuckled.

'You're most welcome.' Adam fetched her rain jacket and held it while she struggled into the still wet garment. Then he opened the sliding glass door.

They stood staring at each other. Adam didn't want her to leave.

'Well…' Libby glanced up at the sky which was till overcast with the threat of more rain.

Adam cleared his throat. 'I know it may be difficult for you, but would you have dinner with me sometime? Not here.' His eyes roamed around his kitchen. 'Out somewhere… a proper meal… in a restaurant.'

'You mean… like a date?' Libby sounded amused.

'Exactly. What do you say?' Adam had never felt so insecure, so anxious about asking a woman out since he was sixteen and asked Angie Ross to go to a movie with him.

'I think I'd like that,' she said tremulously.

'Good, I'll call or text you.'

'Do you have my number?'

'Hell.'

Seeing a pen and a small pad on the kitchen surface, Libby jotted down her number. 'Now I really must go.' She smiled again as Milo strained to get out the door.

As Adam closed the door behind her, he felt like whooping with delight.

Twenty

Libby felt flushed when she arrived home to find Emma and Clancy already there, the reaction from Adam's invitation to dinner still whirling around in her head. She could scarcely believe he'd asked and was even more surprised she'd accepted. It was completely out of character for her to accept an invitation from a man – and one she hardly knew. Though it wasn't exactly true. They'd met a few times. She enjoyed his company. He was a reputable author. But Libby had never imagined herself going on a date ever again.

'Where were you, Mum?' Emma asked. 'I was worried about you.'

Libby shrugged off her still dripping rain jacket and shook it out the door, then slipped off her sodden shoes. 'I doubt I'll be able to wear these again,' she said with a frown, in an attempt to avoid answering her daughter.

'Mum?'

'I took Milo for a walk, and we got caught in the rain. I sheltered with a friend till there was a break in the weather. I'm here now.'

'Milo's all wet,' Clancy said from the floor where she was hugging the dog.

'Oh, Clancy!' Emma was distracted from Libby, who took the opportunity to go to the bedroom and change out of her damp clothes into a fresh pair of pants and a tee-shirt.

'How was your day, Em?' Libby asked when she returned.

'Okay.' But Emma appeared distracted.

'What's up?'

Emma sat down and, with a wary glance at Clancy who was still busy with Milo, said, 'Kate asked me if I was interested in taking on a permanent position.'

'At *Kiddie Korner*?'

'Where else?'

Libby didn't respond immediately. It was a surprise. She fully expected Emma and Clancy to return to Brisbane in January. It was what she'd arranged with Matt. Emma was always talking about her life being in Brisbane where all her friends were. But this was an opportunity for her to have a fresh start. Clancy could begin school here in Bellbird Bay and Libby could watch her granddaughter growing up.

'How do you feel about it?' she asked.

'I don't know. It's not something I ever contemplated, but... Oh, Mum, seeing Matt again, knowing he's with someone else, I don't know if I could bear to be in the same city as him. This could be a godsend.'

'You're very welcome to stay here.' Even as she spoke, Libby regretted the offer. But what else could she do? Emma was her daughter. She couldn't let her try to find the sort of accommodation she'd be able to afford on the salary Kate would be able to offer.

'Thanks, Mum. It would be a big step. And there's the house in Brisbane, our home. Clancy's never lived anywhere else.'

*

At the library next day, Libby couldn't help checking her phone. She felt like a young girl with her first boyfriend, waiting for his call or text, her stomach churning in expectation of hearing from him. She knew she was being foolish. Adam had said his agent was coming to town on the weekend. He'd no doubt be busy preparing for the visit. He'd have more on his mind than his invitation to dinner. Had she been too quick to accept? Should she have played coy? It was so long since she'd been on a date – not since the early days of her and Bernie's relationship – and back then they'd been uni students together, sitting beside each other in classes. It had been impossible to avoid him.

Her confusion was compounded by the fact the library had chosen this week to promote Adam's books. It must be a coincidence as, to Libby's knowledge, no one on the library staff apart from her and Grace, knew he was in town. But it meant that everywhere she went, his face – albeit a younger version of the man she knew – was staring at her, a reminder she was waiting to hear from him.

'Something bothering you?'

Libby and Grace were seated on the tiny veranda outside the library staff room. The rain had passed, and the sun was shining, proclaiming the downpour of yesterday to be a thing of the past. Grace was eating a salad she'd brought from home, while Libby, who'd been in too much of a rush to prepare lunch that morning, had bought a sandwich on her way to work.

'What makes you think that?' she asked.

'You've been like a cat on hot tin roof all morning. I swear I was expecting you to explode when Rachel asked you to fix up the display. Is it something to do with Adam Holland? Have you met him again?'

Libby bit her lip and took a swig of the sparkling mineral water she'd bought with her sandwich. 'I saw him yesterday,' she admitted. 'Milo and I got caught in the rain. He saw us and offered us shelter till it passed.'

'So? I'm sorry Ted and I weren't home, or you could have sheltered with us.'

'I could have gone home.' This was what was bothering Libby. Adam's home was only a few houses up from her own.

'Is that what's bothering you?' Grace peered at Libby.

'Not really. He invited me out to dinner, Grace, on a date.'

To Libby's surprise, her friend chuckled. 'It'll do you good, Libby. You've been holed up all by yourself for too long.'

'But...'

'I know how you feel, believe me. I felt exactly the same when Dot tried to set me up with Ted. But...' her eyes took on a dreamy expression, '...he is exactly right for me. It's never too late to have a second chance at love. Oh,' she said, holding up her hand to prevent Libby from speaking, 'it may not be the same as first time around. How could it be? We're no longer in the first flush of youth when everything was new and exciting. But it can be just as thrilling, and just as real.'

'Grace!' Libby was horrified. 'We're not talking about me falling in love. For one thing, it's only a dinner date. For another, I'm not on my own. I have Emma and Clancy living with me.' *And they might decide to stay.* Libby still wasn't sure how she felt about their continuing presence.

'So why are you getting your knickers in a knot?' Grace asked. 'Ask yourself what your husband would think about it. It's what I did when Ted and I...'

'And what did you decide?'

'He'd want me to be happy. Russ would have hated me to refuse the opportunity to find love again.'

It hadn't occurred to Libby to consider what Bernie might think. Now she tried to imagine his reaction to her meeting his favourite author, to going to dinner with him. All she could see was a stupid grin on his face, encouraging her to go ahead.

'You may be right,' Libby sighed. But it didn't change the fact she was a bag of nerves thinking about it.

Twenty-one

Adam knew he should have contacted Libby. But he'd been caught up with trying to complete the first draft of his novel before Julian arrived, hoping if he presented him with a complete manuscript, his agent would see the value of the new series.

And he'd finally done it.

Adam grinned to himself as he typed *The End*. He'd dedicated the book to Greg. If it hadn't been for him, Adam would never have come to Bellbird Bay, never have decided to write this book, never have met Libby Walker. He'd still have been in Canberra, churning out one more political thriller, spending time with Yvette, and wondering if there was more to life. He had a lot to thank his old friend for. He hoped, wherever he was, Greg knew the influence he'd had on him.

Now all he wanted to do was relax. But first, the ocean was calling to him. He changed into a pair of board shorts and, slinging a towel over his shoulder, headed down to the beach.

It was late afternoon, and the beach was deserted, as was the ocean. No surfers sitting out on the waves today – and no sign of Libby and Milo. Adam stifled his disappointment and, throwing the towel down on the sand, made his way into the water, starting to swim as soon as it reached his thighs. He swam out for a way, then turned on his back to float. Gazing up into the seemingly endless stretch of blue sky, it was easy to imagine he was the only person in the world.

Adam stepped out of the water and picked up his towel. He was about to climb up to the boardwalk when he saw something out the corner of his eye which stopped him in his tracks. The child's toy looked familiar, but he didn't know any children other than… Libby Walker's image floated before his eyes. Had little Clancy been playing with the now sodden blue bear one of the times he'd seen her? He picked it up and carried it home, intending to dry it out before seeking its owner.

Fuelled by his writing achievement and energised from his swim, Adam poured himself a beer when he returned home, then, still in his board shorts, he rubbed his hair dry with his towel, took his phone out to the deck, and called Libby.

*

Adam had been on tenterhooks all morning waiting for Julian to arrive. He'd drafted an outline of the new book plus some ideas for the next two in the series and, although he was happy with them, he was still unsure what his agent's reaction would be.

Julian had texted his arrival time and arranged to meet with Adam for lunch. After trying to work out what to serve, Adam had decided to take him to the surf club, confident they'd be able to enjoy a good lunch there. And it would provide an appropriate background to pitch his new series to his agent.

Now, he was standing outside the tall white building, the scent of the ocean in his nostrils, a light breeze ruffling his hair as he waited for Julian to arrive. Being Saturday, the nearby esplanade was filling with the lunchtime crowd, and there was a cacophony of noise coming from the direction of the beach interspersed with calls from the surf lifesaver's tower reminding swimmers to swim between the flags and be careful of the rip.

A slight figure, dressed in an outfit more appropriate to the city than this seaside town, came into view, heading towards him, his easy gait proclaiming him to be in no hurry. Julian English's outfit never varied, the grey pants teamed with a white shirt, blue tie bearing the monogram of his old school and an outdated black cord jacket. Adam always supposed Julian imagined it gave him an artistic appearance.

'Julian, good to see you.' Adam held out his hand.

'What on earth are you doing here?' Julian looked disparagingly at the surf club into which several locals were now making their way. They were dressed in shorts and tee-shirts, or, like Adam, in jeans and the open-necked, short-sleeved shirt he'd donned in deference to this lunch. 'And you've gone native, I see.'

'Hardly. As to the club...' Adam glanced up at the now familiar façade of white painted brick, the surf club logo prominently displayed above the door, '... the food's good here and we can talk privately on the deck.'

'Hmm.'

Adam led the way into the building, signed Julian in and ushered him up the stairs and into the open restaurant with views over the ocean.

'So this is where you've been spending your time?' Julian asked, when the two men were settled at a table with glasses of beer, having both ordered the club's popular burger and chips.

'Not exactly.' Adam took a swig of beer. 'But it's a lovely spot. Don't you agree?'

'Hmm,' Julian said, again, gazing around and giving a shudder. 'Not my scene, and I didn't think it was yours either. How long did you say you were staying here?'

'I didn't. But I need to stay until after Christmas. I have been getting some writing done.'

'Good, good.' Julian rubbed his hands in delight. 'We need another release to accompany the TV pilot. What's Phil Hanlon up to now?'

Adam cleared his throat. 'I haven't written another Phil Hanlon thriller. This one...'

Julian didn't let him finish. 'What do you mean?'

'Hold on, Julian. Let me finish.'

'This had better be good.' Julian took a gulp of beer and folded his arms.

'I've been inspired by these surroundings.' Adam waved his hand around to encompass the stretch of sand and sea below them. 'In my new series, the hero is a journalist who seeks to solve crime in a seaside town much like Bellbird Bay.' He waited for his agent's reaction.

'What the hell are you thinking? Don't you realise you have thousands of readers waiting eagerly to discover what Phil Hanlon is up to next, readers who have followed you through all nineteen in the series, who...'

'Might be ready for a change?' Adam suggested. 'Let's face it, Julian, Phil was getting a tad stale. I felt I needed to write something fresh and Jay Bolton...'

'The name of your new protagonist, I assume?' Julian said drily.

'It is. I have the first draft ready for you to take a look at and outlines for books two and three.'

'What about the TV series? You stand to make a packet from that if it's successful. They're talking of the entire series. It could go on for years, Adam. Are you ready to throw it all away because of some half-assed idea you want to change tack?'

Adam swallowed down the riposte that *Julian* stood to make a packet out of it, too, and smiled. 'Here's our food,' he said, seeing the waitress coming towards them.

During their meal, Adam could see Julian struggling to refrain from making further comment. As soon as their plates were removed, he broke into a wild tirade, accusing Adam of ignoring their contract and other offences.

Adam listened, remembering he'd heard of Julian acting like this, but, till now, had never been on the receiving end.

'I've done well for you over the years, Adam,' Julian concluded, 'and this is how you repay me.' He shook his head in mock despair.

Adam was surprised at his own calm acceptance of Julian's ranting. He knew the new novel was good. 'Will you at least read it?' he asked, when his companion finally ran out of steam.

'I suppose,' Julian said grudgingly. 'I did plan to be here all weekend, and there doesn't seem to be much else to do in this godforsaken place.'

Adam smiled. Trust Julian to make it sound like a chore, and to dismiss Bellbird Bay so readily. Why couldn't he see the town as Adam did? But Julian was too much of a city dweller to appreciate the coastal beauty and the peaceful ambiance Adam had discovered here.

*

Adam was glad he'd arranged to see Libby that evening. Two hours of Julian's company was about as much as he could stomach in one day. He sometimes regretted signing with him, but he was tied into a long-term contract, and Julian had done a lot for his career over the years. Also, he couldn't face the hassle of finding someone else to represent him. Libby would be a welcome relief from his agent's disapproval. But at least Julian had agreed to read the novel with the working title, *Wave of Death*.

Adam hummed to himself as he showered and dressed for the evening, choosing a new pink shirt to team with a pair of beige pants and, after a moment's hesitation, patting on a few drops of the aftershave Yvette had given him for his birthday.

After an internet search of the surprising number of eateries in town, he'd settled on an Italian restaurant. *The Firenze* on the esplanade was within walking distance, and the menu looked good. He just hoped Libby liked Italian food. He loved it and, in Canberra, often ate at a small family-owned restaurant close to where he lived. He and Greg had often gone there together, so it was partly as a farewell gesture to Greg that he'd chosen it.

Adam was feeling slightly nervous as he walked down the boardwalk to Libby's house. Libby wasn't like one of the women who had passed through his life in the past few years, and she was nothing like Yvette. He hadn't heard from her since their last fraught phone call. He could only assume she meant what she said when she told him they were finished, and he had no wish to change her mind.

To his relief, Libby was waiting at her gate. There would be no chance of experiencing her daughter's disapproval. There was no sign of her or of Milo.

'Hello.' Libby sounded more nervous than Adam felt.

'You're looking lovely,' he said, as he took in the soft colour of the dress she was wearing. It emphasised the grey of her eyes which, in this light, had the colour of a light mist.

'Thank you.' Libby smiled. 'I thought it better to wait out here. Emma…'

'She knows you're having dinner with me?'

'Of course. I can't hide anything from her. I told her about your kind invitation and…' She bit her lip. 'Well, suffice to say, she was not well-pleased.' Her lips tightened. 'But I don't intend to allow her to rule my life. So, here I am, and I plan to enjoy our evening together.'

'Where are we going?' Libby asked as they began to walk down the boardwalk.

'I hope you like Italian food.'

'I love it. Bernie and I went to *The Firenze* a few times before he...' Libby paused for a moment, then continued. 'The food is really good, I particularly like their garlic bread, and the cannelloni is to die for. Have you eaten there before?'

'No. You have the advantage of me there. But I tend to frequent a small Italian restaurant in Canberra. This one will have to be good to compete.'

'I think you'll be pleased.'

The conversation had taken them all the way down to the esplanade.

When they entered the restaurant, Adam was glad he'd had the foresight to make a booking. Being Saturday evening, almost all the tables were occupied. They were led to a small table in the back corner of the room which was filled with chatter and were met with the strong aroma of garlic and spices reminiscent of the restaurant Adam frequented in Canberra.

'Will you have some wine?' Adam asked, when they had been supplied menus.

'Yes, thanks.' Libby appeared more relaxed now they were seated, and Adam was beginning to feel more comfortable, too.

With Libby's approval, Adam ordered a bottle of chianti, and they both ordered entrées of cannelloni with a serving of the garlic bread Libby loved. Then she ordered a spaghetti carbonara, while he chose the pepperoni pizza.

'To getting to know you better.' Adam held up his glass.

Libby held hers up too with a smile. 'Sounds good to me.'

'You mentioned your agent was visiting this weekend,' she said. 'You're not dining with him? Well, obviously not,' she added, self-consciously.

'Hopefully he's spending the evening reading my latest manuscript,' Adam said with a grin. 'We had lunch together, and I fear I didn't meet his expectations.'

'He wanted another of your political thrillers?'

'As I expected,' Adam said ruefully. 'But at least he agreed to look at the new one, and I'm hoping he'll like it.'

'What will you do if he doesn't? Can he refuse to... do whatever it is he does with your books?'

'Unlikely. He's made a good living from my work over the years. About to make a heap more, if this television deal goes ahead. I can't see him passing up the chance for more of the same – unless he really hates it.'

During the meal, which was delicious, proving equal to any Adam had eaten in Canberra, he asked, 'You enjoy living here?'

Libby appeared surprised. 'I love it,' she said. 'We always planned to retire to Bellbird Bay, and when Bernie died, there was nothing to keep me in Brisbane.' Her mouth turned down. 'I thought Emma was settled, but…' she sighed, '…things changed.'

'You'll stay?'

'Of course, but I'm not sure what Emma will do. She's been offered a full-time position in the childcare centre here. It doesn't pay much, but I expect Matt will want to sell their Brisbane house. He's in real estate so will be aware of the value of it.'

'How will that affect you?'

Libby sighed again. 'To be honest, I'm not quite sure. I was just getting used to living by myself, developing a routine. Having Emma and Clancy here has turned everything around, and while I love their company…'

'Your life's not your own?' Adam guessed.

'You've hit the nail on the head.'

*

Libby couldn't believe how well the evening was going. Although she'd been eagerly awaiting Adam's call, when it did come, she almost refused, aware of what Emma's reaction would be.

She knew she was flushed when she walked into the kitchen after the call, and when Emma asked, 'Who was it?' she was tempted to tell her it was just a friend. But that would be the coward's way out, so she'd steeled herself to reply, 'It was Adam Holland. He's invited me to dinner on Saturday.'

The expression on Emma's face was priceless. Libby wished she had her phone handy to take a photo.

'I suppose you said, "Yes"?'

'Why wouldn't I?'

'Dad...'

'Your dad wouldn't want me to stop having a life. It doesn't mean I've stopped loving him, Em. I could never do that. And I'm not looking for another relationship. But it's nice to be invited out, and Adam is your dad's favourite author. I think he might be pleased.'

'Pleased?' Emma snorted, before storming out of the room.

There hadn't been any more said about Libby's dinner date, and Emma had kept out of the way while Libby was getting ready, making more noise than necessary with her preparations for her and Clancy's meal.

Libby had begun to wonder if it was all worth it, if she should have given Adam a polite refusal.

Now, she was glad she'd come. Like all the other occasions when she'd been in Adam's company, he immediately put her at her ease. He was so easy to talk to, not what she'd have expected from a famous author, though she didn't know what that might have been. He was an interesting companion and interested in her, too. And, although she tried to tell herself he was like a ship passing in the night, that he'd be returning to Canberra and his life there after Christmas, she couldn't stifle the thrill that she was sitting here having dinner with him right now.

'Sorry?' Libby realised Adam had been speaking while her thoughts were wandering.

'I was asking you if your granddaughter has lost a toy – a blue towelling bear.'

Libby gasped. 'How did you know?' The old blue bear was Clancy's favourite cuddly toy, the one she slept with every night – until the last few nights when Blue Bear, as she called it, couldn't be found anywhere. It had originally belonged to Emma and had been her favourite, too, given to her by Libby's mother when Emma was only a baby. He was almost a family heirloom.

'I found it on the beach. The poor thing was in a sorry state. I washed it off and it's drying on my deck as we speak.'

'Oh, Clancy will be delighted. Blue Bear's an old one, but a favourite.'

'Blue Bear. I like it.' Adam chuckled.

'It was Emma who originally christened him when she was much younger than Clancy is now, and the name stuck. Thanks so much for rescuing him.'

'I can drop him off to you tomorrow… if it's all right with you.'

'Perfectly.' It might even make Emma warm to him, Libby thought, but decided not to get her hopes up. Her daughter could be very stubborn at times, and she seemed to have taken against Adam – or at least Libby's friendship with him.

When it was time to leave, the sensation of Adam's hand in the small of her back gave Libby a sense of security and comfort she hadn't experienced since Bernie's death, even before then. The last months prior to her husband's death, Bernie had been too ill to accompany her anywhere. There was something about a man's hand – this man's hand – that sent a glow through her entire being.

They walked slowly up the boardwalk together, stopping only when they came to Libby's gate. A glimmer of light showed through the plantation shutters indicating Emma was still awake, no doubt waiting for her mother's return.

As they stood facing each other, Libby felt her heart lurch, wondering if he was going to kiss her.

He didn't, merely putting a finger under her chin and saying, 'I enjoyed tonight. I'd like to do it again.'

Too suffused with emotion to speak, Libby nodded.

'I'll drop Blue Bear in tomorrow.'

'Thanks,' Libby said, then greatly daring, added, 'Why don't you join us for breakfast?'

Twenty-two

As Libby expected, Emma was sitting on the sofa. The television was on with the sound turned down and she was leafing through the colour supplement from the weekend paper. She dropped it to her lap when Libby walked in.

'How was your evening?' she asked in a tone which indicated she really didn't want to know – or hoped it had been a disaster.

'I had a nice time. He's an interesting companion. And guess what? He found Blue Bear on the beach.'

The look of relief on Emma's face immediately disappeared to be replaced with one of annoyance. 'Why didn't he bring him back? It took ages to get Clancy to sleep without him.'

'He was on the beach, so Adam washed him and he's drying. He'll bring Blue Bear around tomorrow morning.' Libby glanced warily at her daughter. 'I've invited him to breakfast.'

'You've what? Why did you do that, Mum? You know how I feel about him.'

'I do. But this is my house, Em, and it's my life. I can invite my friends here any time I want.' She saw her daughter's eyes widen, her mouth open, as if about to speak.

'Now, if you don't mind, I'm rather tired and I'm going to bed.' Without another word, Libby walked out, too annoyed to say more lest she might say something she'd regret.

But once in her bedroom, Libby felt guilty. Emma was just being Emma. Her daughter's emotions had always been close to the surface…

and her father's death combined with Matt's betrayal had left her bereft. It was only natural she wanted to protect her relationship with her mother – and this seemed to entail keeping strange men at bay. The trouble was, Libby thought, as she undressed and brushed her hair, Adam wasn't a strange man. He was a friend, one Libby intended to see more of.

*

Next morning Libby awoke early, pleased to see the sun shining through the window, the now familiar sound of bellbirds greeting her ears.

Dressed in a pair of white pants and a pink shirt, she was in the kitchen feeding Milo when Clancy came running in. 'Can we have pancakes, Grandma?' she asked. 'Mummy says that man is coming to breakfast.'

Surprised Emma had already told Clancy about her invitation to Adam, Libby said, 'That man is called Adam, Clancy, and he has a surprise for you.'

'Ooh, I love surprises.' She crouched down next to the dog, who ignored her as he hoovered up his breakfast.

When Emma walked into the kitchen, Libby was already mixing the pancake batter. 'When is he going to arrive?' she asked, wrinkling her nose to indicate she hadn't forgiven Libby for inviting Adam to breakfast.

'Soon, I expect. Could you set the table on the deck? It will be lovely out there this morning.' Libby dropped the first batch of pancake mix onto the pan. Pancakes had always been a favourite Sunday breakfast when Emma was growing up. Libby hoped choosing to make them today might put her daughter in a better mood.

The pancakes were almost ready when Libby heard the sound of the gate opening and closing, then Adam's voice at the door calling, 'Good morning!'

'Good morning,' she said, her heart giving a little leap at the sight of his smiling face.

He was carrying a bunch of flowers, which he handed to her, and the blue bear.

Clancy's eyes lit up at the sight of her favourite toy.

'I believe this belongs to you,' Adam said, stooping down to hand the bear to Clancy.

She smiled shyly as she took the bear and hugged him to her chest. Then she hesitated before hugging Adam, too.

Libby smiled, then frowned as she saw Emma's lips turn down. 'Thanks, Adam,' she said, in an attempt to pre-empt anything Emma might say. 'Hope you like pancakes.'

'I love them. Can I do anything to help?'

'We're good. I'll just put these flowers into a vase and get everything out to the table. We're eating on the deck; it's such a lovely morning. You must have been up early to get these flowers.'

Adam shrugged and looked embarrassed.

Breakfast was a cheerful affair with Adam sharing stories of his life in Canberra and, to Libby's delight, Emma unbent sufficiently to join in. She was sad when, breakfast over, Adam rose to leave.

'I'm sorry I have to rush off,' he said. 'I need to catch up with my agent this morning to hear what he thinks of my latest book.' He checked his watch. 'I promised to meet him at *The Bay Café* at ten. It's where I usually have breakfast and we planned to have it there together. But this has been much nicer. Thanks so much, Libby. And lovely to spend more time with you and Clancy too,' he said to an astonished Emma who, for once, was lost for words.

At the gate, out of sight and earshot of the others who had gone inside, Adam took Libby's hand. 'I really appreciate sharing your family breakfast. I hope I can return the favour soon... once Julian has gone back to Canberra.' He frowned, clearly thinking about his agent's reaction to his writing.

'I'm sure he'll love it,' Libby said, the warmth of his hand on hers sending waves of pleasure through her body.

'I hope you're right. Till later?'

'Later,' she agreed, before returning inside.

*

Adam was smiling as he strode down the boardwalk. It had been a wonderful breakfast – both the food and the company – and he felt on top of the world. But his mood changed, his steps slowing when he saw Julian already seated at a table outside the café, the dog-eared manuscript lying in front of him. *Did he hate it?*

'Good morning, Julian.' Adam took the seat opposite. He ordered coffee and stared at his agent, trying to gauge his reaction, but the man's face was impassive.

'Let's eat first,' Julian said, as the waitress appeared with a plate piled with bacon, eggs, tomatoes, mushrooms, hash browns and toast for him, and Adam's long black. 'You're only having coffee?'

'I already ate. I had breakfast with a friend.' Adam was glad he had. He knew he wouldn't have been able to eat anything as he waited for Julian's assessment. He sipped his coffee and watched Julian warily as the other man tucked into his *big breakfast* without speaking.

'Not bad for a small town like this,' Julian said, finishing his meal. 'Another coffee?'

'No, thanks.' He waited while Julian ordered another for himself then tapped a finger on the sheaf of papers that was Adam's new book.

'It's damned good, Adam,' he said, allowing his face to relax into a smile. 'I was a bit concerned when you told me you'd taken a new direction and abandoned Phil Hanlon for a coastal journalist. But this Jay Bolton…' he tapped the manuscript again, '…he ticks all the boxes. I think your readers are going to love him.'

Adam let out the breath he'd been holding. *Julian liked it!*

He made a couple of plot suggestions, ways in which Adam could tighten the writing up, then said, 'You mentioned you have a couple of others in mind?'

'I do.'

Julian listened intently while Adam outlined what he had in mind for the next two books in the series. 'Great stuff,' he said. 'Email this manuscript and outlines for the next two and I'll get in touch with your publisher. I'm pretty sure they'll be keen to offer another contract. If not, there are a few others I can approach. When do you get back to Canberra?' he asked, taking out his credit card. 'I'll get this.'

'I'm not sure.' Adam had been trying to figure it out himself. When he arrived in Bellbird Bay, he'd fully intended to leave again once he'd scattered Greg's ashes. Then he decided to stay till after Christmas and New Year. Now, he found he was in no hurry to leave. This small coastal town had found a place in his heart… and there was Libby Walker.

'Well, don't leave it too long. Your publisher wants to arrange a series of talks to coincide with the release of the latest Phil Hanlon novel and with *Summernats* in January,' he said, referring to the annual car festival held in Canberra

Adam sighed, regretting he'd used the setting of the 2020 car fest and horrendous bushfires for his last Phil Hanlon novel, and wondering how he could get out of this. He hated author talks at the best of times and, although he'd written about it, he wasn't a fan of the event. 'I don't…' he began.

'You need to do this, Adam. A new contract may well depend on it. I know you've managed to avoid most in-person events in the past, but the publishers are becoming more insistent. If you want your new series to receive the same marketing as your new releases have had in the past…' Julian didn't need to finish the sentence.

'When is the damn thing again?'

'January sixth to ninth. The plan is to release the book on the second, so ideally, you'd be back immediately after New Year to start the promotion.' He gazed at Adam expectantly.

Adam sighed again, feeling trapped. 'I'll see,' he said. 'How long do you intend to stay in Bellbird Bay?'

'Stay here?' Julian shuddered. He checked his watch. 'My plane leaves in a couple of hours.'

'Do you need a ride to the airport?'

'No, I have a taxi booked. Take care – and make sure you're back in time for the round of promotions. By the way, I like the drugs link in the new book. It's a different angle but works well. Good research, or did you come across a drug ring in Bellbird Bay?' he joked, before walking off, leaving Adam wishing their meeting could have gone differently.

The café had begun to fill up, and Adam noticed a couple of other customers giving him a strange look, so decided it was time for him to leave, too. But he didn't feel like going home. Instead, he fetched his car and drove along the coast till he found a sign to the Botanic Gardens.

He spent the afternoon wandering along the pathways, stopped in the café for lunch, then took a leisurely drive home, planning to call Libby to tell her his good news.

But, when he arrived at his front door, everything else fled from his mind. The door stood ajar, and when he went in cautiously, he found the living room in chaos and his laptop gone.

Twenty-three

Libby felt a sense of loss when Adam left. She'd enjoyed his company over breakfast, enjoyed cooking for a man again, the appreciation he'd expressed in her cooking. Now she was alone again with Emma and Clancy, both of whom seemed to be spoiling for an argument.

'It's a lovely day,' she said, when she'd cleared the breakfast things and loaded the dishwasher – without any help from her daughter. 'Why don't we go out?'

'Where?' Emma sounded bored.

Libby wanted to shake her daughter, tell her it was time she got herself together and started to think about the future, her future and Clancy's. But wasn't that what she was doing considering Kate's offer of a position at *Kiddie Korner*?

'Have you thought any more about the position at *Kiddie Korner*?' she asked.

'I don't know, Mum. It's not what I'm used to, and we do have the house in Brisbane. All our things are there, our friends, too. If we stay here, we have you…' Her voice trailed off, leaving Libby to conclude her company fell far short of what Emma would prefer. She was in two minds how to reply. While if Emma and Clancy decided to stay in Bellbird Bay, it would disrupt her life here, she had grave doubts about their ability to remain living in their house in Brisbane, sure Matt would have other plans for it.

'Can we go to see Santa?' Clancy asked. 'Some of the other kids at *Kiddie Korner* said they were going to see him this weekend.' She looked pleadingly at her mother and grandmother.

'I don't know.' Emma looked at her mother. 'In Bellbird Bay? Already?'

'I don't know either, but I can find out.' A quick call to Kate, who ran the childcare centre elicited the information there was a Santa located in the shopping centre on the outskirts of town. It wasn't one Libby frequented, preferring to shop in the smaller neighbourhood stores closer to home.

'You're on the ball,' Kate said. 'He only arrived yesterday. It's really beginning to feel like Christmas. It's only five weeks away. It'll be here before we know it. I'm having the children make decorations next week, then we'll really know it's about to happen.'

Kate's words reminded Libby she hadn't given any thought to presents for either Emma or Clancy. Emma was easy. They always gave each other books or book tokens. But she wanted to make this Christmas special for Clancy, so she and Emma needed to get together to plan how to do it.

At the shopping centre, they found themselves in a crowd of parents and children, all intent on seeing who could make the most noise as they queued to enter the enclosure where the man, dressed in a Santa outfit that had seen better days, was seated on a chair decked out to resemble a throne. It was pretty tacky, Libby thought, but Clancy was entranced and couldn't wait till it was her turn to meet him, hopping up and down with excitement. Even Emma seemed to have forgotten her earlier bad mood when faced with Clancy's delight.

The encounter over, with the requisite photo taken of Clancy standing by the jolly man's side, they headed to a nearby ice cream outlet while they waited for the photo to be ready.

Afterwards, they wandered around the shopping centre, pausing to admire the Christmas decorations in the various shop windows. Noticing Emma gaze admiringly at a bright red dress in one of the shops, Libby said, 'You'd look lovely in it, Em. Why don't you try it on? Clancy and I will wait for you.'

'Are you sure, Mum?' Emma looked happier than she had in days.

Libby nodded. 'We'll be happy here, won't we, Clancy?'

The little girl nodded then began to pull Libby towards a window in which there was a display of toys including a large jigsaw. 'I could do that one, Grandma,' she said. 'The ones they have in the childcare centre are for the babies.'

Libby was mentally adding it to the Christmas list she was forming in her head, when a flustered Emma joined them.

'You won't believe what he's done now,' she said, her eyes filled with tears. 'I was so humiliated.' She was shaking.

'Calm down, Em.' Libby took her daughter by the arm and led her to one of the seats provided for elderly and disabled customers. They were neither, but Libby judged this was an emergency. 'Now what's wrong?' she asked when they were all seated, Clancy withdrawing into silence at her mother's distress.

'The dress was perfect,' Emma said, her voice breaking. 'I decided to buy it, but when I gave the assistant my card, it was declined. It was so embarrassing.'

'You expected there to be enough on the card?'

'It's our joint account. There should be over twenty thousand in it. Then I tried the credit card. It was declined, too. It's all Matt's doing. He must have…' She broke into sobs. 'How could he?'

Libby had been afraid of this. She'd heard of cases where the husband had either emptied the accounts or blocked the wife's access to them. But she hadn't expected Matt to do it, or to act so quickly. 'You need to see Sharon again tomorrow. Find out what can be done to reinstate your access. You should check about the house, too.'

'The house?' Emma raised her eyes to meet Libby's. 'You don't think…?' She looked horrified.

'I'm not thinking anything at the moment, but you need to get advice from your solicitor. Now I can do one thing, Wait here.' Leaving Emma and Clancy staring after her in surprise, Libby strode over to the dress shop, returning a few minutes later with a large carry bag. 'Here's your dress, Em. You deserve something to make you feel better.'

'Oh, Mum!' Emma kissed Libby on the cheek. 'You didn't need to…'

'Yes, I did. I'd like to wring Matt's neck for putting you in this position.'

The incident had spoiled their trip, so Libby suggested they go home, stopping on the way for lunch at *The Pandanus Café*, where Emma managed to pull herself together sufficiently to eat an egg white omelette, and Clancy dug into a bowl of sweet potato wedges, while Libby chose an open sandwich of avocado and fetta on rye bread.

Once home again, Emma disappeared into her bedroom, shutting the door firmly behind her. Libby wanted to comfort her daughter, but the closed door brooked no interference. Instead, she took pity on Milo who, having been shut in all morning, was eager for a walk. 'Shall we take Milo to the beach, Clancy?' she asked her granddaughter.

'Mummy?' Clancy asked, clearly still disturbed by Emma's earlier distress.

'I think Mummy needs to be on her own for a bit. Why don't you fetch your hat and get Milo's lead for me?'

A few minutes later, they were on the beach, the little girl and the dog running through the shallow water as if they hadn't a care in the world, and leaving Libby to ponder what Matt was up to. It was clear her son-in-law was under the influence of the new woman in his life. Even though she had never warmed to him, this was beyond anything he'd have worked out by himself. He must realise how it would affect not only Emma, but also Clancy. And he loved his daughter. *Or*, she thought, her suspicions aroused, *was this his way of persuading Emma to allow Clancy to spend Christmas with him? Had he been too willing to give into her refusal to his demands? Had this been his intention all along? Surely he couldn't be so devious?*

'Look, Grandma!'

Clancy's shout brought Libby out of her musings to see the girl pointing up to the boardwalk where a couple of police officers were standing outside one of the houses. A quick glance indicated it was either Grace's house where Adam was currently staying or the one next door to it. Whichever it was, the occupant might need some assistance.

While not wanting to intrude into something which was none of her business, but eager to be neighbourly if help was required, Libby called to Milo, fastened his lead and began to climb up the steps from the beach.

She reached the top, just as the police disappeared from sight, to see Adam standing by his gate, running a hand through his hair and looking bewildered.

Twenty-four

Adam was in shock as the police car drove off, after the officer advised him not to touch anything and instructed him to find somewhere else to stay that night to enable their forensic team to check out the house. It seemed there had been a few break-ins like his in the past few weeks, though not in this neighbourhood, and police suspected a gang of youths who had infiltrated the town from the city and were attempting to deal drugs in the local high school.

He had walked outside and was standing at his open gate trying to consider his next move, but unable to think straight, when he saw Libby, Clancy and Milo heading towards him.

'What's happened?' Libby asked. She was out of breath, as if she had climbed up from the beach too quickly. 'I saw the police from the beach.'

'I had a break in.'

'Oh, no! There's never been anything like that around here.' She gazed down the deserted boardwalk. 'Did they take much?'

'Only my laptop, and some loose change I had lying around. I don't have anything of value here.' He saw her expression. 'All my work is stored on the cloud. So I haven't lost anything and, without access to my Dropbox account, no one can access my stuff. It's just damned inconvenient.' He frowned. 'And the police don't want me to be here until they've had time to check the place out. I thought I'd see if I can get a room for the night at the B&B up the way. My agent was staying there.'

'Stay with us.'

From the expression on Libby's face, the invitation came out without any thought.

'I couldn't. I'll be fine in the B&B.'

'Nonsense. What are friends for – and you did say we were friends. Clancy can bunk in with me or her mum, and you can have her room. Okay with you, Clancy?' she asked the girl who had been following the conversation avidly.

'Yes, Grandma,' she said with a smile. 'Will you tell me a story?' she asked the still befuddled Adam. 'You write books, don't you? I heard my mummy and grandma talking about you.'

'Don't bother Adam now, Clancy,' Libby said. 'He's had a shock. Some bad people broke into his house. But perhaps he'll agree to read you a story later if you're very good.'

Adam sent Libby a grateful look. *Was there no end to the understanding and compassion of this woman?*

'Thanks,' he said, suddenly too exhausted to refuse.

'Now,' Libby said, becoming organised, 'are you able to bring anything with you – personal items like toiletries and a change of clothes?'

Adam looked down at the clothes he'd put on that morning, full of excitement at having breakfast with Libby and her family and nervous about what Julian might think of his book. 'I guess so,' he said. 'They didn't go into the bedroom or ensuite. Won't be a minute.'

*

Libby knew her invitation to Adam to stay the night would annoy Emma, but she couldn't leave the poor man to face Ruby in her B&B. It was better he stay with them, where he could at least have some home comforts. Although she had heard *Headland View* was known for its comforts too, it also had Ruby Sullivan, and he was in no state to face the weird woman or hear one of her predictions.

By the time Adam reappeared carrying a small satchel, Libby was fully prepared to face her daughter's objections.

To Libby's surprise, when they reached her house, a delicious spicy aroma greeted them. Milo pushed his way inside ahead of the others, his tail waving like a flag as usual as he made his way straight for his food bowl and stood over it, guarding the empty bowl from all comers.

'Can I feed Milo, Grandma?' Clancy asked and, not waiting for a reply, went to the cupboard for the packet of dogfood.

'I decided to cook away my annoyance with the scumbag I married,' Emma said, her back to the new arrivals. 'I…' she turned and saw Adam standing behind Libby. 'What's he doing here?'

'It's a long story and I think a glass of something strong is called for,' Libby said. 'Let me show you to your room first, Adam.' Leaving an astonished Emma in the kitchen, Libby led Adam through the hall to the room where Clancy had been sleeping.

'Your daughter…' he began.

'She'll get over it. It's not just you. She had a bad experience today which has influenced her mood and made her more bloody-minded than usual. I'll explain later. You should be comfortable here.'

'Thanks,' Adam said again, putting his bag down. 'But I would have been…'

Libby put a finger on his lips, realising as she did so, how intimate the gesture was. She blushed as she dropped her hand to her side. 'I'll leave you to get settled. I'll be in the kitchen.'

What had possessed her to touch Adam like that? Libby could try to excuse her behaviour by telling herself it was in the heat of the moment, but what heat, what moment? They had been standing in her granddaughter's bedroom. The door was open. Clancy could have seen them. Emma could have seen them. That would really give her something to rage about.

Emma was still fuming when Libby returned to the kitchen. 'Mum, what's *he* doing here?' she asked again.

Libby took a deep breath. 'The poor man's had his home broken into. He has nowhere else to go,' she lied, ignoring the large number of hotels and motels in town, not to mention the caravan park and Ruby's B&B.

'That's no reason to have him here,' Emma hissed. 'Especially since…'

At that moment, Adam walked in and, seeming to sense the atmosphere, stood still as if ready to flee.

'Take a seat, Adam,' Libby said, ignoring the glare from her daughter. 'Whisky?' She took three glasses from the cupboard and poured a measure into each. It wouldn't do Emma any harm and might calm her, too.

'Clancy?' Emma asked when Libby handed her a glass.

'She's watching television with Milo. She's quite happy. I think we all need this. It's been quite a day.'

'Thanks.' Adam knocked back his drink.

'What will you do?' Libby asked him, when Emma had gone back to the stove, her expression still one of disapproval.

'Buy another laptop. Tidy up the mess. And hopefully be able to forget it happened. I'm not the first person to have my work equipment stolen and I won't be the last.'

'Your laptop was stolen?' Emma asked, suddenly expressing interest. 'Anything else?'

'Not that I could see. I'll be able to tell better when the police have finished with the place. I'm not the tidiest of people, so it may take some time.' He managed a chuckle.

'You seem very philosophical about it,' she said. 'I'd be climbing the wall if I thought someone had been going through my things. What do the police think?'

'A gang of youths looking for drugs or anything they can sell.'

'Hmm. Well, dinner's ready. Mum, can you make sure Clancy washes her hands?'

Libby went off to organise her granddaughter and make sure Milo was settled and wouldn't interrupt their meal. When she and Clancy returned to the kitchen, Emma was serving up their meal.

Clancy's continual chatter while they ate prevented the conflict which Emma seemed to be harbouring, and Adam had the sense to stay silent, only speaking to praise Emma on the meal, a compliment she accepted with bad grace.

As soon as the meal was over, and Libby had insisted on doing the clearing up, Emma took Clancy off to have her bath. 'She can sleep with me tonight,' she said, pointedly, 'And I'll turn in now, too. I have a lot to think about.'

Libby went over to Emma and gave her a hug. She wanted to tell her everything would be all right but knew she had no basis to offer that comfort. 'We'll see what we can work out tomorrow,' she whispered, before Emma pulled away.

'Another Scotch?' Libby offered, when she and Adam were seated on the deck, the sun dropping below the horizon and sending rays of pink and gold across the sky. She felt exhausted, as if the day had lasted for ever.

'Thanks. I can't thank you enough for your hospitality,' he said. 'I'd have been fine in a motel, but this...' He gestured inside to the cosy house which Libby had decorated in shades of blue and cream to match the beach and the ocean, and which was scattered with various mementoes of her and Bernie's life together.

'It's nothing,' she said, knowing it was more than that. The sight of Adam, looking so distressed had tugged at her heartstrings. She'd wanted to help him, to take away his pain.

They sat in silence, each clutching a glass of tawny liquid, the only sound the distant pounding of the ocean on the shore. It felt comfortable. His company was soothing. There was no need to speak.

This was what Libby had missed, this intimacy with another human being, this sense of being at one with the world.

Twenty-five

Next morning, Adam awoke to the sun streaming in through white plantation shutters and the cackle of a pair of kookaburras. *Where was he?* His eyes roamed around the room, the cream paint providing a perfect background to the flower prints on the walls. There was a pile of children's toys sitting on the floor under the window and a couple of Dr Seuss books lying on the bedside table. He blinked.

Then he remembered. The break-in. He was in Libby's house. Last night they'd sat on the deck in the moonlight. Nothing had happened – yet everything had happened. They'd barely spoken, yet their silence had meant more to him than hours of Yvette's chatter.

He lay still for a few moments, remembering how it had been, how he had felt an intimacy with Libby he'd never felt before with a woman. It had felt good, something he wanted to experience again, to see if it had been a trick of the night air or was something he could recapture. Had Libby felt it, too? He hoped so, but... Adam sighed.

He'd never had any trouble attracting women, quite the opposite. Greg used to tease that they buzzed around him like flies. But, never before, had he felt this tentative about forming a relationship.

Hearing voices and the sound of a radio playing coming from the other end of the house, Adam rose and, wrapping a towel around his waist, found his way to the bathroom. After a brief shower, his head felt clearer. He returned to the bedroom and pulled on the clean clothes he'd brought with him. Then he made his way to the kitchen.

'Why are you still here?' Clancy pointed at him with her spoon, milk dripping from it onto the table. Although her words matched those of her mother the previous evening, her tone was one of curiosity, rather than disapproval.

'Adam stayed in your room, sweetheart. Remember? That's why you slept with your mummy,' Libby said.

'Oh!' Satisfied, Clancy went back to spooning up her cereal.

'Coffee or tea, Adam?' Libby asked from where she was standing by the bench.

'Coffee, thanks.' She looked so fresh and businesslike in a pair of white pants and dark blue shirt. It was difficult to realise this was the same woman he'd spent those special moments with the night before. *Had he imagined it?*

'Help yourself to cereal and fruit, or would you prefer toast?' Libby placed a steaming mug of coffee on the table.

'Thanks, I usually have breakfast at *The Bay Café*. There's no need...' But he pulled out a chair and sat down.

'Why would you go all the way down to the esplanade when we have breakfast right here? I have to be at the library this morning, and Emma will be taking Clancy to *Kiddie Korner*, but you're welcome to stay for as long as you like.'

'Thanks,' Adam said again, feeling embarrassed by Libby's kindness, and wondering where her daughter was. *Was she deliberately keeping out of his way?*

At that moment, Emma arrived in the kitchen and, barely glancing at Adam, said, 'Clancy, we need to go soon. Finish your breakfast and clean your teeth.' She seemed to be on edge.

When Clancy slid out of her chair and disappeared, Emma turned to Adam as if suddenly noticing him. 'Good morning. Will you be going back to your own house today?'

'Em!' Libby said, a warning note in her voice.

'I was just asking, Mum.'

'It's okay.' Adam picked up his mug and took a sip. The coffee slid easily down his throat, giving a welcome caffeine buzz. 'I hope so. I plan to speak with the police as soon as I can. I'll be out of your hair as soon as possible.'

'Sorry about Emma,' Libby said, when, after a fuss with bags and shoes, Emma and Clancy finally departed. 'She's pretty tense today.

She has to talk with her solicitor again. I wish I could go with her, but I have to work.' A pulse twitched in the corner of her eye. 'I hope the police finish with your home. Not that I want rid of you…' she smiled, turning back into the woman Adam remembered from the deck. 'I enjoyed…' she blushed.

'I did, too. You say you have to work this morning. Can we meet for lunch? I can fill you in on what the police say and I should have a new laptop by then. It won't take me long to set it up.'

Libby hesitated for only a moment before saying, 'That would be nice. I don't often get the chance to go out to lunch.'

'Where would you like to meet – or shall I come to the library?'

'The library… no. There's a nice little café nearby. It's called *The Greedy Gecko*. I can meet you there at one, if that suits you.'

'Perfect.' It would give Adam time to do all the things he intended. But he wondered why Libby seemed so insistent he not meet her in the library, promising himself he'd find out later.

Before she left, Libby handed him a key. 'Just in case,' she said with a smile. 'I'd hate to think you had nowhere to go if the police take longer with your place. See you at one.'

Left by himself, Adam brewed another cup of coffee and took out his phone to check his emails. There was one from the police officer he'd spoken to yesterday, telling him he could collect his keys from the police station any time after ten. The others were unimportant, apart one from his publisher which he decided to read later. It was no doubt about the promotions Julian had mentioned, and Adam didn't need to be reminded.

He debated waiting around till he'd collected his keys but was keen to purchase a new laptop. Yesterday, he'd been told there was close to no chance of *his* being recovered. 'It has probably already been sold on,' the officer had said, apologetically, sounding as if he was repeating something he'd said many times before.

So, having picked up his car, he made his way to the shopping centre on the outskirts of town. Once there, he was amazed at all the signs of Christmas, from the large Santa in his grotto to the Christmas carols blaring through the loudspeakers. It was quieter in the Apple store, and he quickly chose a replacement for the stolen computer – a newer model which left his credit card a lot lighter. But, he consoled himself, he'd be able to recoup most of the cost from his insurance.

He learned nothing new at the police station, apart from the news he could now return home. He pocketed his keys and went back to his car, the drive home taking only a few minutes.

The house, although empty, felt strange. Adam went from room to room to inspect it, but couldn't see anything unusual, or anything else missing. Perhaps it was the smell which indicated others had been here. He opened the windows, placed the new laptop on the table, and began to set it up with all the programmes and applications he needed for his work. When he finished, it was time to meet Libby. Making sure all the windows and doors were securely locked – had he left any open yesterday? – he set off again, a spring in his step at the thought of seeing Libby again.

*

Libby could see Adam was already there waiting for her, sitting at a window table, his head bent over his phone. She thought again of how she had felt the previous evening, how her heart had lurched with pleasure – and something more – when their eyes met. There had been an unspoken connection. She was sure she hadn't imagined it. But this morning, in the cold light of day, in her kitchen, he had seemed different, distracted. Had it been Clancy's presence, or Emma's, when she appeared, tense at the prospect of meeting with Sharon again? She had flinched when Adam suggested meeting her in the library. *What if he saw the display of his books, thought she'd deliberately set it up, orchestrated it to force him into some sort of event?*

'Hi, you found the place okay?' Libby dropped into the seat opposite.

Adam half rose with a smile. 'It was easy. Good morning?'

'Busy, but yes,' she said, suddenly feeling awkward. Last night things had been so comfortable between them. *Where had it all gone?* 'Have you ordered?' she asked.

'I was waiting for you. What do you recommend?'

'Anything, really. I've only been here a few times, but I've always enjoyed the food.' Stop, she told herself, you sound inane.

'Libby,' Adam said, 'I... last night... it felt special to me.' His eyes twinkled. One side of his mouth lifted into a lopsided grin. 'I hope...' His eyes met hers.

Libby felt a glow of something she thought she'd forgotten, flow through her. She put her hands to her cheeks which she knew must be turning red. 'Me, too,' she said in a strangled voice. 'It was… good.'

'Are you ready to order?' the waitress's voice broke through the awkward moment.

'Can we have a few more minutes?' Adam asked, but the moment was gone.

They picked up the menus and studied them, before both choosing a Caesar salad with a long black for Adam and a cup of peppermint tea for Libby. Then they looked at each other and laughed.

After an enjoyable lunch, during which Libby learned Adam was now free to go home and his new laptop was ready for use, and Adam discovered more about Libby's daughter's problems, Libby felt they had become more comfortable with each other again.

'I envy you, you know,' he said, when they had finished eating.

'You do?' Libby was surprised. What was there about her messy life to invite his envy? He was a famous author. Surely he was happy and fulfilled, satisfied with his life?

'Your family,' he said, as if surprised with himself. 'I don't have anyone.' He looked down at his empty plate. 'I did once – mother, father, sister. A regular family.'

'What happened?'

'One day, when I was around twelve, my mother and sister left. I never saw or heard from them again. And Dad died some time back.'

'Oh!' Libby didn't know what to say. Although Emma often drove her to distraction, she loved her to bits and would go through hellfire for her. And there was Clancy. Her heart filled at the thought of her granddaughter. 'I'm sorry,' she said, trying to imagine what it must be like to have no one to care for.

'I didn't think it mattered,' he said, gazing into space. 'But as I get older…' He gave himself a shake. 'Sorry, here I am rattling on about myself, when you must be worried about your daughter.'

'Yes.' Libby bit her lip. In the enjoyment of Adam's company, she had almost forgotten Emma's predicament. 'I should get home.' But she made no move to leave. It was so pleasant sitting here with him, chatting to someone who she could relate to, someone of her own age, a man she found attractive.

'Of course.'

They rose and exited the café together. Libby had left her car in the library car park, so she said her farewells and headed off, switching her mind from Adam to Emma. As soon as she reached her car, she checked her phone, but there were no messages from her daughter. She didn't know if that was a good or a bad sign.

'Em!' Libby called, when she walked into the house.

There was no reply.

'Em!' Libby called again, walking through the house. But there was no sign of her daughter. She took out her phone and was about to text Emma when she heard a sound on the deck and, hurrying through, saw her daughter standing there staring across the boardwalk.

'Em?' Libby went out to join her. 'How did it go?'

'Where were you, Mum? I came straight home. I thought you finished work at twelve-thirty.'

'I... I had lunch with...'

'Not with Adam Holland? What is it with you and him? Anyone would think you were...' Her eyes widened. 'You're not, are you? You and him?'

'Who I spend time with is my business, Em. Adam's a nice man. He's been kind to me. I enjoy his company. Your dad's been gone for two years. I'm not in my dotage. I'm allowed to have men friends.' *And what if he becomes more than a friend?* Libby trembled as the thought struck her and she remembered the moment their eyes met in the moonlight. 'But you didn't answer me. What did Sharon say?'

'She told me I should have set up my own account as soon as Matt left. She said men often do this as a way of gaining what they want. It gives them leverage, to leave their wife without cash.' She pouted. 'What if he still hasn't given up on the idea of taking Clancy to Fiji?'

'He hasn't been in touch?'

Emma shook her head. 'I'd have told you.'

'Well, perhaps that's not his plan. Have you contacted the bank?'

'Not yet. Sharon said I should, to see if Matt's emptied the account. She said I need to talk to him again, too.'

'Why don't you give him a call now?'

'Now?' Emma looked horrified.

'No time like the present. You don't want the hassle of going to court if you can sort it out between you.'

'Hmm. I'll call the bank first.' Emma took out her phone.

Libby was distracted by Milo pushing his nose into her hand. 'Sorry, Milo. We left you alone all day. I bet you'd like a walk.' The dog whined in reply.

Seeing Emma was still fingering her phone, and had not made her call, Libby said. 'I'm just going to change my shoes and take Milo to the beach. Talk when I get back.'

Wearing a pair of sandals and with Milo at her heels, Libby went across the boardwalk, stopping as always at the memorial bench to Bernie. As she put her hand on the brass plaque, she said, 'Oh, Bernie, I wish you were still here to help me deal with Emma. Our daughter has got herself into a pickle with Matt. I know you didn't like him either, but neither of us imagined he'd behave like this. And I've managed to attract her displeasure, too. You'd like Adam. I can imagine the two of you talking books together.' She gave the plaque a final pat, before heading down the steps to the beach.

Once on the sand, Milo raced ahead, leaving Libby to take off her sandals and walk along in the shallow water. Out here, with the breeze in her hair, the scent of the sea in her nostrils, and the squawking of the seagulls overhead, she felt a sense of release. It was good to be away from the tension which seemed to follow Emma around like a cloud these days. Fortunately, Clancy hadn't been affected by it and remained her cheerful self, unfazed by her mother's moods and eagerly looking forward to Christmas.

Thinking of Clancy reminded Libby of yesterday, of seeing Adam and going up to speak with him to find out what had happened. *Was it only yesterday?* So much seemed to have happened since then, and she now felt so much closer to Adam. What next, she wondered as Milo returned with a stick and dropped it at her feet. *Was Emma right to be worried about her and Adam forming a relationship?*

Libby shivered as an unexpected flash of desire flickered through her.

Twenty-six

The next two days passed uneventfully for Libby. Emma's call to the bank proved unhelpful and, as far as she knew, her daughter hadn't called Matt. Libby had learned to keep her own counsel and not to enquire too closely into Emma's thinking on this issue but had offered to lend her money till it was all sorted out, and Emma had reluctantly agreed.

There had been no word from Adam and, while Libby knew he was a busy author, after their lunch she had expected to hear from him.

Today, both Emma and Clancy were at *Kiddie Korner* again and she planned to do some Christmas shopping before everywhere became too busy. Despite Clancy's visit to see Santa over a week ago, the festive season had snuck up on her. On Friday, they were going to the esplanade to see the lights being switched on on the large Norfolk pine which dominated the square there. It was to be followed by a carol concert, and Clancy was very excited at the prospect of attending both which would entail her staying up long past her usual bedtime.

Libby spent a lovely morning wandering around the shops and by lunchtime, she had managed to find everything she was looking for. In addition to a book voucher for Emma, she'd purchased a bottle of the expensive perfume her daughter favoured, and for Clancy there was the jigsaw along with the latest Barbie doll and a pretty fairy dress with a ruched purple bodice, a rainbow skirt and a pair of multicoloured wings which could be attached to the shoulders. Clancy would love it. Then, on an impulse, she'd bought a book for Adam, one of Martin Cooper's coffee table books featuring scenes along the coast from Bellbird Bay, something to remind him of his time here when he returned to Canberra. By the time she got back to her car, she was exhausted and ready for coffee and something to eat.

Feeling too weary to envisage making lunch for herself, she stopped at *The Pandanus Garden Centre and Café* on the way home intending to lunch there and to enquire about a Christmas tree. Clancy would never forgive her if they couldn't have a tree, and Libby hated the artificial ones, loving the scent of pine needles, even though they tended to make a mess. Milo loved the scent, too, his attempts to lie underneath the tree a few years ago having almost knocked it over.

After managing to organise for a tree to be delivered in a couple of weeks' time, Libby made her way to the café.

'Good to see you, Libby,' Cleo greeted her at the café, 'Been Christmas shopping?'

'How did you guess?' Libby eased herself into a chair and slipped off her sandals, the cool of the paved courtyard providing a welcome relief to her aching feet.

'It's what everyone seems to be doing this week. I'll have to wait till next Tuesday to do mine. I hope the shops haven't all sold out,' Cleo chuckled. 'It's going to be a special one for us.' She grinned.

Libby smiled back. This would be Cleo's first Christmas since she and Will Rankin got together. They were such a well-matched couple. One of the many couples Libby knew here in Bellbird Bay who had found love the second time around. It was almost as if the town possessed some sort of magic air, she mused.

She ordered a salad of greens, pumpkin, eggplant, mushrooms, feta, olives, and hummus with a cup of peppermint tea and leant back to relax.

Libby's meal had been served, and she was taking her first sip of tea when her phone rang. 'Damn!' she muttered then, checking the screen, saw Adam's number and felt a quiver of delight, her tiredness immediately forgotten.

'Adam!'

'Hi, Libby, sorry I haven't called sooner. Things got hectic.'

'I understand.' All her earlier concern disappeared in a flash.

Libby pictured him sitting at his desk in front of the window, raking a hand through his hair, and smiled. 'No worries. Everything good with you?'

'Pretty much.' He cleared his throat. 'I've been shopping, and I bought myself a cookbook and...' there was a pause, '...I wondered if you'd be prepared to risk my cooking and come to dinner tonight.'

'Tonight?'

'Is it too soon? Too short notice?' Adam sounded deflated.

'No, it's just...' Libby thought quickly. She'd planned to cook dinner for the three of them tonight, but perhaps Cleo could provide her with a takeaway meal from here. 'Sure, I'd love to. What time?'

The relief in Adam's voice was evident. Libby heard him exhale.

'Seven?' he suggested.

'That would be perfect.'

'I'll see you then... and Libby...'

'Yes?'

'I'm looking forward to us spending an evening together.'

'Me, too.' Libby's words were almost a whisper.

Libby ate her lunch in a trance, barely tasting Cleo's delicious salad.

'Problems?' Cleo asked, when she came to remove the empty plate. 'You seem lost in a dream.'

'No, it's all good. Cleo, could I ask you a favour? I know you don't usually do takeaway, but I've just been invited out to dinner tonight and...' She didn't need to finish.

'No worries,' Cleo said immediately. 'I often take food home when I don't feel like cooking one more meal. I can put something together for you. Will it be for your daughter and granddaughter?'

'Yes. Thanks. It would be a big help.' *And maybe keep Emma off my back when she hears where I'm having dinner, though that's doubtful.*

'How about a quiche and salad? I can put it together for you now and it'll be fine in your fridge till dinner time.'

'Perfect.'

'Don't tell anyone. If it gets out I'm supplying takeaway, I'll be inundated with requests and won't be able to keep up with the demand,' she joked.

But Libby knew it was true. The food here in *The Pandanus Café* was so good, there would be a line of people waiting every day.

Libby was delighted as she packed the food containers into the car.

That was one thing taken care of. Now she just had to break the news to Emma.

*

Libby examined herself in the full-length mirror in her bedroom, one hand on her stomach in an attempt to still the butterflies which were careering around wildly. She was as nervous as a sixteen-year-old on her first date. She couldn't remember ever feeling this anxious about going to dinner, but there was something about Adam Holland that touched her as no one else had, other than Bernie.

'Am I doing the right thing, Bernie?' she asked her absent husband, seeing the glow in her eyes that had been absent for so long. She examined the orange and pink patterned dress she'd bought on impulse on her way home from the café. Greta, her friend from the book club who owned *Birds of a Feather* on the esplanade, had assured her it was perfect, but now, Libby wasn't so sure. Was it too bright? Did it make her look like mutton dressed as lamb?

She checked her watch. It would have to do. There was no time to change. She gave her hair one last pat, grimaced at her reflection in the mirror and walked out of the bedroom, popping her head into Clancy's room to say goodnight.

In the kitchen, Emma was clearing up after her and Clancy's dinner. 'Thanks for organising dinner, Mum,' she said. 'If that was a takeaway, we should do it more often.'

'Tonight was a favour from Cleo. They don't normally offer it. I...' She peered at her daughter. 'I don't expect I'll be late, but I have my key.' She tried not to remember Emma's outburst when she revealed who she was having dinner with.

'You look lovely, Mum,' Emma surprised Libby by saying. 'I'm sorry I made a fuss. It's just... Dad...'

'I know sweetheart, I miss him, too.' Libby hugged her daughter and the pair stood like that for several moments, before Libby pulled away to see tears in Emma's eyes. While she felt bad about upsetting her daughter, Libby knew she had to make a stand to lead her own life, to forge a future for herself, one which didn't – couldn't – include

Bernie. 'My seeing Adam isn't the end of the world. It's only dinner.' She crossed her fingers behind her back. 'He'll be going back to Canberra before we know it.' *Why did the thought of him leaving fill her with dread?*

The sun had already set as Libby made her way up the boardwalk, the sea glistening eerily in the moonlight. It was so quiet, the only sound the waves lapping gently on the shore.

Libby took a deep breath when she arrived at Adam's gate and saw the beam of light shining out from his kitchen. She was tempted to flee before he saw her, and text him with some excuse. *Was this all a terrible mistake?* But it was too late. The door opened and Adam was standing there, a grin on his face, his eyes twinkling with delight.

'Welcome!'

'Hello.' Libby held out the bottle of wine she'd hastily picked up from her wine rack before leaving home. 'It's a red. I hope it...' Her voice tailed off as she saw the amused expression on Adam's face. *Did she sound as nervous as she felt?*

'It'll be perfect. Come on in.'

Adam led Libby into the kitchen which was filled with a delicious aroma. The table was set with a white cloth and matching blue and white dishes, and in the middle, was a small bowl of rosebuds. Adam had gone to a lot of trouble.

'You look lovely,' he said, making Libby blush.

'You look very smart, too.' She glanced at his freshly brushed hair, the pressed jeans, and the white shirt with the sleeves rolled up to the elbow. He was seriously hot. *What was she doing here? What did Adam expect of her? If he... could she...? Was she ready for a new relationship? Was that what this was?* It was too late to turn back now.

*

Adam hoped his nerves didn't show. When he greeted Libby at the door, he was blown away by how lovely she looked, the bright dress she was wearing making her resemble a tropical bird, exotic, unattainable.

He had a bottle of champagne chilling in the fridge, intending to start their evening with it, to celebrate what he saw as the start of their relationship. But now Libby was here, he began to doubt his earlier confidence. Would she consider it presumptuous? 'A glass of wine?' he asked, unscrewing the top from the bottle of shiraz she'd brought along.

'Thanks.' Libby gazed around, then took a seat on one of the high stools by the kitchen bench. She was perched there, as if ready to fly off at any moment.

Adam filled two glasses, handing one to Libby and holding one up. 'To us. To an enjoyable evening,' he said, taking a gulp from his glass.

Libby didn't speak but raised her glass and took a sip.

The meal went better than Adam expected. After a couple of glasses of wine, both he and Libby relaxed, and his attempt at the tray-baked salmon with olives, green beans, anchovies and tomatoes proved a success with Libby, thanks to the Jamie Oliver cookbook he'd picked up. He'd opened the book almost at random and this recipe looked simple enough for a novice cook like himself to attempt.

Now they had moved to the living room, and he'd risked opening the champagne and poured two glasses to accompany coffee. They were seated some distance apart on the sofa.

'Thanks for a lovely meal.' Libby sipped her champagne.

'Thank Jamie Oliver. I only followed his instructions.'

'Mmm.' Libby smiled. 'This is nice.'

Unsure if she was talking about the champagne or the company, Adam decided to take the risk to move closer. 'I'm glad you came to dinner,' he said.

'I'm glad, too. I almost didn't.'

'What changed your mind?'

'I decided it was time... time to move on. Bernie's been gone for over two years now, and I'm still grieving. But I can't live in the past for ever, despite what Emma might think.'

Encouraged by her words, Adam felt emboldened to move even closer, so close their thighs touched.

Libby didn't move away.

'You know I like you, Libby,' Adam said, tentatively reaching an arm around her shoulders. 'I like you a lot.' They were so close he could smell her scent, a delicate fragrance of roses with a citrus undertone. It suited her perfectly, so different from the spicy perfume Yvette favoured.

'I like you, too, Adam,' she said so quietly he could only just hear. She turned her face to his.

Adam couldn't resist. Putting one finger under her chin, he traced the line of her cheek with another, then his lips found hers.

Twenty-seven

Libby couldn't believe what was happening. Dinner had been amazing, Adam's company entertaining, and now they were seated side-by-side on his sofa drinking champagne. It was such a cliché, but she was enjoying it, enjoying being spoiled and feeling appreciated. When he moved closer, then his arm reached around her shoulder, her stomach lurched, and an unexpected flash of desire shot through her.

When Adam's lips met hers, her body strained towards him. Time stood still. She felt as if she belonged here, as if nothing else mattered but this moment, this sensation, this man.

When he released her, Libby's heart was beating wildly. She was trembling. She put a hand up to her now tousled hair.

'I hope I didn't act out of turn,' Adam said, much to her surprise. 'You... we... it seemed so right. I didn't expect...' He looked so embarrassed, Libby almost laughed.

She reached up to stroke his cheek. It was a long time since she had touched a man's face, felt the roughness of his unshaven cheek against her fingers. It sent shivers down her spine, reminding her of all she had missed and prompting feelings – and desires – she'd thought dead for ever. 'It was lovely,' she said, smiling.

Adam kissed her again.

It was sometime before they drew apart.

'I should go,' Libby said, pushing herself up from where she had been lying on the sofa, unaware of exactly how she had got there. 'Emma...'

'Your daughter... of course.' Adam sounded disappointed.

'It's not... I'm not... I'd love to stay, but...' Libby bit her lip. She knew what she was saying. She was telling him – this man who was only passing through Bellbird Bay, this man who she'd told her daughter was only a friend – that she was willing to go to bed with him.

Adam's eyes widened and a smile touched his lips.

Libby had surprised herself. But life was too short to prevaricate. She was well aware of how it could be snuffed out with very little warning. She was here. Adam was here. They liked each other.

'Do you really mean...?' he asked, forcing Libby to blush and wonder if she'd been too forward, if she'd misjudged the situation. Then he added, 'I'm sure we can work something out,' and grinned.

*

Emma was noticeably silent at breakfast next morning, which Libby took to be a good sign, and Clancy more than made up for her mother's silence by her excited chatter about the lighting of the tree and the carol service in the evening.

Libby was glad she was scheduled for a shift at the library that morning. She was still buoyed up with the memory of the night before and didn't want it to be ruined by derogatory comments from her daughter.

'When will you be home?' Emma asked, as Libby was on her way to the door.

'Sometime in the afternoon. I promised to have lunch with Grace when we finish at the library. What plans do you have?'

'Can we go to the beach, Mummy?' Clancy asked, forestalling Emma.

'I suppose so. You'll be here for dinner *tonight*?' she asked Libby.

'Of course.' Emma's remark was pointed, but Libby refused to be drawn or to let it spoil her mood. 'See you later. Have a good day, both of you. Love you, Clancy.'

The library was busy all morning, giving Libby little time to reflect on what had happened with Adam. But she couldn't help the frisson of joy she experienced whenever she remembered how it had felt to have his arms around her, his lips on hers.

By the time her shift ended, she was glad to be able to get off her feet. Lunch with her friend was exactly what she needed.

'Where shall we go?' Grace asked, when they were collecting their bags. '*The Greedy Gecko*'s closest, or would you prefer somewhere else?'

'That'll be fine.' Libby couldn't wait to give her feet a rest. She'd been standing on them all morning answering queries and helping people find books. Sometimes she wondered if their clients had ever heard of the internet or understood how to use the library catalogue.

But when she and Grace were seated in the café and had placed their order, all Libby could think of was having had lunch here with Adam only a few days earlier.

'What have you been up to?' Grace asked, peering at Libby. 'You have a glow about you that wasn't there last time I saw you. If I didn't know you better, I'd think... You haven't, have you? You and Adam Holland?'

Libby felt herself redden. 'No...oo, but...'

'Do tell.' Grace leant forward. 'I promise it won't go beyond me.'

Libby hesitated. Despite what Grace might promise, Libby knew she'd tell Ted. She'd never been able to keep a secret from Bernie. That's what marriage was about... sharing things. She sighed. She missed Bernie so much, even as she was slipping into a relationship with Adam.

'We had dinner last night,' she said at last. 'He cooked.'

'Ahh.' There was a wealth of meaning in Grace's utterance.

'It's not what you think. We didn't...' Libby blushed again.

'Methinks the lady doth protest too much.'

'We kissed. That's all.'

'I guess it was a good kiss?'

'Mmm.' Libby smiled at the memory. 'Now, I don't intend to say any more about it. Are you and Ted going to the tree lighting tonight?'

Their meals arrived, and the conversation turned to the evening's entertainment but, from time to time, Libby caught Grace giving her speculative glances out of the corner of her eye. She ignored them. She didn't intend to share her innermost feelings with anyone, not even Grace, who, of all her friends, would best understand her confused emotions.

*

By the time Libby reached home, Emma had unbent sufficiently to ask about the evening event, and Clancy was so excited she had trouble sitting still, making both Libby and Emma laugh affectionately.

'You need to be very good and stay close to your mummy and me,' Libby told her. 'There will be lots of people there and we don't want to lose you.'

'I promise,' Clancy said with a delightful grin.

Clancy danced down the boardwalk to the esplanade between Libby and Emma, holding their hands tightly, too excited to walk. They were a happy trio. Over dinner, Emma had attempted to apologise for her earlier outbursts about Adam.

'I suppose he's really a nice man, Mum,' she said. 'I'll try to be nicer about him. I just find it hard to accept…'

'That I can move on with my life?' Libby smiled gently. 'Life doesn't stop when a loved one goes out of it. It's something *you* need to accept, too, Em. Matt's gone. You need to make a new life for yourself. Whether it's here or back in Brisbane is your choice. But you need to realise your and Clancy's future will be different to the one you imagined.'

'Hmm.'

But Emma didn't disagree. Libby hoped this was a sign her daughter was willing to change, and her heart lifted as they made their way down to where the crowds were already gathering around the large Norfolk pine which dominated the beachfront. It was one of the few which had survived, a recent bout of a fungal disease having resulted in several of the others which bordered the foreshore having to be removed, as they presented a danger to both people and the neighbouring Norfolk pines. This was the largest and had served as the local Christmas tree all the time Libby had been here.

'Look!' Clancy pointed to the decorations which seemed to have appeared on the tree as if by magic. She hopped up and down, beaming with delight.

'Libby!'

Libby turned to see Grace and Ted behind her, along with their children. Aaron was carrying the small Isla in his arms. There was no sign of the older boy.

'Zack's off with his mates,' Ted explained. 'We're evidently not cool enough be seen with at an event like this.' He chuckled. 'I guess we were all like that at his age.'

Libby hadn't been looking for Zack. She was hoping to catch sight of Adam, sure he'd be somewhere in the crowd, which was now growing in readiness for the crowning moment. She hadn't been able to stop thinking about him. Last night had been eye-opening. It had shown her that her emotions were not dead, that she was still capable of desire, and she desired Adam Holland.

But, despite searching the crowd, there was no sign of him. She tried to swallow her disappointment and join in the excitement, but part of her wished he was there with them.

Suddenly there was a blast of music, the microphone crackled, and the mayor began the countdown.

Everyone joined in.

'Ten, nine, eight, seven, six, five, four, three, two, one.' There was a blinding flash as the tree lit up. Everyone cheered, and Clancy screamed with joy.

Then a group of musicians, who were seated under the tree, began to play carols and the air was filled with the sound of happy voices singing together. It brought tears to Libby's eyes as she remembered previous Christmases when she and Bernie had attended carol services at their local church. They had always gone there together on Christmas Eve for the midnight service, returning home to drink glasses of port and open their presents before heading to bed to snuggle up together.

'You, okay. Mum?' Emma asked, linking arms with her.

'I'm fine. I was just thinking about your dad.'

'He'd have loved this.'

Libby nodded, too overcome to say more.

Emma squeezed Libby's arm, and Libby squeezed back, glad they were on the same page again. But thoughts of Bernie didn't change the fact that she was developing feelings for his favourite author. She hoped her daughter could understand that and accept it.

'Okay?' Grace asked, too.

'Yes. I just had a moment...'

'Carols have that effect on me, too. Christmases past.'

The two women met each other's eyes with a shared sadness and a small smile of acceptance. They both knew what it was like to lose a loved one, to decide to move on, but to be beset with memories of the past.

Twenty-eight

On the day the Christmas lights were to be turned on, Adam spent the morning trying to get his head around the email from his publisher which he'd finally opened. He couldn't believe it. He re-read the email three times before it sunk in, the words dancing before his eyes and making him blink. Could it really be true? But it was there in black and white.

We have received an email from a person purporting to be your sister, requesting contact details for you. How do you wish us to proceed?

His heart beating madly, Adam picked up his phone and pressed the speed dial for the publisher. Five minutes later, he collapsed onto the sofa, the phone clutched to his chest. It was her. It was Alison. After all this time, his little sister was trying to contact him. He looked at the details he'd jotted down. It wasn't much – an email address and her name. She called herself Alison Wells, not Holland. Wells was their mother's maiden name, so that figured. But where had she been all these years, and was his mother still alive? He had so many questions, he didn't know where to start.

The words of a song from one of his favourite movies pulsed through his head. He'd start at the beginning, and that was to email her to check she was who she said she was, not some misguided fan who had somehow found a way to get close to him. It had happened before, but never like this. Who could have known he had a sister, her name was Alison, and his mother's maiden name? No, she had to be the real deal.

He brewed a strong coffee, then sat down to compose a reply to the woman. It felt strange to be writing to someone who had been part of his life but who he hadn't seen or heard of for over forty years. In his mind she was still the younger sister who followed him around, who tried to join in on his games with his mates. She was now a woman in her fifties. She could be married, have children. She could even be a grandmother. Adam leant back in his chair. How would it be to have nieces and nephews, grandnieces and grandnephews, an entire new family? It would take some getting used to. But first, he had to make contact with Alison.

Adam laboured over the words. It was important he got it right. This wasn't a novel. It was real life... his life. Finally, after several aborted attempts, he was satisfied.

His phone pinged with a text just as he pressed *Send* on the email. Picking it up, he was surprised to see Yvette's number on the screen. He sighed. What did she want? On their last call, she'd clearly told him it was over, saving him the trouble of ending things between them.

I'm sorry.

The words, coming so soon after the contact from Alison, almost made him laugh. Two voices from the past arriving within minutes of each other, though this one was in the more recent past. And, unlike the one from Alison, this was one he could choose to ignore.

Adam stood up and stared out the window. Now he'd sent the email, it would be difficult to think of anything else till he received a reply. He wished there was someone he could share it with, someone he could tell that his long-lost sister had contacted him. Libby was the person who immediately came to mind. Libby with her soothing manner, her willingness to listen without judgment. But she knew very little of his past, a past he'd hidden for years. And what if it wasn't his sister?

He looked again at the message from Yvette.

I'm sorry.

He hesitated. After last night with Libby, he was tempted to delete it, but knowing she deserved a reply, even if it wasn't exactly clear what she was apologising for, he pressed her name, still on his speed dial.

The conversation with Yvette did nothing to change his mind about her. While he could understand she now regretted her angry words, and accepted her apology, he told her as kindly as he could, that their relationship was over, taking the blame for the ending of what had been, for him, at least, a long-term affair.

Adam felt bad when he finished the call, but he hoped Yvette had accepted the inevitable end to their relationship. It had been fun, but he had never given her any reason to believe it would lead to anything more permanent. He conveniently forgot his own earlier musings in that direction. Since meeting Libby Walker, he knew no other woman could match her in his affection.

Knowing he'd be unlikely to hear from Alison any time soon, and unable to settle to writing, Adam set off down the esplanade without any clear plan. When he found himself outside the surf club, he decided to go in. Maybe a beer would help settle him. Ignoring the fact he could have had one at home, he headed upstairs to the bar.

The same dark-haired barman as before served him. He took his beer out to the deck, grateful he was the only person there at this time of day. It was too early for the lunch crowd.

But he had barely taken his first swig of the amber liquid when he heard a voice at his elbow.

'Hey, Adam, mind if I join you?'

Looking up, Adam saw Martin Cooper. Although he'd have preferred to be alone, he knew it would be rude to refuse, so he nodded.

Martin hooked a chair and took the seat opposite. 'Good to see you again,' he said, before taking a sip of beer. 'Great stuff. I needed that. Had a difficult morning trying to get just the right angle on a shot I wanted. Nothing like what I used to get up to.' He chuckled. 'I know I must be getting old when I find myself burnt out with a local shoot.'

'Happens to us all.' Adam gazed down into his beer.

'Going to the tree lighting tonight?' Martin asked. 'Should be a good turn. Hope to get a few good shots there too. For my sins, the local paper has commandeered my services for the event.' He gave a sigh, but Adam guessed he wasn't too concerned about it.

'I hadn't thought about it,' he said honestly. He wasn't a big fan of community events. In Canberra, with Yvette, he'd been forced into attending a lot of such affairs, when he'd have preferred to stay home with a good book and a glass of his favourite tipple. But this one… He could bet Libby would be there with her daughter and granddaughter. 'I might give it a go,' he said.

'Having lunch?' Martin asked. 'I'm meeting Will and you're welcome to join us.'

Adam was about to reply when his phone buzzed. Glancing at the screen, he saw an unfamiliar number. His stomach churned. 'Excuse me. I need to take this,' he said to Martin, rising and moving away from the table.

'Hello? Adam Holland here.' He could hear the tremble in his voice.

'Adam? Is it really you? It's Alison.'

'Alison, Ali!' The voice was older, more mature, but Adam could still recognise his ten-year-old sister. 'It's really you. Why…'

'It's a long story, and one I'd prefer to tell face-to-face. Can we meet?'

'Where… where do you live?' Adam's pulse raced.

'I live in Perth.'

His heart plummeted.

'But it so happens, I'm in Brisbane for a few days. Could you…?'

'I can drive down today,' he said, the words tumbling over each other in his excitement. This was his little sister, the sister he hadn't seen for over forty years. He didn't want to waste another minute, afraid she might disappear again.

'Really? That would be wonderful. I'm staying at The Emporium. Can you drive to South Bank, and I'll give you directions from there?'

'Anywhere.'

She chuckled, the sound taking him back to his childhood, to the pair of them playing together in the backyard of their old weatherboard home in Western Sydney. 'Text me when you get there.'

'Give me a couple of hours.'

'Drive carefully.'

'I will.'

Adam stared at the phone in disbelief that he had been speaking to his sister.

'Adam, is everything okay?' Martin was looking across at him with concern.

'Better than okay. I'm sorry. I need to go. Thanks for the lunch invite. Another time, maybe.'

He headed off, almost running back up the boardwalk to his accommodation where he picked up his keys and, taking the car from the garage, set off down the highway.

The snarl of traffic hit as soon as Adam entered the outskirts of the city, making him realise how quickly he'd become accustomed to the peace and tranquillity of Bellbird Bay. Did he really want to return to Canberra after Christmas, to face the daily grind of traffic heading through the city, when he could easily work from the house overlooking the ocean, with the scent of the sea and the sound of seabirds? And Libby, he thought, remembering the promise of the evening before, a promise he fully intended to make good.

But he was here in the city now, a city with which he was unfamiliar. His satnav took him directly to South Bank, an area he'd heard about, where there was a man-made beach close to the Brisbane River. He parked in the underground car park and sent a text to Alison. She replied immediately with directions to her hotel. Adam headed out to discover several walkways filled with cyclists, walkers and others out for a jog. He followed Alison's directions, easily finding his way to Grey Street and the hotel.

Adam stood outside and took a deep breath before entering the foyer and looking around. Almost immediately, an elegant woman with grey-streaked hair rose to greet him. Alison. He'd have recognised her anywhere. Her features were a feminine version of the face he saw in the mirror every morning. She came forward and gave him a kiss on the cheek.

'Adam,' she said. 'At last.' She reached out both hands.

Adam grasped her hands in his, too moved to speak. He felt his eyes moisten. This was a moment he'd never dared to hope for.

They stared at each other, drinking in each other's features.

Alison was first to recover. 'I think we both need a drink.'

Settled in a quiet corner of the hotel bar with glasses of white wine, they stared at each other again.

'Little Ali,' Adam said in wonder. 'Where have you been. I tried to find you, but...' He shook his head. 'Mum?'

Alison shook her head sadly. 'She passed a few months ago. That's why... Is our dad still alive?'

'No. he's been gone for years.'

'Oh!' Alison bit her lip. 'I wish I'd known.' She took a gulp of wine.

'When you and Mum left, it was awful. Dad...' Adam remembered those horrendous days when his father had shut himself up in his room, and Adam, at the tender age of twelve, had to fend for himself. Things had got better over the years as they'd formed a means of getting along, but as soon as he turned eighteen Adam had left home, only returning from time to time.

'Mum couldn't stay. We heard the arguments, but we didn't see the rest. Mum told me later about the abuse – physical and emotional. She thought you'd be okay. You were the son he'd always wanted, but she knew she had to get away and take me with her.'

'He had a strange way of showing it,' Adam muttered, almost to himself. How different his life might have been if his mum had taken him with her, too.

'We went to Perth,' Alison continued. 'It was as far from Dad as we could go. Mum knew no one there. She was terrified he'd try to find us.'

'You've been there all this time?'

Alison nodded. 'It's a good city. We had a good life there. When I was old enough, I looked for you, though Mum warned me never to contact you, lest Dad found us. I've followed your career – my famous big brother.' She grinned.

'And you? What happened to you?'

The drinks were replenished, food ordered and eaten, and the hours passed as the two caught up on the years they'd missed. It was growing dark when they finally ran out of things to say.

Adam discovered that, like him, Alison had eschewed commitment, preferring to lead the single life. She lectured in women's studies at a university in Perth and was attending a conference in Brisbane.

'How long will you be in Queensland?' he asked. 'Can you fit in a trip to Bellbird Bay? I'd love to show it to you.'

'I'm due to fly back after the conference ends on Sunday,' she said. 'Classes are over, but I have a batch of online assignments to mark. But if this Bellbird Bay is as lovely as you say it is, I'd love to see it – and spend more time with you. It's been too long.'

Adam agreed, and they made arrangements for Alison to fly to Bellbird Bay to spend Christmas with him. That settled, they hugged each other, and Adam went off to find his car for the drive back up the highway.

All the way home, Adam's mind was reeling from the realisation he had just spent the afternoon and part of the evening with his long-lost sister. Little Ali was back in his life. It was a lot to take in. He fumed at the realisation of what his mother had suffered at the hands of his father, and wished he'd known. Though what could a twelve-year-old boy have done to prevent it? He couldn't believe his dad had wanted him to stay; the man had never shown him any love, never indicated he was the son he'd always wanted. Maybe the loss of his wife and daughter had affected him more than he knew. Scenes from the past flitted through Adam's mind as he tried to make sense of what Alison had told him.

It wasn't till he saw the lights of Bellbird Bay, that Adam forced himself back to the present. The crowds on the esplanade were dispersing as he drove through, reminding him of the ceremony he'd intended to attend. It all seemed so unimportant in the light of what he'd heard, what he was trying to come to terms with. But he was sure of one thing. He needed to see Libby Walker.

Twenty-nine

Libby awoke to another glorious day. She tried to dismiss the niggle of disappointment in the back of her mind, telling herself there was no reason for Adam to have been at the event the previous evening, that he probably had more important things to do. But the niggle wouldn't go away. Had she frightened him off? He had said they could work something out, but what if he was only humouring her.

Hearing Emma and Clancy already in the kitchen, Libby forced herself out of bed and into the shower, the impact of the water helping to knock some sense into her. Community events such as the one they'd enjoyed weren't everyone's cup of tea. No doubt Adam had his reasons for not being there. She was feeling better when she joined her daughter and granddaughter, who were already having breakfast.

'We walked down to buy croissants, Mum,' Emma said, 'and there's one for you, if you'd like it.'

'They're yummy, Grandma,' Clancy chimed in. 'We took Milo with us and he…' She ran out of breath.

Libby looked across to where a placid Milo was lying in his usual sunny spot by the window. His food bowl was empty. 'You fed Milo, too. Thanks. And a croissant would be lovely, Em,' she said, wondering what had happened to put Emma in such a good mood. Last night they'd all been too tired to talk and had gone to bed as soon as they got home.

She didn't have to wait long to discover the reason.

'Mum, would you mind if Clancy and I went out for the day? Mel and Aaron invited us to…'

'We're going out on a big boat,' an excited Clancy finished for her.

'Sounds lovely.' Libby raised her eyebrows at Emma.

'I got talking with Mel when you and Grace were chatting. She hasn't made many friends here yet, and we got on. We talked about how men can be… *bastards*,' she said quietly, a crease appearing on her forehead. 'Aaron isn't Isla's dad. Her birth dad let Mel down. Anyway, they're going out on a boat belonging to a friend of Aaron's today and she asked us along.'

'A friend of Aaron's. Won't he mind?'

'No. Aaron texted him. It's all good. It's what we need, Mum. A day away from everything.'

'Right.' But Libby was perplexed. *Did Emma feel the need to get away from her, too?*

'You don't mind?'

'Of course not. I can find lots to do.'

But once Emma and Clancy had left, Libby was at a loss. Tempted as she was to contact Adam, to suggest they spend the day together, she couldn't bring herself to do so. In her day, it was up to the man to do the inviting and, although she knew it was an old-fashioned view today, she was inhibited enough to maintain it.

Perhaps she'd stay home and sort out the drawers in her kitchen, something she'd been planning to do for some time, but never had the motivation to start.

Milo had other ideas. The dog rose from where he'd been lying during breakfast to stand at the door, whining and pawing at the glass.

'You want to go for a walk, don't you?' Libby said, a glance outside reminding her of the glorious day and how silly it would be to spend it cooped up inside. Making a sudden decision, she changed into her swimsuit, wrapped a sarong around her waist, threw a towel, a book and sunscreen into a bag, popped on her hat and took Milo's lead from its hook. 'Come, boy,' she said to the dog, whose tongue was now hanging out in anticipation of a run on the beach.

The stretch of beach was busier than Libby had expected. As she climbed down the steps, Milo leaping beside her, what had looked like clumps of rocks from above, revealed themselves to be groups of sunbathers, unaware or uncaring of the damage the sun could wreak on their skin.

Dropping her bag in the shade, Libby released Milo and walked along in the shallows, while he ran ahead, moving in and out of the water, and keeping out of reach of the waves. When they were both tired of this, they retreated to the shade, Milo to have a nap, while Libby took out her book.

But the book didn't prove as engrossing as Libby had hoped and she soon dropped it to gaze out at the ocean, a hand over her eyes to protect them from the sun. It was still mid-morning, too early to go home for lunch, and the water looked inviting, so she decided to have a swim, then dry off before returning home.

Wisely, Milo chose to stay with her belongings, as Libby headed into the ocean. She swam out through the waves, relishing the sensation of the seawater on her skin, then turned to float on her back, looking up into the clear blue sky, filled with gratitude to be living in such a beautiful place. She was about to turn over and swim back to the shore, when she became aware of a shadow close by.

'Hello, there.'

Adam's voice in her ear took Libby by surprise. It was all she could do to stay afloat. 'Adam?'

He laughed and gestured to the beach.

They swam back side-by-side.

'I was just thinking of you, and here you are. It's as if I conjured you up,' Adam said when they reached the shore together and began wading out of the water. 'Your daughter and granddaughter?' He glanced up the beach.

'Just me and Milo today. Emma and Clancy have gone out on a boat with Grace's daughter and her partner.'

'Even better. Just you and me.'

Libby felt a flutter of excitement start to build. What did he mean? It was broad daylight. They were on a busy beach. She was suddenly aware she was only wearing a flimsy swimsuit and Adam... She swallowed hard. With the water dripping from his strong body, he looked like a Greek god.

'It must be around lunchtime. Why don't you – and Milo – join me for lunch?'

'I...'

'I insist. I have something I want to share with you.'

Her interest piqued, Libby agreed.

They walked back up the beach together. Libby dried off and wrapped her sarong around her again, while Adam went to collect his towel. Her eyes followed him, marvelling at how his tanned body moved so effortlessly. She felt herself grow hot and stifled the thoughts whirling around in her head. They were going to have lunch. That was all.

Sitting in Adam's kitchen, watching him prepare a salad, Libby wished she'd taken time to go home and change. She felt very exposed in only a swimsuit and a loose sarong.

Adam appeared to have no such qualms, moving easily around the kitchen in his damp board shorts which were clinging to his body like a second skin. He hadn't bothered to dry off properly, and there were still droplets of water on his shoulders, tempting Libby to reach up and wipe them off.

Her heart lurched as he turned to see her watching him. 'What did you want to share with me?' she asked, in an attempt to hide what she'd been thinking.

'Later. Let's eat on the deck, shall we? It's too nice to be indoors.'

Libby quickly agreed and carried out the plates and cutlery while Adam took care of the salad. Milo joined them, lying under the table in the hope of some titbits falling his way.

It wasn't till they had finished eating and drinking coffee that Adam satisfied Libby's curiosity.

'A strange thing happened to me yesterday,' he said. 'I was reunited with my sister.'

Libby gazed at him in surprise. 'Reunited? I don't understand.' Adam had only mentioned his sister once, but that wasn't surprising. They had talked more about her family than his. Hadn't he said his mother and sister left when he was young? She suddenly realised she knew practically nothing about his personal life, only what she'd read on Wikipedia and on his website, when they first met and she'd been curious about him.

'It's a long story.'

'I don't have anywhere I need to be.' Libby curled her legs up under her and prepared to listen.

She listened, shocked, as Adam told his story, the tale of his unhappy childhood, broken home and long-lost sister reminding her of the plot of one of the novels she devoured voraciously. When he came to the end, she gazed at him, her eyes wide with astonishment and compassion. 'And you had no idea?' she asked.

'None. I'd given up hope of ever finding Ali. It's like a miracle. Though it's too late for my mother.' He sighed.

Libby realised their coffee had gone cold while he spoke, and the sky was clouding over. She shivered slightly and wrapped her arms around herself.

'Let me…'

Libby never knew what he was going to say, because they both rose at the same time and managed to bump into each other.

Adam's arms went around Libby to prevent her from falling, their faces so close together she could feel his breath on her face and see the wrinkles around his eyes and mouth. The touch of his naked skin on hers sent shivers running through her.

'Sorry!'

'Sorry!'

They both spoke at once, then laughed.

'Let's go inside,' Adam said, his arm still around Libby's shoulders.

Once inside, they turned towards each other as if drawn by some invisible thread. Their eyes met… then their lips.

Libby felt herself caught up in a force beyond her control as their bodies pressed together, their hearts beating as one. She forgot where she was, lost in a tumult of desire.

Thirty

'When does your daughter get back?'

Adam's words roused Libby, who had been enjoying the closeness of his body. She opened her eyes to see the walls of his bedroom and to remember how she got there and what had happened next. She could hear Milo whining outside the door. 'What time is it?' she asked.

'Four o'clock.'

Adam's voice was muffled, his lips on her forehead, tempting her to snuggle down again, but there were Emma and Milo to consider. 'I have to get up. Milo will need to go out, and... Sorry.' Libby kissed Adam's shoulder, marvelling at the knowledge she had made love with this lovely man, this man who wasn't Bernie... and it had been wonderful. And she didn't feel one iota of guilt.

'Happy?' he asked.

'Very.' For just one moment, Libby allowed herself to cuddle up to Adam, then she drew away and slid out of bed.

'When can we do this again?' he asked, as she slipped her swimsuit back on and tied the sarong around her waist. 'You look so delicious like that. I can't believe how...'

'Shh.' She placed a finger on his lips. 'It won't be easy, but...maybe...'

Adam rose, too, and pulled on his board shorts.

Libby's breath caught in her throat. Even though she'd seen him like this before, even though she and Adam had been as close as a man and woman could be, the sight of his body still took her breath away.

As soon as she opened the bedroom door, Milo leapt up on her as if chastising her for leaving him in the kitchen. 'Sorry, Milo,' she said. 'We're going home now.'

'Tomorrow?' Adam asked. 'Ali will be here in less than two weeks, so we won't have much chance then. I'd like you to meet her.'

'Oh!' Libby hadn't expected this. Meeting Adam's long-lost sister sounded serious. 'You mean…?'

'I mean I want you to meet my sister. I… Hell, Libby, you must know this is no casual fling. You mean more to me than that, more than…' He ran a hand through his hair as if unsure what he did mean.

Libby felt herself melt at the emotion in Adam's voice. 'I'd be happy to meet your sister,' she said, 'but tomorrow… I don't know. It will depend.'

'It's Sunday You don't have to work.'

'No…oo.' Libby's mind was working overtime in an effort to figure out how she could evade Emma and Clancy to spend more time with Adam – in Adam's bed, when Milo, realising he was being ignored, barked loudly. 'Sorry, I really need to go. I'll see what I can manage and call or text.' She kissed Adam on the cheek, felt his warm fingers on the nape of his neck as he turned her face towards him for one last kiss, and she headed off, hurrying down the boardwalk with Milo scampering after her.

To Libby's relief, she reached home before Emma and Clancy, and was able to shower and change into a pair of knee-length shorts and tee-shirt. The shock of a cold shower brought her out of the stupor Adam's lovemaking had induced, and she was ready to face her daughter and pretend it had never happened. But it had. And when she looked in the mirror, Libby could see a glow in her cheeks and shine in her eyes that hadn't been there before. She hoped Emma would put it down to her having spent the day in the sun.

Libby had poured herself a glass of wine and was making a salad for dinner, Milo getting underfoot in his delight at being back home, when a smiling Emma and a tired Clancy walked in.

Before Libby could speak, Clancy came over to hug her. 'It was so fun, Grandma,' she said. 'We were on this big boat and… the man…'

'His name's Nick,' Emma corrected her.

Looking at her daughter, Libby noted the blush on her cheeks. She raised her eyebrows. 'Nick?'

'Nick Armstrong. Aaron's boss. It was his boat.'

Wondering if Emma's blush was entirely due to being in the sun, too, Libby asked, 'You had a good day?'

'It was amazing.' Emma hadn't sounded this happy since she arrived in Bellbird Bay.

'And Nick?'

'As I said… he's Aaron's boss. He owns a boat building business. They're friends. They were at school together. It was fun being with Mel,' she added hurriedly.

Libby didn't think it was Mel's company that had brought the blush to Emma's cheeks. Had her daughter found someone to take Matt's place in her affections already? 'Dinner will be ready soon. Salad okay?' she asked.

'Fine, Mum. We're not that hungry. There was a lot of food on the boat. I'll get Clancy into the bath before we eat.' Then, as an afterthought, she asked, 'How was your day?'

Libby gave a sigh of relief. She should have known Emma's activities would take priority over anything Libby might have done. 'Milo and I went to the beach,' she said.

Emma didn't even comment, but hurried Clancy off to her bath.

Alone again, Libby couldn't help reliving her afternoon in bed with Adam. It had been a pleasant surprise to discover how different it was to make love with someone new. She and Bernie had enjoyed a full love life until he was too ill, and he had been her first and only lover. Adam was clearly experienced and knew how to please a woman. She smiled to herself remembering how he had made her feel and shivered with delight.

Dinner passed without incident. Clancy was too tired to say much, and Emma seemed distracted. Libby tried to find out more about the boat trip, but Emma was uncharacteristically reticent, so Libby didn't pursue it. After dinner, Emma took Clancy off to bed, while Libby tried to settle down to read the book of Adam's she'd already started.

But tonight, although well-written, the tale of political intrigue in the capital failed to hold her attention, the image of its author forcing its way between the pages, till Libby closed the book and her eyes.

*

Adam looked at the tangled bedsheets, unable to believe what had happened. He'd spent the best part of the afternoon in bed with Libby Walker. He dragged a hand through his hair, then the realisation he was still wearing the damp board shorts he'd hastily pulled on when they rose forced him into the shower to cool off.

Dressed again, he went into the kitchen and opened the fridge. But he didn't feel hungry. Instead, he pulled out a can of beer and took it out to the deck where he stood gazing at the ocean, remembering…

He was so lost in the memory of the afternoon, he didn't notice the two men walking up the boardwalk until they stopped at his gate.

'Mr Holland? Adam Holland?' one asked. He was a tall thin man wearing a pair of grey pants and a white shirt and tie. *Who wore a tie in Bellbird Bay?* The other was shorter and similarly dressed.

'Guilty,' Adam replied before realising it might not be the most appropriate thing to say.

The two men smiled.

The tall man spoke again. 'I'm Detective Sergeant Joe Baker and this is Detective Constable Miller. We're here about the break-in.' He showed Adam his badge.

'I guess you'd better come in,' Adam said, his earlier mood entirely ruined.

Inside, the two men stood awkwardly in the kitchen.

Adam wondered if he should offer them tea or coffee, but before he could come to a decision, the tall man spoke again.

'We won't take much of your time, but we wanted to let you know we've arrested two young men. I'm afraid there's no sign of your laptop.' He didn't look sorry, only bored at what was no doubt a common occurrence for him. 'The thing is…' he rubbed his chin, '…one of the men we arrested broke down and revealed they had information you knew about their drug deals. He offered that up as an explanation as to why you – and your laptop – were targeted.' He stared at Adam expectantly. Adam stared back at him in astonishment. 'Me? Drugs? No, Sergeant. He's wrong about that.'

'Are you sure, Mr Holland? He seemed very sure, and it's a strange thing for him to state out of the blue. Were you in *The Bay Café* with another man on…' he referred to his notebook. '…Sunday 28th November, the day of the burglary? And were you discussing a local drug ring? If you do have information, we would like to know why you didn't report it.' He closed the notebook with a snap.

Adam's mouth fell open as he recalled his conversation with Julian, and his agent's joking comment about him having local knowledge of a drug ring.

'We were joking,' he said weakly.

'It's not something to joke about, not something we take lightly.'

'No.' Adam was trying to work out how to explain – dealing with the police in real life was much more difficult than writing about it – when the shorter detective picked up the proof copy of Adam's latest novel which was lying on the benchtop.

He gave it a cursory glance, then turned it over and looked from the author photo on the back cover to Adam and back again. 'Adam Holland. You're *this* Adam Holland?' He held up the book. 'I've read everything you've ever written, I'm a big fan.'

His colleague looked at him in amazement.

'He's the author, Joe. He writes thrillers. They're damned good.'

'That's beside the point,' Sergeant Baker said. 'Drugs are nothing to joke about.'

'Of course not, Sergeant. I was with my agent. We were discussing the book I'm writing. It's set in a small coastal town not unlike Bellbird Bay, and the plot includes drug dealing.' Even as he spoke, Adam realised it sounded weak. But it was the truth.

'Hmm.'

But both men seemed to relax.

Adam felt himself relax, too. 'Is that all?' he asked.

'For now,' Sergeant Baker said. 'We may have further questions later.'

At the door, Detective Miller stopped and said, 'I like the sound of your new book. If you need any help with police procedures...' He glanced to where his sergeant was waiting impatiently for him on the boardwalk.

'Thanks. I'll send you both a copy,' Adam promised, glad to be rid of them. He stared after the two men making their way down the boardwalk. He'd often talked with the police in Canberra to get background for his writing, but this was the first time he'd experienced this sort of confrontation. What had they expected of him, he wondered, before heading to his new laptop to write an enhanced version of his experience into the life of Jay Bolton.

Thirty-one

Libby was still suffused with the glow of yesterday's lovemaking when she entered the kitchen next morning to find a cheerful Emma already there with Clancy who was enjoying a boiled egg with toast and vegemite. Milo rose and wagged his tail to show he was pleased to see her, too.

'Good morning, Mum,' Emma carolled from where she was standing by the toaster. 'Breakfast?'

'Thanks, honey. Toast would be lovely, and I'll make some tea.' She checked the electric jug had boiled and dropped a lemon and ginger teabag into a cup.

'You sound happy this morning,' she said to Emma, when they had both joined Clancy at the table.

'I had a call from Mel. She's invited Clancy and me to a barbecue today. She and Aaron live up the coast a bit, close to where he works with Nick.' She blushed, and Libby guessed Nick would be at the barbecue, too.

'That sounds lovely, sweetheart.' She was glad something – someone – had happened to take Emma's mind off her plight. She just hoped this Nick guy was more genuine than Matt, and Emma wasn't heading for hurt again. She felt helpless to do anything to make things better for her daughter, and if Mel along with Aaron's friend could work their magic, so be it.

'Will you be okay on your own again, Mum?'

'Darling, I've been living on my own since I moved up here.' Libby chuckled at her daughter's sudden concern for her welfare. Her heart was pounding, and she was tingling all over at the prospect of another day with Adam. She remembered his tentative 'Tomorrow?' Now she could give him an answer.

Emma seemed to take even longer than usual to get her and Clancy ready to leave.

Libby had sent a brief text to Adam to let him know she'd be free, and he had replied with a thumbs-up emoji and one which signified a kiss. Feeling like a teenager, she sent back a heart, then put her phone in her pocket determined not to look at it again till she was on her own.

Milo, sensing her excitement, was wagging his tail and turning in circles. 'Be patient, Milo,' she said, feeling like spinning around herself, when they were finally ready, Emma telling Libby to have a good day.

'You, too, honey,' Libby said, closing the door behind them. Back in the kitchen, she was about to call Adam when his tall figure appeared on the boardwalk.

'Have they gone?' he whispered with a wicked grin.

'Perfect timing. They've only just left.' Libby's pulse raced at the sight of the twinkle in his eyes. Even Milo seemed pleased to see him, the dog's tail wagging more wildly than ever. 'Coffee?' She tried to calm the mad beating of her heart, hoping Adam couldn't see her excitement.

'Lovely, but let's go out. *The Bay Café* is lovely at this time in the morning. We can take Milo,' he said, as the dog gazed up at him with a pleading expression.

'Sure. I'll just fetch my bag.' *What had she expected? That he'd whisk her off to bed?*

'I have something to tell you.'

'Oh!' Libby's heart fell. *He was going to say it had been a mistake, that he regretted yesterday, that...* She swallowed and pasted a smile on her face. 'Right.'

But Adam didn't seem any different. He kissed her on the cheek, took her hand as they walked down the boardwalk, Milo padding happily alongside, and squeezed her waist when they reached the café. Maybe she was wrong, and it was all going to be all right.

Once they'd ordered a long black for Adam and an iced coffee for

Libby along with two slices of banana bread, Libby asked, 'What do you have to tell me?' her heart thumping madly.

'Yesterday, after you left, I had a visit from two detectives.'

Libby exhaled with relief. It wasn't about her. 'Did they find your laptop?'

'Sadly not.' He grimaced. 'But I'm not worried about that. My new one works well, and I'm insured. They came to tell me they'd arrested the culprits.'

'That's good... isn't it?' she asked, seeing him frown.

'It is and it isn't. One of them gave them the impression I knew about their drug deals. They'd evidently heard Julian and me talking about my novel and assumed...' He dragged a hand through his hair. 'The two detectives wanted to know why I hadn't reported it to them. I felt as if *I* was the culprit. It was a weird feeling, I can tell you.'

'But they believed you?'

'They seemed to, one of them at least. He's a fan of my books.' He chuckled.

Their coffees arrived, and the waitress provided a bowl of water for Milo, who lapped it up greedily before settling at Libby's feet.

'Apart from that, I haven't been able to stop thinking about yesterday,' Adam said, taking Libby's hand. 'I couldn't believe it when I got your text this morning. What's your daughter up to today? Another boat trip?'

'Not exactly. It's a barbecue today, at Mel and Aaron's. But... the guy whose boat they were on yesterday, the friend of Aaron's, Nick. I think he made an impression on Emma. She was a different person last night – and this morning. I just hope...'

'You can't live her life for her,' Adam said gently, rubbing his thumb across the back of her hand and sending shivers down her spine.

'I know, but... she still hasn't had time to get over what Matt's done to her. I'd hate it if she... Sorry to bore you with my problems. I seem to make a habit of it.' Libby bit her lip.

'Nonsense. I'm glad to provide an ear, though I'm afraid I'm in no position to offer advice. Do Grace or Ted know this man, if he's a friend of Aaron's?'

'I didn't think of that. Maybe I can ask Grace when I see her at the library next week. See, you have been of some help.' She smiled.

'Now, enough of our problems. It's a glorious day and we're spending it together. What shall we do?'

*

An hour later, they were gazing down on the most beautiful stretch of beach Libby had ever seen. 'Dolphin Beach,' she said. 'No wonder they were at such pains to save it.'

'Amazing, isn't it? Will Rankin said something about saving it from developers.'

'He's too modest,' Libby said. 'Last year, a bunch of developers wanted to turn it into some sort of mega resort. Will was at the forefront of those who opposed it – and won. I don't know him very well, but from what I do know, he's a pretty humble guy, one who gets things done without bragging about it. He does a lot of good in the community. It's why people hope he's going to stand for council.'

'I didn't realise…' Adam pulled Libby closer. 'Shall we?' He gestured to a path leading down to the beach.

'Let's.' Libby picked up the basket she'd dropped when they got out of the car, the one containing the rug, towels and sunscreen, and Adam collected the picnic hamper from the boot. They'd stopped by *The Greedy Gecko* on the way to purchase one of their deluxe picnic packs for two. It sounded delicious, containing breads, pâté, various cold meats and cheeses, fruit and slices of cheesecake. There were also two mini bottles of sparkling wine. Everything was carefully packed in a freezer bag to maintain freshness and there were disposable plates, glasses and cutlery, and even a small paper tablecloth.

Once down on the beach, Libby let go of the hand Adam had taken to help her down the steep incline and found a shady spot to spread the rug. Then, feeling daring, she slipped off the shorts and shirt she'd donned at home before they set off, to reveal the new, one-piece, blue swimsuit which Sassy had assured her flattered her mature figure.

Turning, Libby saw Adam had taken off his clothes, too. His body was only covered by a pair of navy and red board shorts, leaving his naked chest on view.

'Hey,' he said, 'you look good enough to eat.'

Libby blushed. In an attempt to hide her embarrassment, she called, 'Last one in's a sissy,' and ran into the sea, wading out till the water was up to her knees before diving into the waves.

Adam joined her, and they were soon floating together some distance from the shore.

I could stay here for ever, Libby thought, as the gentle movement of the waves lulled her, helping her to forget everything other than the wide sky above, the cool water underneath and the man she was with.

But they couldn't stay for ever, no matter how enticing the idea was. Hunger won out, and soon Adam said, 'Must be time for lunch.'

Back in their shady spot on the beach, but still in their swimwear, Adam opened the hamper, and they feasted on the delicious tidbits.

'That was special,' Libby said, when there was nothing left but crumbs. 'What a wonderful way to spend a day.'

'The day's not over.' Adam leant over, his lips brushing the nape of her neck.

Libby's breath caught, her body tingling at his touch.

He swept back her hair to kiss her neck.

She trembled.

Then his lips were on hers.

They moved closer, Adam's hand reaching under the strap of Libby's swimsuit to slip it from her shoulder.

'We can't,' she protested weakly. 'Not here.' But her body was saying something different. She was quivering with a desire she hadn't thought she was still capable of.

'There's no one to see us.' Adam's voice was thick with a passion which matched hers, and Libby felt herself succumb to an emotion she couldn't deny.

*

When Libby and Adam returned to Bellbird Bay, and to Libby's house, they were glowing from their day in the sun and their lovemaking. After time spent in each other's arms, they had fallen asleep and, by the time they awoke, the sun had moved around to reach where they were lying.

They were laughing when Libby opened the door to find a disgruntled Milo. In the delight of Adam's company, she had forgotten her poor dog had been shut inside while they had been enjoying themselves.

'Sorry, Milo,' she said, opening the door to allow him outside. The dog gave her an accusing look before heading out.

'Poor Milo,' she said to Adam. 'He thinks I forgot him.'

'You had other, better, things to think about.' Adam drew her towards him, his lips tracing a line from her mouth to her ear and back again.

Libby slid out of his embrace. 'I think what we both need is a shower. I can feel the sand sticking to me.' She blushed at the memory of how her body had become covered with grains of sand. It had been wonderful. She'd never made love in the open air, on a beach, never imagined taking such a risk. Anyone could have come along and seen them. But they hadn't. As Adam had said, they had the beach to themselves. She wondered what Emma would think if she knew what her conservative mother had been up to, then stifled the thought. Emma would never know, must never know. It would remain her secret, hers and Adam's. She glanced at him out of the corner of her eye. He was staring at her so tenderly, she felt herself melt, tempted to drag him to bed and…

'A shower's a good idea,' he said, 'before I drag you off to bed and have my wicked way with you again.' He chuckled.

Had he read her mind?

Despite Adam's pleadings, Libby chose to shower in the ensuite, relegating Adam to the main bathroom. While the thought of showering together was tempting, she knew what it would lead to, and she was aware Emma might return home at any moment. She couldn't risk her daughter finding them in *flagrante delicto*. Then the fat really would be in the fire. Emma might never speak to her again.

As it was, they were barely out of the shower and dressed, when they heard the front door open and Clancy burst in, followed by a smiling Emma.

Emma stopped in her tracks when she saw Adam sitting at the kitchen table, his hair still damp from the shower. Libby was in the process of making tea, and Milo had come back inside and was wolfing down his food.

To Libby's surprise, Emma didn't glower or make some rude comment, but only said, 'Hello, Adam. Looks like you had a nice day, too, Mum. Tea would be nice. I'll just freshen up first.'

When she left, Libby and Adam looked at each other. He opened his mouth to speak, but Libby pointed to Clancy and shook her head. 'Later,' she mouthed.

Emma was still in a pleasant mood when she returned to enjoy tea with them, while Clancy downed a glass of milk then went to talk to Milo.

'I should take Milo for a walk,' Libby said, when tea was over. 'We've been out since morning,' she said to Emma by way of explanation.

'Fine, Mum. I'll see what we have for dinner.' She looked at Adam, one eyebrow raised.

'No,' he said hurriedly, 'I need to get back to my book. It won't write itself, and I have some things to send to my agent.'

He left with Libby and Milo, and they walked up the boardwalk together, but when they came to his house, he didn't stop as Libby had expected, but continued with them up to the headland.

'Does Emma realise my car is still outside your house?' he asked with a laugh.

'She may not have noticed. She did appear distracted – and I haven't seen her in such a good mood since... since yesterday.' Libby laughed, too. 'I think Aaron Crawford's friend, Nick, may have something to do with it. I must remember to ask Grace about him.'

By this time, they had almost reached the top of the boardwalk from where there was an amazing view of the bay on both sides of the headland. Libby released Milo to allow him to wander through the long grass, knowing he wouldn't stray far. He was a good dog.

'I thought it was the two of you.' The voice came from the garden of the house at the end of the boardwalk. The old high-set house was one of the few of its kind in this part of town and had been standing for as long as anyone could remember. Ruby Sullivan was said to have lived here all her life. Now, the elderly woman leant over her gate, gazing at Libby and Adam.

'Hello, Ruby,' Libby said, having met the elderly woman once before when she was having an early morning cup of tea at *The Pandanus Café*. 'Isn't it a lovely day? Been gardening?' she asked, seeing a wheelbarrow behind Ruby.

'I do what I can these days.' She peered at Libby, then at Adam. 'Remember what I told you?' she asked him with a grin. 'You can't escape your destiny.' Then she turned her attention to Libby. 'You need to be careful if you want what's waiting for you. Be patient, and don't jump to conclusions.' Then, muttering to herself, she disappeared into the house.

As the shabby white door closed behind her, Libby and Adam looked at each other.

'What was that about?' he asked. 'She said a strange thing when I met her once before, too.'

'She does that. People tend to ignore her, but I've heard she can be uncannily accurate. Of course, I guess it's always possible to think so in retrospect.'

'Hmm.'

'What did she tell you before?'

'Nothing much.' Adam seemed reluctant to share, and Libby didn't want to pursue it.

'We should be getting back,' she said. 'Emma offered to prepare dinner, and I don't want to upset her and ruin her good mood.'

'Okay.'

Libby attached Milo's lead again, and they walked slowly back down the boardwalk, stopping when they came to Adam's gate.

'Can I see you tomorrow?' he asked. 'Even if it's just for coffee or lunch.'

'Emma and Clancy will be at *Kiddie Korner*, and I don't have to work,' Libby said.

'And I will need to pick up my car.'

'Yes.'

'See you tomorrow, then.' Adam gave Libby a kiss on the cheek and stood at the gate while she and Milo continued their walk home.

Thirty-two

'What's happening today?' Emma asked at breakfast next morning.

Libby was delighted Emma still appeared more content. 'Christmas tree,' she mouthed to her daughter over Clancy's head. 'Surprise.' She gestured to the little girl with a smile.

Emma nodded.

'Good barbecue?' Libby asked. 'Were there many there?'

'Just family… and Nick.' Emma blushed.

'Sounds he's almost like family, too.'

'He's nice, Mum. I think you'd like him.' Emma hesitated.

Libby could see she wanted to say something more. She waited.

'He… he's asked me out to dinner. I… I didn't know what to say.'

'Do you want to go?'

'Yes, but…' She nodded towards Clancy.

'It's time you told her,' Libby whispered.

'I know.' Emma frowned.

'When does he want to see you?'

'On Wednesday. Could you…?'

'Of course.' Libby checked to make sure Clancy wasn't listening, but the little girl was busy spooning up her cereal. 'It will do you good.'

'What about Matt?' Emma looked fearful.

'What about him? He's shown how much he cares about you and Clancy. You don't think he's going to change his mind and come back, do you?'

'No…oo, but…' Emma bit her lip.

'Then what's stopping you? I haven't met Nick, but he can't be all bad if he's a friend of Aaron Crawford. Aaron is Ted's son and Grace…'

'I know, I know. Grace is a friend of yours. I thought Matt was an okay guy, too, and look what happened there?'

'I thought you wanted to go on this date. Are you trying to talk yourself out of it?'

'No.' Emma seemed to make up her mind. 'Thanks, Mum. I'll text him now.' She took out her phone.

Emma and Clancy had no sooner left, than Libby received a text to let her know the Christmas tree was on its way. She hadn't had one delivered here in Bellbird Bay before and hoped it wouldn't be too tall to fit into the living room. She could envisage it sitting by the window, the coloured lights illuminating the view. Then she remembered. When she moved here after Bernie died, she'd given all the Christmas lights and decorations to Emma, deciding they held too many memories and should be passed on to the next generation. She thought of the special ornaments collected over the years, and now regretted her generous gesture. She could buy others, but they would never replace the old familiar ones.

To Libby's delight, the tree and Adam arrived together, the garden centre van arriving at the front door, just as Adam walked in through the deck.

'Just in time,' she said, when she saw the size of the tree. There was no way she could have managed it on her own.

'Will you be right?' the man asked, as he manhandled the large tree onto her front step.

'I will now,' Libby said, as Adam appeared behind her and took hold of the base of the tree while she grasped the top, and together they carried it into the living room where she had already placed a large tub.

Before long, but not without an effort on both their parts, the tree stood upright in the tub, almost, but not quite, reaching to the ceiling.

'Thanks a lot, Adam. I don't know what I'd have done if you hadn't arrived when you did. I wanted to have it set up before Emma and Clancy get home, to be a surprise for Clancy.'

'It looks a bit bare.'

'I know. I want Clancy to help with the decorations. It's half the fun, but…' she bit her lip.

'What?'

'I don't have any. I gave them all to Emma. They're in Brisbane. I need to buy a new collection.'

'No problem. Why don't we go out to lunch and check out the shops? I've been wanting to visit *The Pandanus Garden Centre and Café* again. Maybe I'll see if I can get a wreath for my front door or something. Now Alison is coming to visit, I feel I need to make more of an effort to make the place look festive. We can kill two birds with one stone.'

'What a good idea. I'd love to have a Christmas wreath, too.'

After a cup of tea for Libby and coffee for Adam, accompanied by slices of carrot cake left over from the weekend – and several minutes spent in each other's arms as a reminder of their new-found closeness, they set off.

First, they headed to the shopping centre which, now Christmas was closer, was crowded with shoppers all intent on finding the best bargains, and the line of mothers and toddlers waiting to see Santa was almost out the door.

Libby and Adam pushed their way through the throng and into one of the chain stores where they were faced with a display of everything from artificial trees to lights, strings of tinsel, coloured baubles, Christmas themed tee-shirts and Santa hats.

'This is why I avoid these places at this time of year,' Adam groaned, as yet one more mother trailing excited children pushed past, intent on adding to her already overflowing trolley. 'I try to forget Christmas even exists.'

'Yet here you are.' Libby chuckled.

'You must have put a spell on me. I've heard about women like you.'

'Women like me? Whatever do you mean?' Libby said flirtatiously.

'Women who weave their magic around a man till he doesn't know what he's doing, women who…'

'Oh, look!' Libby pointed to a display of wooden reindeer, small enough to be held in a tiny hand. Next to them was a hanging stand of red Christmas stockings. 'Clancy would love those, and we had a stocking just like that for Emma when she was little. I bought one for Clancy, too, for her first Christmas. It's still in Brisbane, too. Maybe I should replace it.'

'Why not?'

Soon, they were standing at the check-out with a collection of tree ornaments, a box of tree lights, the wooden reindeer and a large red Christmas stocking with *Happy Christmas* embroidered on it in white.

Although happy with her purchases, Libby mourned the loss of the special decorations and ornaments gathered over the years, all of which held special significance for her, and several of which had been made by Emma when she was a child, and proudly brought home from school. And, although the Christmas stocking for Clancy was bright and new, it could never completely replace the one which she and Bernie had chosen together and had embroidered with her name. She sighed.

'Something the matter?' Adam asked. 'Are the crowds too much for you?'

'No, it's... Oh, I'm just being silly. Everything's fine.'

'I think we both need something to eat.'

Libby agreed. So they headed back to the car, where Adam packed their purchases into the boot then drove them to the garden centre.

*

'All ready for Christmas?' Cleo asked as she took their order. The sound of Christmas carols was filtering into the café from the garden centre, providing a festive atmosphere.

'Almost.' Libby smiled at her. 'How about you?'

'I've been so busy here, I've left a lot of the preparations to Will – apart from the food.' She chuckled. 'He's co-opted Owen and Hannah, and they've promised to surprise me. Kerri-Ann will be with us, too,' she said, referring to her daughter's half-sister who had only made her presence known to them a year earlier. 'She's travelling down from Townville with Grace's son, Ben. They've been seeing a lot of each other since she took the job at James Cook University. And Hannah wants us to include Nate in our celebration, which means Ailsa and Martin, too. And we can't leave Bev out, so we'll be quite a crowd.'

'Wow!' Libby couldn't imagine organising for such a large group but was sure Cleo and Will could cope. 'Sounds like a full-on celebration.'

'We're looking forward to it,' Cleo confirmed. 'And it'll be good to have a few days off work. Bev has decided to close the place between Christmas and New Year to give everyone a break. Now, what would you like to order? You didn't come here to hear about my Christmas plans.'

When they had placed their orders, both deciding on the chicken sandwich with salad, and Adam choosing his regular long black, while Libby opted for a beetroot, carrot and orange juice, they sat back and looked at each other.

'Happy?' Adam asked.

'You know I am, but...'

'You're sorry you don't have your old Christmas stuff?'

'I know it's silly. It's only stuff, but it holds so many memories, memories I thought I didn't want. I was wrong.'

'You can always make new ones.'

Adam took Libby's hand, and she had the impression he wasn't only talking about Christmas ornaments.

*

As Adam clasped Libby's hand, he hoped she understood his meaning. He wasn't referring to the Christmas decorations, either the ones she'd lost, or the new ones in the boot of his car. He wanted her to know he was willing to make new memories with her, with her and her daughter and granddaughter, too, if Emma would permit it. Meeting Libby, combined with seeing Alison again had been life-changing for him. Between them, they had broken through the hard outer shell he'd built to protect himself from hurt. Ever since he'd been a child, Adam had had a need to ensure he kept himself safe. At first, it was safe from the arguments between his parents that made him want to hide, then it was safe from his dad's temper when things didn't go his way. By the time Adam left home, the hard outer shell was already forming and his time in war zones only hardened it, made it more impenetrable. Greg had been the only person to see through and to reach the vulnerable Adam hidden inside.

He was ready to move on. Was Libby?

Her answering squeeze of his hand told him she was.

'Sounds as if Cleo will have her work cut out. Quite a gathering,' she said, 'How are you planning to spend the day?'

'I had intended to spend it like any other day, but now there's Alison, we can spend it together. It will be weird after all this time. Our last Christmas together was when I was only twelve and she ten.' Adam's mind went back to that day. It had started out well, the kitchen filled with the aroma of a turkey cooking in the oven, the Christmas tree a branch he and Alison had pulled in from the nearby bush the week before and decorated with home-made garlands of coloured paper. Lunch had been good, but things had gone downhill afterwards, and he and his sister had hidden behind the shed in the yard as they listened to their parents' angry voices and the sound of things being hurled around. His mum and Alison had left a week later.

It had ruined Christmas for him.

'You?' he asked.

'Just the three of us.' She sighed. 'It'll be a very different type of celebration from what we're used to, but…' she took a deep breath and gave a smile, '…I intend it to be one Clancy will never forget.'

'Good for you.'

The sandwiches were as delicious as they expected, and after another long black for Adam and a cappuccino for Libby, they were ready to move on. Heading into the garden centre proper, the carols became louder, and they had to almost shout to make themselves heard. But the atmosphere here was such that everyone was in a merry mood.

Adam and Libby wandered around hand-in-hand till they found the display they were looking for. After much discussion, Libby chose a traditional wreath made from pine branches interspersed with Christmas baubles, while Adam went for a modern version fashioned from wicker, laced with gum leaves and seed pods.

Libby laughed when Adam pointed to the poster advertising wreath-making classes and suggested they could have made their own. 'I don't have a creative bone in my body,' she said.

They were both feeling very cheerful as Adam drove back to Libby's house where he unloaded her purchases and took them inside. Once there, he pulled her into his arms. 'I've been wanting to do this all morning,' he said, 'When does your daughter get home?'

Libby glanced at the clock.

Adam could feel her trembling.

'We have an hour and a half,' she said, a smile playing on her lips. 'The bedroom's this way.' Libby took his hand and led him through the hallway.

Thirty-three

'Good weekend?' Libby and Grace were manning the desk together at the library and enjoying a brief respite from answering queries. 'You were off yesterday, too, weren't you?'

'Yes to both, Grace. Emma was busy, so…'

'While the cat's away?' Grace tapped her nose in a knowledgeable manner. 'You're still seeing my tenant, then?'

Libby felt herself blush. 'He's an interesting companion.'

'I hope he's more than that.' Grace chuckled. 'But don't worry, I don't expect details.'

'Actually, I wanted to ask you about Emma. She met someone when she was with your Mel and Aaron, and she seems a different person. It's so soon after the debacle with Matt – and that's not over yet – I'd hate to see her getting hurt again.'

'I don't know all of Mel and Aaron's friends, but I'll help if I can.'

'It's a friend of Aaron's. His boss. A man called Nick. I don't know his surname.'

'Nick Armstrong,' Grace said. 'I've heard Ted talking about him. He and Aaron were at school together. He was a bit of a troublemaker back then, I understand, some story about taking his dad's boat out without permission and the coast guard having to be called out to save him.'

As Libby's eyes widened with fear, Grace continued, 'Oh, he's changed now, grown up. He now owns a boat building yard up the coast. He's turned into a successful businessman. Never married. Think he's been too busy building up his business. He's been good for Aaron, helped him make a fresh start and build his confidence again. Ted is full of praise for him.'

Libby felt herself relax. He sounded okay.

'Isn't your daughter still married?'

'Yes.' Libby sighed. 'But I'm expecting them to be talking about a divorce after Christmas is over. The only point of contention will be access to Clancy – my granddaughter. I wish I could spare Emma and her the dispute which is bound to erupt as soon as the divorce proceedings start. I doubt Matt will let go easily. And there's the house in Brisbane, too.' She sighed again.

'So, what's happening with your daughter and Nick?'

'Nothing yet. They met a couple of times on the weekend and are having dinner together tomorrow night. But he seems to have made an impression on her. I don't know, Grace…'

'I know exactly how you feel. I've been through it with my two. We want to keep them safe, but we can't protect them for ever. Once they're grown, they have the right to make their own mistakes. All we can do is be there to pick up the pieces.'

'Hmm.' Libby seemed to recall that Grace's daughter, Mel, turned up here on the coast single and pregnant. And she had another daughter, too, and a son. Worrying about one child was quite enough for Libby. It was at times like this she missed Bernie even more, sure he'd have words of wisdom to put her mind at ease.

Talking about Emma reminded Libby she'd forgotten to ask Adam about babysitting with her the following evening. She'd intended to do it when they returned home from their shopping trip and lunch but had been side-tracked – deliciously side-tracked. Then there had been the rush for Adam to leave before Emma and Clancy returned home, though why she still wanted to hide Adam from her daughter, Libby wasn't quite sure.

Adam had left without them making arrangements to meet again, and the evening had been spent with Clancy oohing and aahing about the tree and begging to help decorate it. It had taken till her bedtime to hang the new ornaments on the lower branches, but the tree still looked bare. Libby had underestimated how large it was, when she was choosing the decorations for it.

She slipped off to the staffroom and picked up her phone.

*

'You invited Adam Holland here tonight, didn't you, Mum?' Emma asked. She had taken care of her hair and makeup and was wearing the red dress which had been the cause of the problem with her bank cards. Libby wondered if Emma really had spoken to Matt about them. She hadn't been game to ask.

'You look lovely, honey,' she said. 'That dress really suits you.'

'It does, doesn't it?' Emma twirled around in the middle of the kitchen. 'What do you think, sweetie?' she asked Clancy.

'You look like a princess, Mummy,' Clancy said.

Emma hugged her. 'Be good for Grandma,' she said, then looked at Libby again. 'Mum?'

'Why does my friendship with Adam bother you so much?' Libby asked.

'It doesn't. Well, not as much as it did. I talked with Mel about it.'

Libby bristled at the thought of her personal life being a subject of gossip, but Emma spoke again.

'She understood how I felt. She said her sister was like me when their mother met Ted Crawford. They're all good, now,' she added. 'But Mel told me how much it pleased her to see her mother happy. She said she still loved her dad but loved Ted in a different way.'

While relieved at this change in Emma's mindset, Libby wanted to disabuse her daughter of the idea she and Adam were in love. They had known each other for such a brief time. His life was in Canberra. But hadn't she, in her innermost heart, hoped there might be a future for them together?

'To answer your question, yes, Adam will be dropping round tonight.'

Clancy's ears pricked up. 'Can Adam tell me a story?' she asked. 'He does all the voices.'

Both Libby and Emma laughed. It didn't take much to please Clancy.

*

'This is Nick Armstrong, Mum.' Emma led the tall dark-haired man into the room. 'He wanted to meet you.'

'Good evening, Mrs Walker.' Nick held out a hand. 'I guessed you might want to see who your daughter was having dinner with. I promise I'm not an ogre. Ted Crawford can vouch for me.'

'Nice to meet you, Nick.' Libby felt guilty for her initial fears about him. He seemed to be a perfectly mannered young man, and a little older than she'd imagined. 'Have a good time, both of you.'

Clancy watched wide-eyed, saying nothing. But when the pair had left, she said, 'Mummy says Daddy doesn't love her anymore.'

'Oh, sweetheart,' Libby hugged the little girl. She hadn't realised Emma had already told her about Matt. 'Your daddy still loves *you*. He loves you so much. But sometimes, grownups fall out, and your mummy and daddy have decided they don't want to live together anymore.'

'Where will we live? Will we stay here with you? Will I go to school here?'

Libby bit her lip. She had no answer to this one. 'We'll see. But, before that, we have Christmas to look forward to.'

That seemed to satisfy Clancy, and Libby gave a sigh of relief. But she knew Emma had to resolve matters soon. Clancy was due to start school in January either here or in Brisbane and there was lots to take care of before then – enrolment, uniform and a host of other bits and pieces children needed these days. It was just like when Emma started school.

Clancy had eaten dinner and had her bath, and was settled in front of the television, Milo at her feet, when Adam appeared at the doorway from the deck.

'Reporting for duty,' he said, his eyes twinkling and one corner of his mouth curling up in a way Libby was becoming familiar with. He held out a bottle of wine. 'Thought we could enjoy this later.'

'Thanks.' Libby took the wine and placed it on the bench just in time, before Adam swept her into a warm hug, his lips on her forehead. She gave a wary glance to the doorway. 'Clancy...'

'Okay, I'm not going to ravish you right here... not yet, anyway.' He grinned. 'Where is your granddaughter?'

'She and Milo are watching The Wiggles Christmas show. It should be finished soon, then I'm afraid she's expecting you to read her a story.'

'Happy to oblige. And once she's asleep?'

'Let's wait and see.' But Libby was aware of her heart pounding in anticipation of being alone with Adam again. She thought of what Emma reported Mel saying about Grace. Was she falling in love with Adam? Surely it was too soon?

While Adam was reading to Clancy, Libby fed Milo and ensured his water bowl was full, then she made up a platter of cheese and biscuits to accompany the wine Adam had brought. She was trying to decide whether to take it into the living room or out to the deck, when he reappeared.

'Sorry I took so long,' he said. 'I think she must have chosen the longest book in her collection.' He chuckled.

'No worries. I was just trying to decide whether we'd have the wine inside or out.'

'It looked like rain when I walked down, so the deck probably isn't a good idea tonight. Let's stay inside.'

They took the wine and the cheese platter into the living room where the television was still playing quietly. Libby was about to turn it off, when an image flashed up onto the screen.

'Oh, my. I don't believe it,' Adam said in amazement. '*Miracle on 34th Street*. An oldie but goodie. I watched it when I was a kid.' His eyes took on a glazed look as if remembering happy times.

'Me, too. And it looks as if they've added colour. I remember watching it in black and white.'

'Shall we?'

'Let's'

They cuddled up together on the sofa with glasses of wine, Adam's arm around Libby's shoulders and her hand on his knee, as the introductory music began.

They had been sitting in the same position for so long, Libby was stiff when the movie came to an end. She stretched her arms and legs with a groan. 'I shouldn't have sat still all that time, but it was so good. I'd forgotten most of it.'

'A classic,' Adam said. 'I'm glad we saw it again together. It reminded me...' He stopped.

'Yes?'

'Nothing.' Adam shook his head, clearly unwilling to share those memories, good or bad.

'Coffee?' Libby asked, stretching her neck from side to side. She must be getting old if she could feel like this after only two hours of sitting.

'Sounds good. Can I help?' Adam wiggled his eyebrows, making Libby laugh.

'If you like. There's still some wine left, too.'

'I think I've had enough wine for tonight.' He rose and planted a kiss on Libby's lips, sending quivers down her spine. She wished she could take him to her bed right now, but it was too risky with Clancy asleep nearby and Emma due home.

The coffee had just brewed when she heard the front door opening, and Emma walked in with a smile on her face.

'Did you have a nice time, honey?'

'Lovely. We went to an Italian restaurant on the esplanade. Beautiful food and atmosphere.'

'*The Firenze.*' Libby shared a glance with Adam.

'You've been there?' Emma seemed surprised. 'Nick says it's a favourite of his. He went to school with the guy who runs it. His family have owned it for yonks. He says…' She looked at Libby and Adam who were regarding her with amused expressions. 'Well, he grew up here,' she said by way of explanation.

'Of course he did,' Libby agreed. 'It was nice of him to want to meet me, too. A sign of respect. He seems a decent sort of guy.'

'He is, Mum. He really is.'

'I should be going,' Adam said.

Libby looked at the coffee she was about to serve.

'It's late.'

She knew he was only leaving because Emma had come home and, even if her daughter had changed her attitude to Adam, she still hadn't fully accepted him in her mother's life.

'I'll see you out,' Libby said, making for the front door, away from the door to the deck where Emma was standing.

'The wreath looks good,' Adam said at the door. 'I need to fix mine, too.'

'It does, doesn't it.' Libby touched the wreath gently with one finger. It made the house look ready for Christmas.

'Thanks for a wonderful evening. It's a long time since I spent such a relaxing time with anyone,' Adam said, before sweeping Libby into his arms and giving her a passionate kiss. He hesitated. 'Ali will be here on the weekend. Can you come to dinner on Saturday to meet her?'

'Won't you want some time alone? You must have a lot to talk about, to catch up on.'

'Years. A lifetime.' He gazed into space, lost in thought, then met Libby's eyes again. 'She'll be here till after Christmas. I really want you two to meet.'

'If you're sure.'

'I am.'

He kissed her again, before giving her one last hug and setting off for home.

'He didn't need to leave just because I came home, Mum,' Emma said, when Libby returned to the kitchen to discover her daughter had poured out their coffee and was seated at the kitchen table.

'Our evening was over. We watched a movie and it had finished.'

'I've been thinking,' Emma said. 'It was spending time with Nick. It's made me realise I need to see Matt, to persuade him to allow me access to our account. It's not fair of him to cut me off like he has. And all our old Christmas ornaments are in a box in the garage. The tree would look so much better with them. The new ones you bought are nice, but...'

'I know what you mean.' Libby had tried her best but was disappointed the tree looked nothing like their trees had in the past. It was too perfect. She missed the handmade ornaments Emma had proudly brought home from school every year to take pride of place on their tree, the collection growing and becoming more creative as she grew older, till it had been difficult to tell them from the shop-bought ones.

'I can pick them up, along with more of our summer clothes. We left in such a rush.'

'When were you thinking of going?'

'On the weekend. Saturday, maybe. Nick wants to see me again tomorrow night.' She blushed. 'Can you take care of Clancy again then, and while I'm gone?'

'Saturday?'

'What's the matter?'

'I have plans for Saturday.'

'Oh! But you can change them, can't you?'

Libby thought quickly. She probably could. Although Adam was adamant about wanting her to meet his sister, maybe it wasn't such a good idea after all. 'Of course I can,' she said.

Thirty-four

Adam was on top of the world. Things were going well with Libby. He had found his sister – or she had found him – and his writing was going well. He was well into book two in his new series and the words were flowing. The email from Julian telling him his publisher loved the new book and had offered a contract for the first three books was the icing on the cake.

He couldn't wait to see Libby again and to introduce her to Alison. Bellbird Bay had come to seem like home. He hadn't stopped to wonder what he intended to do after Christmas, after he had fulfilled his promise to Greg. His Canberra unit was still empty, waiting for him. His life was there. But Libby was here. And Alison lived in Perth, on the other side of the country.

Last night had been a game changer for Adam, an insight to what life could be like, what *his* life could be like if he let his guard down. But... doubts began to surface, memories from the past he thought he'd managed to suppress rose up to haunt him. There was a reason he'd avoided commitment, always kept women at arm's length. Alison understood. It was the same for her. Although she – and their mother – had escaped from his father's tyranny, fear of it had followed them around, never permitting them to feel totally secure.

He knew Libby was working today, and, with Alison arriving tomorrow, they hadn't planned to meet again till Saturday. Maybe he'd take both of them to the surf club. He'd come to like the friendly atmosphere of the club and was beginning to be known there. He almost felt like a local.

Thinking of the club made him decide to walk down there when he became sore from sitting in the same position all morning. That was one of the challenges of his chosen career; it was all too easy to spend day after day at his desk.

Once out in the fresh air, the sun beating down on him, the scent of the ocean reminding him he was far from his old haunts, Adam felt energised. He walked smartly down the boardwalk, hesitating only briefly at Libby's gate to see Milo through the full-length glass window. It had taken him a little while, but he was now comfortable with the ungainly animal, and had even developed a soft spot for him.

By the time he reached the surf club, Adam was ready for the beer the barman drew for him after only asking, 'Your usual?'

Adam took his beer out to the deck, his eyes drawn to the wide stretch of white sand marked by the two iconic red and yellow flags, between which a number of enthusiastic swimmers were enjoying the morning sun.

Noticing how the water seemed to change colour from blue to green to a deep turquoise, Adam had a flash of inspiration and took out the notebook he always carried with him. He began to jot down some ideas and was lost in his own little world when he became conscious of someone standing beside him.

'Am I interrupting you?' Will Rankin asked, placing his beer on the table.

'What? No, please join me,' Adam said, although Will had already sat down.

'Here for lunch?'

'No, I…' Adam checked his watch. He hadn't noticed the time. It was almost one. 'Well, I guess so,' he chuckled. 'You?'

'I usually come here at this time, if I can get away. It's my busiest time of the year. But I had a class from the high school this morning so can take a bit of a breather.'

'You must have an interesting life. I'd like to talk with you about it sometime.' Maybe a future Jay Bolton plot could revolve around surfing, and Will would be an ideal source.

'Sure, anytime.'

Will's lunch arrived, the plate filled with a burger and chips looking so enticing, Adam ordered the same.

'You're a bit of a local hero,' Adam said, when his meal had arrived. 'As well as your surf business, I see you're involved in a number of local charities.'

Will looked embarrassed. 'You read that article in *The Bugle*,' he said. 'Don't believe all you read there. But we do have a Christmas fundraiser coming up for Surf Lifesaving. That and Breast Cancer Awareness are dear to my heart. In fact…' he scrutinised Adam, '… you may like to become involved in it.'

'Me? Happy to do anything to help.' Adam took out his wallet, wondering how much he should offer.

Will put his hand on the wallet. I'm not after your money – not yet, anyway. We have an annual event on Christmas Eve to raise money for the local surf lifesavers. It goes to maintenance and replacement of equipment and the purchase of surf boats. It's a lot of fun. You surf?'

'No.'

'But you swim?'

'Yes.' Adam began to wonder what he had agreed to.

'No worries, then. It's a Santa event. The surfers, all dressed in Santa outfits, take their boards out and surf into the beach. The swimmers…'

Adam dreaded what was coming next.

'The swimmers,' Will continued, 'swim out to the headland, then back again. It's a huge crowd pleaser. The town is usually swarming with tourists by then, and many of them take part, too. *The Bugle* gets involved, and the regional television station normally send a reporter and cameraman. You only need to sign up – you can do it online – and organise some sponsors.

He must have seen Adam's doubting expression as he added, 'Some of the swimmers don't worry about the outfit. They just don a Santa hat. They often fall off, of course. It's part of the fun, watching them try to retrieve them. You're in?'

'I guess.' Adam regretted his hasty agreement. It was way out of his comfort zone. But Will and Martin had been good to him, welcoming him into their lives. It was a small way to repay them and was for a good cause.

Will continued to describe previous years' events and the good work done by the surf lifesavers, but Adam had ceased to listen. He was trying to work out if he could manage to swim to the headland

and back. He was a strong swimmer but, in recent years, until coming to Bellbird Bay, his exercise had consisted of running along the side of Lake Burley Griffin before stopping for a coffee.

He was still pondering his ability to make the swim as he made his way back up the boardwalk, so when his phone rang, he failed to check the screen before answering.

'Hello, Adam Holland.'

'Adam. It's Libby.'

Adam stopped walking. Coincidentally he had just reached the viewing platform outside Libby's house, the one where the memorial bench to her late husband was a constant reminder of the time they met. She wouldn't be there now. She'd be in the library. Feeling slightly guilty, Adam sat on the bench, seeing the bronze plaque with her husband's name and dates of birth and death. Such a stark reminder of how a life could be cut short.

'How lovely to hear from you,' he said. 'You won't believe where I am right now.'

But Libby didn't seem interested in where he might be.

'About Saturday,' she said.

He could hear the tremor in her voice. 'Is there a problem?'

'It's Emma. She's decided to go to Brisbane – to pick up some things and speak to Matt. She's asked me to look after Clancy. I'm sorry, Adam, but...' Her voice trailed off and Adam knew she had to put her family first.

His heart plummeted. He'd been looking forward so much to seeing the two women in his life together, hopefully to them becoming friends. Even though they lived so far apart, with social media and Facetime, what was a few thousand kilometres?

'I'm sorry,' Libby said again.

Adam thought quickly. 'What about Friday, then? Ali's plane gets in at lunchtime. You could come to dinner then.' He waited with bated breath. There was silence.

Then Libby said, 'Are you sure? Won't you want more time together first?'

'We'll have that.' Adam knew his sister would be pretty tired after her early start and the five-hour flight, and had planned on her taking a rest in the afternoon. But they'd have a few hours prior to dinner

– and they'd have two whole weeks to catch up, weeks in which he planned to spend time with Libby, too.

'Okay, if you're sure.'

Adam could hear the relief in her voice.

'I am. See you at six on Friday. I'm really looking forward to it.'

When he finished the call, Adam realised he'd have to rejig his dinner plans. Ali might not feel like going out on her first night here. He scratched his head. He had no idea what Ali would feel like. The grown-up Ali was like a stranger to him, but an oddly familiar one. He was looking forward to getting reacquainted with her and to finding out more about what had happened to her in the last forty-odd years.

*

When Friday arrived, Adam was feeling nervous. This was a big deal. His sister was arriving to spend Christmas with him. His sister! And Libby was coming to dinner.

He started his day as usual with breakfast at *The Bay Café* and the realisation he'd need to change his ways while Alison was staying with him. It was unlikely she'd want to traipse down to the esplanade every day for breakfast. Then he headed home to change for a swim. If he was going to take part in this fundraiser of Will Rankin's and didn't embarrass himself, he needed to get in some training.

It was glorious out on the water, and Adam made more progress than he anticipated. Maybe he wouldn't do too badly on the swim. He turned on his back and floated for a time, then swam back to the shore, satisfied with his effort.

There would be no writing this morning, Adam decided. He had to tidy the house, ensure the bed in the spare room was made up, and organise dinner. He flicked through the Jamie Oliver cookbook but didn't give himself much hope of repeating the success he'd had cooking for Libby last time, especially in his current frame of mind. A barbecue was a much better option. Even *he* couldn't go wrong with steak and salad.

A quick trip to the shops provided what he needed, and Adam grinned to himself as he added a couple of bottles of Moet & Chandon to his basket in the liquor store. Tonight, was going to be a celebration, not a time to watch his budget.

All too soon it was time to meet Alison's plane. Checking himself in the mirror, Adam reminded himself this was his sister he was meeting. He wasn't about to go on a hot date. He remembered how he used to tease Ali about her fear of spiders and how she always wanted to keep up with him whether he was climbing the tree in their backyard or chasing after his mates.

She was too old to tease now and had done well for herself. She lectured in university, something he could never aspire to. But perhaps he had done just as well in his own way, he thought, remembering the new contract Julian had told him about.

The airport was busy – lots of interstate travellers coming to the coast for Christmas – and it took Adam so long to find a place to park, he had to hurry into the terminal to avoid being late.

He arrived just in time. He saw Alison as soon as he ran through the door. She was standing near the baggage collection, staring around. She smiled when she saw him.

'Hey, good to see you again. You made it.' Adam hugged her.

'Good to see you again, too. I can scarcely believe it.' She grinned, a grin so like the one he remembered from the ten-year-old Ali, his heart bloomed for her.

'Let's get your luggage and go home. You must be exhausted. Did you manage to sleep on the plane?'

'Not a lot. I dozed off from time to time, but not a real rest.'

'Well, you can have a bite to eat, then sleep all afternoon if you like.'

'When am I going to meet your lady friend?' Her lips turned up on one corner the way he knew his did. His heart bloomed again. He had a family again. After all these years, he was part of a family.

'Libby's coming to dinner tonight. I hope it's not too soon for you.'

'Of course not. I want to meet the woman who appears to have captivated my big brother.' She grinned and nudged him with her elbow in the way he remembered her doing when they were kids.

Back home, Adam put a quiche into the oven and mixed up a salad while Alison prowled around the house.

When he went to tell her lunch was ready, he found her at his desk, reading some pages he'd printed off the night before. *Damn, he'd forgotten they were there.*

'This is good, Adam.' She looked up, her eyes twinkling as they met his. 'It's different. I have all your Phil Hanlon books – apart from the one coming out next month, of course. But this has a different feel. I like it.'

'I can let you have one of my author copies of the latest,' he said. He was thrilled at her praise. It meant more to him than all the plaudits from reviewers

'Sorry, I can't keep my eyes open any longer.' Alison pushed her chair back from the table. 'Lunch was delicious, but now I need to get some shut-eye if I'm to be awake enough to make conversation tonight.' She gave Adam a peck on the cheek and disappeared through the hallway.

Adam cleared up the dishes, then went to his desk, intending to re-read what he'd written the day before. But before he did, an idea occurred to him. This Christmas fundraising. The image of multiple Santa-suited surfers rose in his mind's eye. It would be quite a scene, one worthy of gracing the pages of a Jay Bolton novel. What if one of the participants was killed, his body, still clothed in his Santa costume, found floating in the ocean?

Adam fired up his computer and began to write.

Thirty-five

The library was unusually deserted, giving Libby too much time to think. Adam's sister would have arrived by now. She wondered what she was like, if she resembled Adam, if she was married, had children. Adam hadn't mentioned any other family, so perhaps she was alone. She could be divorced or widowed like Libby. All she knew was that Alison was two years younger than Adam, lived in Perth and taught in a university.

That, alone, put her out of Libby's orbit. Marrying young, she'd never made much use of her own degree and had long ago forgotten what university life was like. She pictured Alison as one of those serious, mannish women you saw on television spouting forth about some issue or other, someone with very definite views. What on earth would they talk about? How could she hope to compete in conversation with someone like her?

Libby was glad when the day was over, but when she arrived home, it was to discover the tension which had dogged Emma, and disappeared when she met Nick, had surfaced again – with a vengeance.

'What am I going to say to Matt, Mum?' she demanded, almost as soon as Libby walked in. 'What if…'

'There's no sense in worrying till you get there. He does know you're coming?'

'Yes. I texted him. I'm to meet him at the house.' Emma glanced over to where Clancy was busy colouring in a book of Christmas scenes.

'Clancy will be fine with me. We'll find lots to do. You just need to concentrate on picking up the things you need and coming to an agreement with Matt. You plan to stay overnight?'

'I suppose so. I thought I could check in with Claire, too,' she said, referring to a friend and neighbour who had a daughter the same age as Clancy.

'That's a good idea. You must have missed talking with your friends.'

'Mmm. We talk on Facetime and text, but it's not the same. It's been good to meet Mel.'

'And Nick?'

Emma blushed. 'He's helped me see how I need to come to some agreement with Matt, like Sharon said. But I'm not looking forward to it. As long as he doesn't bring April along.' She scowled.

Libby sympathised with her daughter, wished there was more she could do, but there were some things Emma had to work out for herself. And she had her own worries to contend with.

Later, dressed in a pair of white pants teamed with a pink and white tunic top, Libby examined herself in the mirror. How did she look? Was this an appropriate outfit to wear to meet Adam's sister? She didn't remember feeling this nervous when Bernie took her home to meet his parents. But, back then, she'd been twenty and invincible. She sighed and walked out of the bedroom.

'You look lovely, Grandma.' Clancy ran over to give her a hug.

'Bless you, sweetheart,' Libby replied.

'She's right, Mum. You've made more of an effort than usual.'

Why did Emma's compliment make her feel as if she normally didn't take any care of her appearance? 'Thanks, Em. I won't be late,' she said as usual, giving Clancy a kiss.

Libby enjoyed her walk up the boardwalk to Adam's. There was only a week to go till Christmas and many of the houses were decked out in Christmas lights, giving the entire boardwalk a festive appearance. She must remember to tell Emma to look out the Christmas lights she'd given her, the garlands she and Bernie used to string around the garden. They could use them on the deck. Clancy would love it.

She reached Adam's gate almost before she was ready and, pushing it open, could see two matching grey heads through the window.

'Here you are.' Adam greeted her with a hug and a kiss on the cheek.

'You're looking lovely,' he said, steering her inside to where a woman, a feminine version of Adam, was seated with a glass of sparkling wine.

She rose at Libby's arrival, her hands outstretched. 'You must be Libby. I'm so glad to meet you. Adam has told me all about you.' She kissed Libby on both cheeks, French style.

'Good to meet you, too,' Libby said, surprised by the effusive welcome and by the naturalness of the woman who looked nothing like Libby's preconceived idea. She was almost as tall as Adam, with the same angular features, her short, greying hair brushed back from her face, and was dressed simply in a pair of jeans and a loose white shirt.

Adam watched their greeting, seemingly delighted to see them together. 'We're celebrating our reunion,' he said. 'A glass of champagne?' He picked up the bottle of Moet & Chandon with one hand, a glass with the other.

'Yes, please.' Libby needed something to help her recover from her surprise. She took a gulp of the sparkling wine, enjoying the fizz of the bubbles.

Libby and Alison sat together on the deck chatting, while Adam expertly cooked the steak, interrupting the women's conversation from time to time to add some anecdote or make a joke. It was a friendly group. Libby felt at ease in Alison's company, as if she'd known her for years. They found they had a lot in common – besides Adam – enjoying the same books and music.

Adam carried the cooked steaks inside to where the salad was already on the table. He refilled their glasses and was proposing a toast. He'd got as far as, 'To the two most important women...' when there was a loud knocking on the front door.

'What the...' he said, laying down his glass. 'Don't wait for me,' he said as he went to answer the door.

Libby and Alison exchanged amused glances and started to eat.

There was the sound of agitated voices from the hall, Adam's deep one and another, lighter, female voice, then Adam returned to the dining room followed by an elegant blonde.

'This is Yvette,' he said, running a hand through his hair, and looking embarrassed. 'She's driven up from Canberra.'

'Well, isn't this nice.' Yvette glanced around the room, before taking a seat. 'Won't you introduce your two friends, Adam?'

'Eh, this is my sister, Alison... and Libby.'

There was an amused expression in Alison's eyes, but Libby face had turned red, and her chin was trembling.

Yvette! Was she the woman Adam said he was involved with in Canberra? But he'd said it as if it was in the past. It must be her. She'd driven up from Canberra. You didn't do that unless... What was she doing here? Libby's eyes flitted around the room seeking an escape.

The evening had been going so well. Alison had been much easier to talk to than she'd expected, someone who could become a friend. And Adam had been on top form. Libby looked down at the barely touched plate of steak and salad. There was a lump in her throat. She felt sick. Adam was speaking, but she was too distressed to make sense of what he was saying. 'I need to...' She rose and, with an apologetic smile to Adam and Alison, slipped out of the room and almost raced through the kitchen and out the door onto the boardwalk before anyone had time to realise what was happening.

'Why are you back so soon?' Emma asked, from where she was seated on the sofa with her iPad. 'Is something wrong?'

'Yes. No. I'm going to bed. I'll see you in the morning.'

Libby closed the bedroom door behind her and stood shaking. What a fool she'd been, imagining she meant anything to Adam, imagining there might be some sort of future for them together. Instead, she'd been what she'd heard called a parenthesis in a movie she'd seen recently – a diversion, someone to take to bed while he was here in Bellbird Bay away from his real life in Canberra. And now his Canberra life had come to join him. The three of them must be laughing at her right now. She had never felt so humiliated.

How was she going to face Adam again? Libby made up her mind. She'd get away, go to Brisbane with Emma. Clancy could come, too. It would at least give her a few days' respite, time to consider how she was going to cope with the embarrassment.

*

There was an awkward silence as Libby disappeared out the door.

'Libby?' Yvette asked as Adam stammered an explanation and gazed at Libby's empty chair in despair.

'What are you doing here, Yvette?' Adam asked. 'I told you... I thought you understood me when I said it was over.' He dragged a hand through his hair again.

'I thought... if I came to Bellbird Bay... if we could talk face-to-face...' Suddenly, Yvette's confident manner crumbled. 'Who was that woman?' Her eyes went to the door through which Libby had exited. 'Is she...? Are you...? Oh, I should never have come, but I thought... I hoped...' she took out a tissue and patted her eyes.

Adam rubbed the back of his neck. He didn't know what to do. He had never been able to cope with a woman's tears. He looked at Alison, searching for an answer... anything to calm the situation.

'Yvette,' Alison said, immediately taking charge. 'You've had a long drive. You're distraught. You must be hungry.' She fetched an empty plate, loaded it with an extra piece of steak and handed it to Yvette. 'Adam, do you have any brandy?'

Adam shook his head. 'Whisky do?'

'Fine.'

Adam poured a glass for Yvette, surprised how quickly she calmed down once she'd taken a few sips.

'I'm sorry,' Yvette said. 'I've interrupted your evening.' She peered at Alison, then back at Adam. 'I didn't know you had a sister.'

'It's a long story.'

'And not one for tonight,' Alison said. 'You'd better stay here for the night. You can have my room.' She met Adam's eyes. 'I can sleep on the sofa.'

'The one in the room I'm using as my study folds down into a bed,' Adam said. 'I can sleep there.' He felt as if everything was careering out of his control. The evening he'd looked forward to so much was turning into a nightmare.

By the time Adam was tucked up in his study, the two women having already retired, he was trying to process what had happened, why Yvette's arrival had sent Libby scurrying away, and how Alison had managed to resolve at least one part of the problem. He picked up his phone and pressed Libby's number... but there was no reply.

Next morning, things didn't look any better. After a breakfast where no one said very much, Yvette headed off, presumably back to Canberra, after apologising to Adam and hoping they could stay friends. He felt bad about what had happened between them. They had had some good times together, but now his thoughts were filled with Libby Walker.

'I didn't imagine my big brother was such a lady killer,' Alison said with a grin, over their second cup of coffee which they'd taken out to the deck.

'Don't!' Adam remonstrated. 'I never intended this to happen. As far as I was concerned, it was finished with Yvette.'

'And Libby? I liked her.' Alison gazed at him over the top of her cup.

'I need to see her, sort things out.'

'Good idea. I'd say you have some explaining to do.'

'I'll go now.' Adam laid down his coffee and, opening the gate, walked down the boardwalk. But there was no reply at Libby's. As he stared at the empty house, a short bark attracted his attention and, turning, he saw Milo standing at the fence separating Libby's yard from Eddie's, a sure sign Libby had left town.

Thirty-seven

After a restless night, when Libby looked at herself in the mirror next morning, the result of her lack of sleep was evident, her eyes puffy with dark circles. She looked a mess and only managed to disguise her appearance with a careful application of makeup. She pulled on a pair of jeans and a shirt and went into the kitchen where Emma and Clancy were already eating breakfast.

'Mum, you look…'

'Don't say it. I know what I look like. I didn't get much sleep. How would you like me to come to Brisbane with you today? Clancy and I can do some fun things while you take care of what you need to do.'

'Ooh, Grandma, can we go to the pool at South Bank and see the Christmas lights?'

'I don't see why not. Em?'

'If you want.' Emma peered at her mother. 'Did something happen last night?'

'I don't want to talk about it. When did you intend to leave?'

'As soon as we finish breakfast. What about Milo?'

In her distress, Libby had forgotten to consider her furry companion. Hearing his name, Milo's ears pricked up.

'I'll check with Eddie. I'll do it now.'

Libby went outside, then through her neighbour's gate.

Eddie was seated on the bench under the window with a cup of tea. 'You're an early bird, Libby,' she said. 'What's up?'

'I'm off to Brisbane with Emma today. Can you look after Milo till we get back? We'll be gone overnight.' She wished she could stay away till after Christmas, till Adam had gone back to Canberra, back to his real life.

'No problem. But what's the matter with you? You look like death warmed up.'

So much for her careful application of makeup. But Eddie was always very perceptive. Libby collapsed onto the bench next to Eddie. 'Oh, Eddie, I've been a fool. I thought Adam Holland was interested in me. How could I have been so stupid, to imagine a famous author would be interested in someone like me?'

'I don't think you're a fool. It looked to me as if he was.' She put a hand on Libby's arm. 'What happened?'

Libby's eyes moistened as she recounted the scene in Adam's house the previous evening, finishing with, 'So you see, Eddie, it was all a game to him, and I...'

'I only met him a couple of times, Libby, but he didn't strike me as someone who'd toy with anyone's emotions. Maybe you got it wrong.'

Libby shook her head and patted her eyes with a tissue. 'No. You didn't see the woman from Canberra. She was so glamourous. She made me feel like a frumpy middle-aged hag.'

'You're hardly that.' Eddie chuckled. 'Adam Holland would be lucky to get you.'

'Thanks, Eddie. You're a good friend, but I think you're wrong about that.' Libby rose. 'I'll bring Milo round.'

By the time Libby had settled Milo with Eddie, Emma and Clancy were already in the car waiting for her. She quickly locked up and they set off.

Libby was glad that she didn't need to make conversation during the drive. Clancy kept them occupied singing along with her from a Wiggles CD and playing I spy. But it was a relief when they arrived in the city and reached the familiar neighbourhood.

'It all looks just the same,' Emma said, as if she had expected it to change in the short time she'd been away.

When they reached the house, there were two cars parked in the driveway.

'Is that Matt's?' Libby asked.

Emma bit her lip. 'We didn't arrange to meet till twelve. I thought I could look out the Christmas things first.'

'What do you want to do?' Libby asked, as a woman in her mid-twenties dressed in designer activewear stepped out, turning to call to someone inside the house, before getting into the red Kia parked beside the black BMW, and reversing down the driveway.

Emma immediately accelerated and drove off. 'The bastard!' she yelled, oblivious to Clancy's presence.

'Was that...?' Libby asked.

'April bloody Clarke. The bitch is living there. Matt has moved her into our house.' Her jaw tensed as she drove away from the house which had been her home.

'Sorry, Mum,' Emma said, glancing over her shoulder to where Clancy seemed oblivious to what was happening, busy with the copy of *Hop on Pop* she'd insisted on bringing with her and from which she was now reading aloud.

Libby wanted to say something to comfort her daughter but was at a loss as to what she could say to make things better. Her own troubles faded to insignificance in the light of Emma's agony.

'I'll drop you and Clancy at South Bank and go back to confront him. I can't believe he's moved her in... to our house.' Her lips tightened. 'Nick said...'

Libby waited.

'He said Matt might try something like this, but I didn't believe him. How wrong can I be?'

'Are you sure you want to go back there... on your own?'

'It's still my house, Mum. It's in both our names. I have every right to be there. But I guess we can't stay there tonight.'

'No.' They had planned to spend the night in the house before Emma caught up with her friend next day. 'We can book into a hotel,' she said. 'I'll arrange it while you're with Matt.'

'Thanks, Mum. I still can't believe it.'

As soon as Emma dropped Libby and Clancy off, the little girl took her grandma's hand and pulled her towards where crowds of families were already enjoying the manmade pool. It was a feature of Brisbane which Libby had always loved. Clancy soon shed her shorts and tee-shirt and was paddling in the shallow water while Libby found a shady spot to sit and watch.

She took out her phone, her forehead creasing and her heart racing at the sight of several missed calls from Adam. She had nothing to say to him.

Living in Brisbane, she and Bernie had never had any need to stay in a hotel, but she remembered Adam mentioning the one his sister had stayed in, right here on South Bank. Keeping one eye on Clancy, she googled The Emporium. It was a bit pricy, but she reckoned she and Emma deserved a bit of spoiling this weekend. She booked them in for the night.

Clancy soon became bored with the pool and led Libby to a playground where she played happily on various pieces of equipment before deciding she was hungry.

As they ate lunch, chicken nuggets for Clancy and a ham and tomato sandwich for Libby, Libby wondered how Emma was getting along with Matt. She checked her phone, but there were no new messages. Then, just as she and Clancy were about to go for a walk, the phone pinged with a text.

On my way. Pick you up in 30 mins. Em.

Libby replied with a smiley emoji. 'That was Mummy,' she said to Clancy. 'She'll be here soon.'

The rest of the day passed swiftly.

After booking into their hotel, they wandered around South Bank again till it became dark, then, at Clancy's pleading, they drove through the city and surrounding suburbs to see the Christmas lights, before Clancy's eyes began to close.

Libby waited till Clancy was asleep before asking her daughter about Matt.

'He's completely under her thumb,' she fumed. 'I knew she must be behind him cutting me off from our account.' Her lips tightened and she took a gulp from the glass of wine she was drinking. 'But I told him it was hurting Clancy and he seemed to see sense. At least April stayed away while I was there. I couldn't have borne it to have seen her lording it over *my* house. He plans to put it on the market when everything opens up again after January and I agreed. I don't want to live there again, Mum, not after…' She shuddered.

'And the money?'

'Matt said he's closed the account. He wrote me a cheque. I'll set up an account of my own on Monday.'

Libby was tempted to make a comment but didn't, reasoning it was none of her business. But she was glad when Emma added, 'We talked about Clancy too and agreed to meet again after Christmas and put what Sharon called a parenting plan in place. Matt seems to have changed his tune a bit. I got the feeling April isn't too keen on his spending time with me or Clancy. I'll talk with Sharon again, too, Mum. I need to make sure Clancy and I are okay. I'm going to file for divorce as soon as I can. I know I'll have to wait awhile. Sharon said we needed to be apart for twelve months.'

'I think that's a good idea, Em,' Libby said, pleased Emma was thinking ahead, even though she hated to think of her daughter having to go through that process. 'You know you can stay with me for as long as you like.'

'Thanks, Mum, but I think Clancy and I need our own place.' She took a deep breath. 'I think I will take up Kate's offer. Now I'm beginning to make friends in Bellbird Bay, where there are no memories of Matt, where I know I'm not going to bump into him and his new...' She sniffed.

'I'm glad, honey. It'll be good to have you close by, and Bellbird Bay is a good place for Clancy to grow up.' As she spoke, Libby wondered how much meeting Nick Armstrong had influenced Emma's decision, but she'd never ask.

'I don't think I want to catch up with Claire tomorrow, after all,' Emma said, when she had finished her wine and they were getting ready for bed. 'She'd want to know all about Matt and me and... I don't think I can talk about it, not yet. Can we drive back to Bellbird Bay after breakfast?'

'Fine by me,' Libby said. Emma had managed to collect all the things she needed, and the car boot was filled with the box of Christmas ornaments and the rest of her and Clancy's clothes. There was nothing to keep them in Brisbane.

But when she closed her eyes, even though she understood Emma's desire to leave the city, she wished they could stay in Brisbane for a little longer. She loved Bellbird Bay, but right now, there were too many memories, memories of Adam Holland. She should have known he was still involved with someone in Canberra. A man like Adam Holland wasn't for her. She should have known better. But it had been good, for a little while, to be able to pretend, to pretend she could attract the famous author, that they might have a future together. He'd be gone soon. The past few weeks had been an excursion into a world she had no right to enter, something she'd tuck away to take out from time to time just to remind herself of what might have been.

Thirty-eight

'Adam, sit down. You're like a bear with a sore head, the way you're pacing up and down. You'll wear a hole in the carpet.'

'You sound just like our mum.' Adam chuckled at his sister's words. 'I think I can remember her saying that before...'

'It was one of her favourite sayings,' Alison agreed. 'Fancy you remembering.'

'I remember a lot about her.' Adam stopped pacing and did sit down on the sofa next to Alison. 'Dad wasn't much of a conversationalist. I had a lot of time to think – about her, and you. I missed you both.'

'Poor you.' Alison put a hand on his arm. 'I missed you, too. There was no one to tease me. It was lonely in Perth to start with. Then I made new friends, and it started to feel like home. But I never stopped wondering about you. Then, one day, I saw a book in a bookshop window. It had your name on it. And when I went in and picked it up, there was a photo. I recognised you straight away. It was like looking at a masculine version of myself. It was as if I'd found you again, even though I didn't dare try to contact you till Mum died. She was too afraid of Dad. I couldn't risk him finding us.'

'Mmm.'

'It's Libby, isn't it?'

'What?'

'The reason you've been unable to sit still, to settle to anything. Where do you think she's gone?'

'Eddie said she's gone to Brisbane. God knows when she'll be back. But I don't expect she'll leave Milo for long.'

'Milo?'

'Her dog. A big shaggy brute who thinks everyone's his friend.'

'Right. Eddie didn't know when she'd be back?'

'I didn't ask. I was too surprised to find her gone.' He took a deep breath. No need for Alison to know about the times he'd tried to call her. 'But you're here and it's a lovely day. I promised to show you Bellbird Bay, so let's do it.'

*

The day passed quickly. Adam took Alison to all his favourite haunts including Dolphin Beach where he told her of his plan to scatter Greg's ashes there.

'He must have been a special friend,' she said, seeing a tear in the corner of Adam's eyes and hearing how his voice broke when he spoke about him.

'He was a good mate,' Adam agreed. 'We went through a lot together, had each other's backs in a few hairy situations. He was too young to die.' He brushed a hand across his eyes. 'It's the least I can do for him.'

'Maybe I'll look for a job in Canberra,' Alison said, when they were walking down the boardwalk for dinner at the surf club.

'Canberra?'

'Where you live, dummy. You'll be going back there when you've fulfilled your promise to your old mate, won't you?'

'I suppose.' Adam realised that, since he'd met Libby, since they'd become close, returning to Canberra had become less attractive and the thought of staying here in Bellbird Bay had begun to take root.

'Or were you considering a move – to Bellbird Bay?' Alison glanced at him in amusement.

She'd read his mind. Adam remembered how she used to be able to do that when they were kids. It had annoyed him then. It still did. He didn't reply.

When they entered the surf club, the first person Adam saw was Will Rankin, followed by Cleo, Martin and Ailsa. The four were standing at the bar chatting with the dark-haired barman who Adam now knew was Ailsa's son, Nate.

All looked surprised to see Adam with Alison.

'Friends of yours?' she asked.

'I should introduce you.' Adam led Alison across and introduced her to the two couples and Nate.

'Your sister,' Will said. 'That explains it. The likeness,' he added after a brief pause.

'You must join us for dinner,' Ailsa said with a smile. 'We've reserved a table on the deck and I'm sure we can fit in two more.'

Adam was about to refuse, when he saw Alison's pleased expression. She had always been more of a social butterfly than he had, even at the age of ten. It was a surprise to him she'd never married. But he wasn't one to talk. Their parents' marriage had had a similar effect on her and, like him, she'd avoided commitment.

The conversation during dinner flowed smoothly with Alison learning more about Bellbird Bay, including the ensuing fundraiser in which Adam now regretted having agreed to take part.

'It sounds like fun,' she said. 'I definitely want to see you all dressed up,' she said to Adam with a wink.

'Only the hat,' he retorted. 'I could never swim all that way fully clothed.' But he could see a wicked gleam in her eyes and wondered what she was planning.

Their meal was almost over, Martin pouring the final drops of wine into Ailsa's glass when they were joined by another couple.

'Hi, Grace,' Cleo said. 'I didn't see you earlier.'

'We just arrived. Looks like you're having quite a party.' Grace looked enquiringly at Adam and Alison.

Adam remembered she was a friend of Libby's, probably wondering what he was doing there with another woman. *Sometimes this town was too small for comfort.*

'Meet Adam's sister,' Ailsa said before Adam could speak. 'She's here for Christmas.'

'How lovely.'

When the introductions were over, Grace spoke again. 'It's Christmas I wanted to talk about. I guess you folks are having a big family reunion.' She nodded to Ailsa and Cleo. 'What are *your* plans, Adam?'

Adam rubbed his chin, knowing that with Alison here, his plan to spend Christmas Day like any other had gone out the window. He was still trying to formulate a reply, when Grace spoke again.

'I'm planning a family Christmas. Our yard is plenty big. Why don't you and your sister join us?'

Alison beamed. 'That sounds lovely, doesn't it, Adam?'

'I guess so.' Then, realising how ungracious he sounded, he added, 'Thanks so much, Grace. It's very kind of you to include us in your family celebrations.'

'Good. That's settled. Christmas lunch at twelve, but come along anytime. Libby not here tonight?' She glanced around.

'She's in Brisbane,' Adam said. Grace would learn soon enough why she'd left town.

'Well, enjoy the rest of your evening.' She and Ted smiled at the group before heading to another table close to the edge of the deck.

'Isn't that kind?' Alison asked Adam. 'You seem to have made a lot of friends here.'

'Grace is my landlady,' he said. 'She works in the library.'

Alison said nothing, but Adam could see her making the connection. Libby worked in the library, too.

'We all belong to the same book club,' Ailsa explained, 'and Grace and Ted live along the boardwalk from Adam and Libby, and Martin's sister. It's a small world.'

Adam rubbed a finger along the inside of his collar. It *was* a small world. Bellbird Bay was a small town. And it was becoming too small for comfort – unless he could persuade Libby that Yvette meant nothing to him.

Thirty-nine

Libby was glad to get to work on Tuesday morning. The library was one place where Adam was unlikely to appear, especially after she'd finally told him about the display of his books. For such a successful author, he seemed strangely reluctant to accept recognition.

'Good weekend?' asked Grace, when they met for morning tea. It was what they normally asked each other at the beginning of each week. 'I hear you went to Brisbane.'

'Who told you that?' Libby knew how quickly news got around in Bellbird Bay, but this was ridiculous. Eddie was the only person she'd told where she was going.

'Ted and I bumped into Adam at the surf club on Saturday. We met his sister. She seems lovely, and they're so alike, aren't they?'

Libby muttered something non-committal. The last thing she wanted to talk about was Adam and his sister. Alison was lovely. It would have been good to get to know her better. But that wasn't possible now.

'Before I forget,' Grace said. 'What are you doing on Christmas Day?'

Libby relaxed. This was something she *could* talk about. 'I want to make it special for Clancy,' she said. 'It'll be her first Christmas without her dad and will seem a bit strange to her. We have a tree, and Em brought all the old Christmas decorations and ornaments back from Brisbane. I plan to string the lights around the deck and maybe have lunch on the beach.' She hadn't broached the idea with Emma yet, but it might help Clancy come to terms with there only being the three of them.

'You must come to us,' Grace said. 'We have a big yard and it'll be a family affair. Emma and Mel are already friends... and Nick Armstrong will be there, too. Mel says he's very taken with your daughter.' She gave a conspiratorial grin.

'Oh, Grace, that's kind of you.' It wasn't what she'd planned. But Libby knew Emma would jump at the chance to spend Christmas with her new friends, and Nick would be an added incentive. It was good to hear he was interested in her, too.

'Good. Lunch will be at twelve and we'll probably end up on the beach afterwards, at least the younger ones will.'

'Thanks.' Libby picked up her cup to take it to the dishwasher when Grace spoke again.

'I've invited Adam and his sister, too.' She gave another grin and winked before leaving the staffroom.

Libby almost dropped her cup. Adam was going to be at the Christmas lunch she'd agreed to attend. It was too late to change her mind, would entail all sorts of explanations, and Emma would never forgive her. Libby could only hope the group would be large enough to enable her to avoid him.

*

Later that afternoon, Libby was on the deck struggling with a long strand of Christmas lights, hoping the ladder wouldn't collapse, when she heard Adam's voice.

'I seem to be making a habit of rescuing you.'

She turned quickly and felt the ladder wobble, then stabilise. When she looked down, she could see Adam was steadying it. Biting her lip, Libby went back to her task and, having the fixed the lights to her satisfaction, slowly descended the ladder, almost ending up in Adam's arms. She took two steps away and folded her arms, glaring at Milo who was greeting Adam enthusiastically.

'What are you doing here?' Libby tried to stifle the trembling in her legs. Adam still looked good, still had the power to turn her legs to

Maggie Christensen

jelly. But he wasn't for her. She steeled herself to resist the temptation to fall into his arms.

'We need to talk, Libby.'

'I have nothing to say to you. I guess you didn't expect your *friend* to arrive when she did, but, it's okay, I understand.' She blinked back the tears.

'Libby, I need to explain. Can we go inside?'

Libby was about to shake her head, when she saw two figures coming towards them up the boardwalk. She didn't want anyone to see them here arguing. Without another word, she led Adam inside. Milo followed them in and flopped down, his head on his paws.

Once in the kitchen, Libby folded her arms again, as if to ward Adam off and to keep her emotions in check. 'Well?' she said.

'Can we at least sit down?'

Libby shook her head, too upset to speak. How dare he force his way into her house like this? She conveniently forgot she had led him inside.

'Yvette…' Adam dragged a hand through his hair.

Libby's stomach churned at the sound of the woman's name.

'She… we… It's as I told you, Libby. It's over. I have no idea why she turned up here in Bellbird Bay. She's gone now… back to Canberra. She won't be back.'

Could she believe him?

Libby felt the tightly coiled anguish in her heart begin to ease. She gazed at Adam, at the honesty in his eyes, the mouth which had given her so much pleasure.

'Please believe me, Libby. I'd never hurt you. I meant what I said when I told you what we had was no casual fling. I've never felt this way for a woman before. I'm falling in love with you.'

Libby saw a shocked expression appear on Adam's face as he said the words. Then he grinned, one side of his mouth curling up in the way she found so endearing. 'I love you, Libby.'

Libby felt her lips turn up into a smile, then widen into a grin which matched his. *Adam Holland loved her!*

Milo gave an encouraging bark.

Libby laughed.

'Dare I hope you care for me a little?' Adam asked. 'I know it may be too soon for you, but I hope that…'

Libby didn't allow him to finish. Giving in to the impulse she'd stifled earlier, she took two steps forward into Adam's waiting arms.

Forty

The beach was swarming with people – locals and tourists, all of whom had come along to see the fun and enjoy the sight of the surfers and swimmers who had chosen to step out of their comfort zone for such a good cause. From what Libby could determine, it was an annual event which drew many to Bellbird Bay for the express purpose of participating either as a surfer or swimmer – and it attracted a throng of onlookers.

Those surf lifesavers who weren't participating, plus many of the high school students who took part in Will Rankin's classes, were wandering among the crowd shaking collection cans to collect last-minute donations. It was eight o'clock on the morning of Christmas Eve in Bellbird Bay, and everyone was in a festive mood.

For once, Libby wasn't standing with Emma and Clancy. Both had chosen to join Nick, Mel and Aaron who, with little Isla, were cheering on Ted and Zack, both of whom were among the surfers. Instead, she had joined Alison, and they had found a prime position with a good view of the swimmers.

As the swimmers made their way to the starting point, Libby laughed when she saw what Adam was wearing. The board shorts covered in tiny Santa figures with surfboards were perfect for the event but where had he got them? She glanced at Alison who was doubled up in laughter and knew she was the culprit.

'I dared him to wear them,' Alison gurgled. 'Adam hasn't changed He never could resist a dare. Aren't they cute?'

Libby nodded. Adam did look cute in the shorts and a red Santa hat. He fitted right in with all the others getting ready for the event.

The mayor, also dressed for the occasion, sounded the starting horn and they were off, some surfers failing at the first hurdle of riding their boards, some dressed in ankle-length gowns. It was all good fun, but Libby could see many participants took it seriously, determined to complete the course.

To her surprise, Alison produced a bottle of champagne and two glasses.

'It's one we didn't drink last week,' she said with a grin. 'This seemed like the appropriate time to open it.'

Libby glanced across to where Emma was standing with Nick, Mel, Aaron and Grace, and Clancy was sitting on the sand with Isla. Deciding she wasn't needed there, she took the glass from Alison. 'What a good idea,' she said. Who'd have thought, when she left the dinner table so hurriedly, and in such distress, that today, less than a week later, she'd be watching Adam leap into the ocean in such a ridiculous outfit and enjoying a glass of champagne on the beach with his sister.

'To many more occasions like this.' Alison raised her glass.

'I'll drink to that.' Libby clinked glasses with Alison, a warm glow suffusing her.

But, despite the wine and the jollity all around, Libby gazed worriedly out to sea, trying to identify Adam among the red-capped swimmers heading towards the headland, then back again, barely noticing the surfers who were the main attraction, and only breathing evenly again when she saw Adam – minus his cap – walking up the beach.

'Well done!' she said, joining Alison in hugging the dripping swimmer who looked exhausted.

'Champagne?' Alison asked, as Adam collapsed onto the sand.

'Not now. Maybe later.' Adam was breathing raggedly. It was a few minutes before he managed to recover and held up his hand for a glass.

There was a loud cheer as the last swimmers and surfers reached the shore. Then people began to drift away.

'Lunch at the club?'

Libby looked round to see Ailsa and Cleo behind her.

'We're meeting the guys there. It's going to be quite a celebration. The Christmas surf and swim raised more than ever before this year. We'll grab a table, and you can join us.'

'If I ever recover,' Adam groaned. But he was already breathing normally and was halfway through his glass of bubbly. 'You have my gear?' he asked Ali.

'Right here.' She produced a pair of khaki shorts and a blue shirt, which he donned quickly, his board shorts already dry.

'It's a pity to hide them,' Alison said as the tiny Santa figures disappeared.

Adam gave her an affectionate scowl.

Once Adam was dressed, they made their way to the surf club to join the others. They found the place thronging with people, many still wearing the outfits they had surfed or swum in. It appeared that today the normally strict dress regulations had been relaxed and anything was acceptable.

During lunch there was much good-hearted teasing about Will's outfit which included a fake white beard, and Adam's board shorts. But their meal over, Adam became more serious.

'It's time,' he said, as they were making their way up the boardwalk. 'Will you come with me, Libby?'

Libby knew to what he was referring. His promise to Greg hadn't been far from his mind since early morning. For him, it was a sacred trust.

'Alison?' she asked, expecting him to want his sister there, too.

Adam shook his head. 'Ali has some last-minute shopping to do – secret Santa stuff.'

Alison grinned and gave Libby a wink.

'I'd love to come, if you're sure.'

Adam nodded. 'Greg would approve. He'd like you.'

*

The sun was shining brightly as they drove along the coast to Dolphin Beach. Once there, Adam unpacked a blanket from the car with a bottle of sparkling wine and two glasses. Then he carefully took out the urn containing Greg's ashes.

Libby watched as he walked slowly down to the edge of the water, stood, head bowed for several minutes, then opened the urn and tossed the ashes into the ocean, his eyes following them as they were swallowed up by the waves. Then, carrying the empty urn, he made his way back up the beach.

When he reached Libby, she enveloped him in a warm hug, feeling the tears on his cheeks from farewelling his old friend.

They toasted Greg with the wine, as Adam shared stories about his friend and some of the exploits they got up to when overseas.

'You know, Eddie thought you and Greg were a couple,' Libby said. 'For a while there I thought you were gay.'

'Greg would have loved that,' Adam replied. 'Greg was but not me.' He pulled Libby into his arms. 'He was delighted when gay marriage became legal, always sure his soulmate was out there somewhere and one day he'd find him. He never did. But I did, Libby. I found mine, I found you.'

Libby felt a rush of joy. How could she ever have doubted Adam? He had helped her find a new reason for living. But now he had fulfilled his mission, the reason he had come to Bellbird Bay, what did the future hold for them?

Adam pulled Libby into his arms, his lips on her hair. 'I can't live without you, Libby. I've extended my lease on Grace's house. I'm planning to stay in Bellbird Bay. I may have to return to Canberra briefly. My publisher wants me to do some events in January, and I should do something about my unit there. Maybe you can come with me?' He nuzzled her neck. 'Mmm?'

Libby thought her heart would burst. All her fears and worries disappeared. She loved Bellbird Bay. She loved Adam. And now she could have both – and Emma and Clancy, too. Life couldn't get any better.

Forty-one

Libby turned over in bed to look at the face on the pillow beside her on Christmas morning. Last night they had all attended a Christmas Eve party at Mel and Aaron's, and Mel had talked Emma and Clancy into staying overnight. Grace had winked at Libby and Adam, making Libby think she'd had a word with her daughter.

'Merry Christmas,' Libby whispered in Adam's ear.

'Merry Christmas.' Adam opened his eyes and pulled Libby closer, their lips meeting.

'It's not much,' Libby said as she handed over the book she'd wrapped carefully in shiny gold paper. 'I bought it before…' she blushed.

'You are the only Christmas gift I want or need.' Adam kissed her again, before producing a tiny silver-wrapped box. 'For you.'

Libby slipped out of Adam's arms to unwrap her gift, surprised and delighted to discover a pair of beautiful silver and opal earrings in the shape of a heart. 'Oh, Adam! They are beautiful.' Libby was overcome with the thoughtfulness of the gift, regretting she hadn't bought him something more personal.

'Beautiful earrings for a beautiful lady,' he said, kissing her again.

They were interrupted by the sound of Christmas carols coming from another part of the house.

'Sounds like the troops have arrived,' Libby said, swinging her legs out of the bed and pulling on her robe. 'We must join them. I want to see Clancy open her presents.'

They followed the sound to the living room where Clancy was dancing around.

'At last, Grandma,' she said. 'Mummy said I wasn't allowed to open anything till you came. Look what Santa left me!' She pointed to the pink bicycle which was leaning against the wall. It had pink and white streamers coming out of the handlebars and a white basket. 'I'm going to learn to ride it really soon. Now can I open my presents, Mummy?' she asked.

There was a knock at the door leading in from the deck, and Alison appeared carrying several large parcels. 'Merry Christmas,' she said, dropping the parcels under the tree. 'Hope I'm not too late.'

'Grandma and Adam just got up,' Clancy said in a disapproving voice. Libby blushed, and everyone laughed.

Once all the presents had been opened, Clancy delighted with the iPad from Matt, at which Emma rolled her eyes, they enjoyed a breakfast of croissants provided by Alison. Then, when the Christmas wrappings had been picked up, and Clancy had had her first lesson on her new bike, it was time to walk up to Grace and Ted's for lunch.

Before they left, Libby slipped out and crossed to the viewing platform. Taking a seat on the bench, she stroked the metal plaque.

'Merry Christmas, Bernie,' she said, a break in her voice. 'I hope that, wherever you are, you know how happy I am. I'll always love you. You'd like Adam. He's good to me. But I'll never forget you. You'll always be my first love.' She kissed her fingers and pressed them to Bernie's name. Then, with one last, lingering look at the words engraved there, she returned home.

*

Grace had put on a sumptuous spread. In addition to the traditional turkey there was a selection of seafood from prawns to salmon, plus several varieties of shellfish Libby didn't recognise. 'Ted has connections with the owner of one of the fishing boats,' Grace said by way of explanation. For dessert, there was a variety of Ruby's cakes which she had purchased from *The Pandanus Café* and a selection of cheeses. There was enough to feed an army for a week, Libby thought when she set eyes on the overflowing table.

It seemed Milo thought so, too, taking up a spot underneath the table in the hope of rescuing whatever dropped to the ground. Earlier, when everyone was wishing each other Merry Christmas and sharing gifts, he had raced around madly, followed by Clancy and a toddling Isla who tried to catch his flailing tail.

Meanwhile, Grace's cat, Tiger, glared disapprovingly at Milo from his perch on a bench.

The wine and beer flowed, and there was juice and milk for the two littlies and Zack, though Libby thought she caught sight of him sneaking a drink of beer.

By the time the meal was finished, all Libby wanted to do was lie down, preferably in a quiet shady spot and close her eyes.

But her hosts had other ideas.

'Who's for a game of beach cricket?' Ted asked, to a resounding cheer from Aaron, Nick, Mel and Zack.

'It's a tradition,' Grace explained to Libby, as they followed the others across the boardwalk and down to the beach.

The game of cricket came to an abrupt halt when Milo grabbed the ball and ran off with it. Zack gave chase, Clancy trying desperately to catch up, while the other players collapsed onto the sand in gales of laughter.

Sitting in the shade, Libby dropped her head onto Adam's shoulder.

He slid his hand under her hair and stroked her neck. 'Happy?' he asked, pulling her in for a kiss.

'So happy,' she said, as the shouts of the others faded into the distance. 'I'm so glad we met and...' She was forced into silence as Adam kissed her again.

'This has been the best Christmas ever,' Adam said, gazing into her eyes.

The End

If you've enjoyed Libby and Adam's story, a way you can say thank you to me is to leave a review on Amazon and/or Goodreads. A few words will suffice, no need for a lengthy review. It will mean a lot to me and help other readers find my books.

The next book in the series,
Finding Refuge in Bellbird Bay is Bev's story.

Thirty-five years ago, tragedy forced *Bev Cooper* to cut short her university studies and seek refuge in her hometown of Bellbird Bay. Today, as the owner of the thriving Pandanus Garden Centre and Café, Bev has moved beyond the past and is happy in her solitary existence.

Following the tragic death of his son's wife, *Iain Grant* takes early retirement and moves with his devastated son and granddaughter to the peaceful coastal town of Bellbird Bay hoping it will provide the change of scene they all desperately need.

When Iain's son accepts a position at Bev's garden centre, the pair find themselves drawn into each other's lives. But as they begin to enjoy an unexpected attraction, issues from the past threaten to derail their growing relationship.

Will the healing atmosphere of Bellbird Bay work its magic and provide a second chance in life, or will Bev find it too difficult to put the past behind her and enjoy her own happy ever after?

A heartwarming tale of family, friends, and how a second chance at love can happen when you least expect it.

You can order it here https://mybook.to/FindingRefuge

From the Author

Dear Reader,

First, I'd like to thank you for choosing to read *Christmas in Bellbird Bay*. I hope you've enjoyed this trip to Bellbird Bay as much as I've enjoyed writing it. I'm really enjoying writing about my fictional town in the part of Queensland where I live and populating it with characters who I hope you will come to love. It's the fourth book in this series, but like the others, can be read as a standalone.

If you'd like to stay up to date with my new releases and special offers you can sign up to my reader's group.

You can sign up here

https://mailchi.mp/f5cbde96a5e6/maggiechristensensreadersgroup

I'll never share your email address, and you can unsubscribe at any time. You can also contact me via Facebook, Twitter or by email. I love hearing from my readers and will always reply.

Thanks again.

Acknowledgements

As always, this book could not have been written without the help and advice of a number of people.

Firstly, my husband Jim for listening to my plotlines without complaint, for his patience and insights as I discuss my characters and storyline with him, for his patience and help with difficult passages and advice on my male dialogue, and for being there when I need him.

John Hudspith, editor extraordinaire for his ideas, suggestions, encouragement and attention to detail, and for helping me make this book better.

Jane Dixon-Smith for her patience and for working her magic on my beautiful cover and interior.

My thanks also to early readers of this book – Helen, Maggie and Louise for their helpful comments and advice. Also, to Annie of *Annie's books at Peregian* and Graeme of *The Bookshop at Caloundra* for their ongoing support.

And to all of my readers. Your support and comments make it all worthwhile.

About the Author

After a career in education, Maggie Christensen began writing contemporary women's fiction portraying mature women facing life-changing situations, and historical fiction set in her native Scotland. Her travels inspire her writing, be it her trips to visit family in Scotland, in Oregon, USA or her home on Queensland's beautiful Sunshine Coast. Maggie writes of mature heroines coming to terms with changes in their lives and the heroes worthy of them. Maggie has been called *the queen of mature age fiction* and her writing has been described by one reviewer as *like a nice warm cup of tea. It is warm, nourishing, comforting and embracing.*

From the small town in Scotland where she grew up, Maggie was lured to Australia by the call to 'Come and teach in the sun'. Once there, she worked as a primary school teacher, university lecturer and in educational management. Now living with her husband of over thirty years on Queensland's Sunshine Coast, she loves walking on the deserted beach in the early mornings and having coffee by the river on weekends. Her days are spent surrounded by books, either reading or writing them – her idea of heaven!

Maggie can be found on Facebook, Twitter, Goodreads, Instagram, Bookbub or on her website.

https://www.facebook.com/maggiechristensenauthor
https://twitter.com/MaggieChriste33
https://www.goodreads.com/author/show/8120020.Maggie_Christensen
https://www.instagram.com/maggiechriste33/
https://www.bookbub.com/profile/maggie-christensen
https://maggiechristensenauthor.com/

www.ingramcontent.com/pod-product-compliance
Lightning Source LLC
Chambersburg PA
CBHW030624120726
47904CB00006B/2021